A Roman Road to Freedom

A First Century Christian Novel

JEANETTE STAHLHEBER

Cover design: Nada Orlic
Editor: Maureen A. Campanile
Formatter: Jennifer Hiott
Illustrations: Yoko Matsuoka
Author photo: Chris Robinson

Ebook ISBN: 979-8-9914645-2-9
Hardback ISBN: 979-8-9914645-1-2
Paperback ISBN: 979-8-9914645-0-5

First Edition

Scripture Index is located at the end of the book.

Published by Jeanette Stahlheber
www.jeanettesrelaxingreads.com

DEDICATION

Dedicated to my amazing husband, Sean, who encouraged me to turn my just-for-fun short story into a novel; my children, Flynn, Titus, and Annora, who make sure my imagination never ceases; my three babies, who I am eager to reunite with in heaven one day, David, Topaz, and Tobiah; and of course, God who has never left me or forsaken me.

CONTENTS

PREFACE

This is a fictionalized account of the early church and Christ-followers, who were at this time referred to as believers in "the Way." Peter, Paul, James, John, and Matthias were all real and active members, as described in the Bible. However, because I was not there, their conversations in the book are fictional. Most importantly, though, EVERY word in this book that is attributed to Jesus is quoted verbatim from Scripture.

Thank you for reading, and I hope you enjoy!

CHAPTER 1

Rome

AD 46

Octavia turned and glanced over her shoulder as she slipped from her home. She barely noticed the predawn light beginning to illuminate the impressive columns and landscaping of her domus. She could see her slave, Esther, keeping watch near the entrance, prepared to distract any of the other slaves if they happened to come Octavia's way.

The silence of the morning strengthened Octavia's resolve, and as she took a deep breath, she felt the bag of coins she had carefully concealed into the folds of her stola and clutched the larger bag of items at her side. She set out for the nearest market to her home, avoiding the other Romans, mostly slaves, bustling through town on their early morning errands.

She hiked further from her home and made her way to the market, focused on her mission. As she slipped through side streets, she prayed, "God, please provide the one I need and help him to agree."

Every detail had to work in her favor, and she knew that God's blessing was the only thing that could save her from destitution. As she walked up to the market area, she skirted the vendors and affected a disinterested air, one that she had perfected in her life among the upper echelon of Roman society.

Octavia drew herself to a stop where the various carts and horses waited with their slave drivers. She drew a few coins from her bag and walked up to a slave with an essedum cart hooked up to four horses. She was in a hurry, and this was the fastest vehicle that could take her to the other side of the city. The slave was a young man, probably around her twenty-three years. He glanced at her with little curiosity.

"Do you need a ride?" he asked.

"Yes," replied Octavia in her disinterested tone, "I need a ride to the market outside of the Colosseum."

Octavia knew that this was the easiest part of her plan, and yet the blood roared in her ears. She prayed that the man could not sense her nervousness. Fortunately for Octavia, the man, in an equally impassive tone, gave her the price and took the coins from her hand as she held them. He offered her his arm as she climbed into the cart, not even noticing the slight tremble in her hand.

He climbed in the cart after her and soon had the horses moving in a quick trot down the road toward the Colosseum. As Octavia clutched her bag in her lap and held her anxiety at bay, she considered the change in her life since Esther had been hired by her husband eight months prior. It nearly took her breath away to think about how much had changed since then. Esther had been such a timid and yet kind slave, unlike any that Octavia had ever experienced.

The rest of the slaves in the home had taken her late husband, Festus's attitude of disdain toward Octavia. While they avoided doing anything beneficial for their mistress except if it was commanded by the master of the house, Esther was different.

She only ever regarded Octavia, Festus, and the other slaves with an amiable spirit. She was obviously of Jewish heritage, and Octavia had heard some of the kitchen slaves talking about how her parents had been taken from Jerusalem and enslaved when the Roman army was victorious over her homeland.

One evening, after Octavia had said something that angered Festus, Esther had gently tended to Octavia's bloody lip. Octavia had finally asked Esther why she was so kind even when it was not required of her.

Esther paused for a moment before answering, "My God has told me to be kind even to my enemies and to patiently endure hardships even when I have done nothing to deserve them."

Octavia could not have been more shocked at this response. From that day forward, Esther answered all of Octavia's questions, and they even attended church services in some believers' homes when they had an excuse to sneak away. Octavia now had the greatest gift she could imagine—salvation from her life of sin. She hoped that God had a good life in store for her here in Rome in addition to her eternity.

Octavia was roused from her musings as the horses began to slow, and she could see the marketplace coming into view under the imposing structure of the Colosseum. She quickly alighted from the essedum using the driver's arm for balance. The slave went to tend to his horses without a backward glance toward the relieved Octavia.

Stepping quickly out of the way of another cart, she walked around the market until she found another essedum to take her to Trajan's Market. If anyone tried to retrace her steps, they would have a difficult, if not impossible, task ahead of them. She smiled before she slid the impassive face of nobility back into place.

This essedum was driven by an older slave who barely even glanced at her before taking her fare and helping her to board his cart. The ride took considerably longer than the first, and she found herself nodding off to the sound of the wind rushing past her. The sleepless night she had spent praying with Esther for God's favor was catching up to her.

When the horses came to a stop, Octavia awakened with a jerk of alarm before quickly composing herself as the driver turned toward her. It would not do to draw any attention, which might cause anyone to remember her. Her goal of the day was to blend into the vastness of Rome, where people minded their business unless someone made it easy to do otherwise.

She stepped out of the essedum and walked to the slave market at a measured pace. Once again, she prayed for God's favor and kindness toward her. Steeling herself for the task ahead, she walked up to the market where the slaves who were for sale that day were chained to one another. She stayed back in the crowd as she perused the first slaver's offerings. Most of the slaves he had were women and children, and he had a few older men. No one was suitable for her needs, so she walked on to the next slaver's booth.

The second vendor offered some men closer to her age, but they wore angry, hardened faces. One had a terrifying scar over his milky eye. He caught her looking at him and turned his good eye to stare at her leeringly. She quickly turned her head and walked around the corner of the market where the last two slavers held their prisoners.

As she stood near a group of customers who were inspecting some of the women slaves, her gaze caught on a group of three young men standing in chains. The man on the left of the group stared angrily at the buyers walking around the market while the man on the right kept his sad eyes fixed on the ground. The slave in the middle, however, had his eyes closed and looked as if he was speaking to himself.

As Octavia stared at his lips, it almost appeared as if he had said, "The valley of the shadow of death." As she continued to stare at his mouth, it seemed more and more like he was reciting a song of the Israelite King David, one of the few passages of the Jewish Bible that Octavia had memorized; however, she noted that his appearance was clearly that of a Roman and not a Jew.

Octavia looked around and noticed that the slaver was engrossed in a conversation with the patrons interested in the women slaves, so she cautiously approached the group of men, trying not to draw unnecessary attention.

Using her best cultured tone, she quietly commanded the murmuring man, "Look at me, Slave."

As his eyes raised to meet hers, she was surprised to see no fear or anger but only peaceful resignation in his gaze.

"Do you have a family?" she asked quickly.

"No, I do not have any family," he answered.

"No wife or children?"

"No."

"Are you a follower of the Way?" she demanded.

He looked back and blinked, obviously taken aback. He did not glance around at the audience that Octavia knew was hanging onto their every word, but his cheeks flushed as he answered, "Yes."

The sad young man beside him gasped in shock at this admission. Octavia nodded and maintained her neutral expression even as she rejoiced inside.

The slaver, apparently finished with his business with the other buyers, walked up at this moment and gazed curiously at Octavia, clearly unsure if she was there to purchase or just to entertain herself by speaking with his slaves.

"How much are you asking for this man?" Octavia asked in her most businesslike voice.

As Augustus, the slaver, led the woman away to his booth to work out his price, Julius stared in shock, wondering what was happening. How did that Roman woman know that he was a follower of the Way? He was a Roman citizen as well and would not have known about Christ but for his Jewish neighbors where he had owned his property. They had come to believe that Jesus was the long-awaited Messiah and had led Julius through their beliefs in the Bible and the Son of God, who had come to bring salvation to the world.

As persecution by the Pharisees became increasingly prevalent in the Roman countryside, his neighbors had moved their family to Samaria. While the Roman emperor did not condemn this new religion, Romans often were ostracized for the belief that there was only one God instead of the many that were commonly worshiped.

Julius thought that he was safe alone on his farm, but then he was kidnapped by slavers who had no legal right to take him. He still was unsure if he was taken because he was singled out as a member of the Way or if these unscrupulous slavers had seen a man alone and knew they could overpower him and sell him as a slave without consequence.

He had heard of such things being done, of course, but had not considered it that much of a risk until it had happened to him. No doubt, his home was now owned by some rich nobleman who cared nothing of its former owner.

That thought brought his mind back around to the wealthy Roman who appeared to be holding her own as she bargained to own his life. It did not seem as if she was angry that he admitted to being a follower of the Way, but he was entirely unsure of her motives. The slaves near him had inched away from him as if being near him put them in increased danger of wrath from the gods.

Just then, he saw the woman hand Augustus a small bag, and he handed her the scroll that Julius knew gave her the rights to his service and his life.

Octavia felt the relief flood her body as she clutched the potential key to her freedom, hoping the slave would listen to her and be amenable to her pleas. She had never been able to convince a man to do anything for her. She couldn't convince her father not to barter her away as a wife to an old, bitter nobleman, and she hadn't been able to convince her husband that she was even slightly worthwhile. She clung to the hope that this time would be different. But first, she had to get this slave away from here without anyone noticing them.

She watched as Augustus unchained her new slave from the others, and she commanded the man to follow her without a backward glance.

Julius followed the woman who had purchased him, not knowing where they were going or what she would require of him. He knew that God was in control of his life, and he prayed a quick prayer for a favorable mistress. He noticed that she was quite beautiful with pale marble-like skin, a lovely, almost regal face, and the countenance of one accustomed to getting what she wanted. What struck him as he answered her questions was the startling green of her eyes and the intensity he saw in them.

Soon, she drew to a stop beside a litter and its four slaves. She gave one of the men the name of an inn and paid him. Then she climbed inside. She waved at Julius with one elegant hand, and he followed her and folded his long legs into the litter. He braced himself as the four men picked up the vehicle. The woman stared impassively in front of her and held herself in such a stiff, upright position that he was uncomfortable just looking at her.

Julius instantly realized that staring was impertinent and shifted his gaze to the inside of the litter, which was embellished with an assortment of colorful blankets and cushions for the comfort of the riders. As he sat, he could hear the unevenness of the woman's breathing and realized she was not as at ease as she was trying to portray. It made him curious about her and why she was alone, purchasing a slave early on a weekday morning when most noble women would still be in bed.

Soon, they arrived at the inn the woman had specified, and he braced himself once again as they were lowered to the ground. He opened the flap, stretched out of the litter, and then extended his hand to his mistress, who took it and allowed him to assist her out of the ride. He realized that they were on the edge of Rome, and the inn was in a field of golden wheat that was almost ready for harvest. The image of his own wheat that he should be preparing to harvest popped into his head before he shook the melancholy thought away.

His mistress walked with a determined yet refined gait toward the inn with Julius right behind her. Then, for the first time since she had questioned him at the market, she turned and acknowledged him.

"Walk beside me, and when we get inside, ask for a room," she commanded quietly as she handed him some coins.

Julius started for a second and nodded in agreement. He hoped that she did not intend to use him for worldly passions. It was common for slaves to be used in such a way, but it was a sin against his God, and if that was her intention, he would kindly explain that to her. Not that he could do anything to prevent her from punishing him for his refusal, but he would trust his God with the results.

He followed her instructions and purchased a room with the money his mistress gave him. Then, they followed the innkeeper to their room.

Octavia was trembling with anticipation and fear as they walked down the corridor to the temporary quarters. She was trying so hard not to let it show, but her new slave kept giving her surreptitious glances, proving she was not fooling him with her calm portrayal. She hoped that he did not think she was bringing him here for a liaison, but she could not risk breaking her silence until they were alone and could speak in complete privacy.

As the innkeeper opened their door, Octavia walked inside and looked out the window at the field of wheat that nearly vibrated in the bright sunshine and breeze. She could sense that her new slave followed her into the room, and she heard him close the door. She turned to see him standing in the entry and just then realized how tall and well-built he was. His face was chiseled, and he was quite muscled from whatever work he had been used to doing.

Suddenly, the enormity of her request felt overwhelming, and she dropped to a seat on the bench in front of the window. She hid her face in her hands as she tried to contain the tears that threatened to pour out and never stop.

"Are you alright, Mistress?" he asked with concern.

Octavia wiped away the few tears that had managed to escape and quickly composed herself.

"Yes. Please take a seat," she said as she motioned to the bed. "I will sit here. Before I explain my actions, can you please tell me about yourself?"

Julius sat upon the edge of the bed and told her the story of who he was, how his mother, father, and two siblings had died of the plague that had swept through the empire five years earlier. He spoke of owning a small farm in the countryside outside of Rome. Then he recounted how he became a believer and how he was kidnapped last week and sold to Augustus for the market.

Octavia stared at him forlornly as he told his story, and when he was finished, she said, "I'm sorry for the misfortune that has befallen you. I think you will find that we are, in some ways, quite similar. We both want our freedom. I have a large request for you, and I hope that you will listen to my story before you make any judgments."

"I can agree to that," said Julius as he looked at her expectantly.

Octavia sighed and began to recount her story.

"My name is Octavia Metelli. My late husband passed away almost a month ago. He was much older than me, and he hated me. He told me throughout our marriage that no one else would want me as a wife and that if he died before me, I would have no choice but to sell myself in the streets." Octavia glanced up and saw Julius wince in anger and sympathy.

"He stipulated in his will that if I remarried within one month, I and my new husband would keep his estate and possessions. If I do not remarry, I will get nothing and will be out on the street."

Her shoulders slumped as she continued, "He did this as a final joke on me. He made it seem as if there was hope for me not to be put out, but he charged his friends to prevent anyone from marrying me. They hover around me always, making sure no one can court me. They have used bribes, threats, and rumors to keep any potential suitors away.

"All of the slaves in the house, except my dear Esther, were on my husband's side and continue to mistreat me. They spy on me and report to his friends. I devised a plan to evade all the spies and make a last attempt this morning to find a husband.

"I am a believer as you are, and I cannot marry another blasphemous man. I determined that if God willed, maybe I could find a slave who believed in Christ and would consider marrying me."

Octavia looked up into his astonished eyes, "I want you to know that regardless of your choice, I have every intention of giving you your freedom today. I hope that you will consider my offer of marriage, as unconventional as it may be, but after we leave this inn, I will take you to the magistrate's office and free you.

"If you do decide to marry me, I will be as good of a wife as I can be. I will never make any mention of how we came to meet. I would tell everyone that we met at a market. If you find me as detestable as Festus did, we can be married in name only. I can make myself invisible to you and stay in my rooms. I am hoping to have children if that is agreeable to you, and I would allow you to run the estate and your family how you like."

She took a deep breath and continued timidly, "I am hopeful that you would not find the idea of marriage to me an awful proposition. It can give us both the freedom we so desire. If you agree, we can marry at the magistrate's office." Her words came to a halt at this as she looked pleadingly at him.

Julius stared at Octavia. He had initially been fooled by her self-assured and commanding presence in the market, but it was clear that she was quite desperate, and he looked into her beseeching eyes as he considered his options.

If he was emancipated right now, he would have no money and likely no home to go back to. Even if he did return home, he would not be safe there for long. Marriage to this stranger would give both of them freedom. They were both believers in the Way, so nothing would morally prevent their union. And ever since his family had passed away, he had been increasingly lonely.

He began to nod as he scrambled for the right words to say. "I do not find the idea of marrying you anything but appealing. I would also like children and would be pleased to have such an agreeable wife as you appear to be."

Octavia wilted in relief, and tears once again filled her eyes. Julius quickly walked over to her and knelt in front of her.

"It's going to be okay. I will take care of you. We will get married today, and when we return to the house, we will get better slaves to replace the ones who were cruel to you," he assured her comfortingly.

Octavia looked up into his eyes and tearfully thanked him.

She handed him the large bag she had been carrying. "These are new clothes for you. If you agree, we should make a stop at the baths before we go to the magistrate. That will give no one cause to question your suitability when we arrive home."

Julius felt like a new man after he had bathed and changed into a fresh tunic that he assumed must have been Festus's. He could hardly believe that he was about to be a free and married man.

CHAPTER 2

For Octavia, the next few hours of getting a new litter, going to the magistrate's office, freeing Julius, and marrying him, passed by in a blur. Her relief at the success of her mission was the only thing keeping her from falling into an exhausted slumber. By the time they were married, it was already midday, and they ate a quick meal at a market near the magistrate's office.

Afterward, they took a litter back to the domus that Octavia had left that morning in desperation. Now, she returned in triumph and exultation. She watched Julius take in their home, and she considered it with fresh eyes. The sprawling domus took up a city block and was surrounded on two sides by a large olive orchard. A row of massive columns surrounded the front of the home and formed a porch. As they alighted from the litter and walked into the entrance, Julius reached down and held her hand.

Esther was eagerly waiting for her mistress, and when she saw Julius, her eyes lit with excitement and hope. Octavia introduced Julius as her husband to Esther and the slaves who had gathered upon their arrival. The other slaves looked at each other in shock and dismay as the newlyweds moved into the atrium of the domus.

Julius glanced around the large, rectangular atrium with its open ceiling, the numerous curtain-covered entryways, and the large impluvium. This pool collected the rainwater that slid down from the sloped roof. Her new husband immediately took charge and asked for all the slaves to be brought before him.

When all fifty slaves were assembled in the common room, he asked for the household manager. The portly slave, Julian, stepped forward and sneered as he looked at Octavia. Julius looked down upon the man and glared at him, making him drop the sneer from his lips and begin to cower slightly.

Julius then addressed the assembly, "I have been told by my new bride how she has been treated in this, her own house, by her slaves. I am sure you can understand that I cannot trust any of you with the care of my wife or home, knowing how you have behaved in the past. Esther will remain in our service, but none of the rest of you will.

"All those of you who have the money to buy your freedom will be taken to the magistrate's office to do so now. The rest of you will pack your belongings, and you will be taken to the market to be sold to your next master. I hope that master will be more careful about how he allows his slaves to treat his family."

As he spoke, the faces of the slaves showed shock, anger, and, for some, shame. Octavia could not have been more pleased with her new husband, and she took his hand encouragingly. He squeezed it and looked down at her with a smile.

After they removed the former slaves from the domus and had acquired a new cook, they returned home and ate the dinner that the old kitchen staff had already prepared. Julius was exceedingly pleased to see how happy his new wife was at this change in her fortunes. He would search for new slaves for the rest of the positions in the home tomorrow, but for now, they could make do with the cook and Esther.

As they walked back into the atrium, Julius realized that he did not even know in which room they would be sleeping. He looked around at the doorways branching off the common area. Octavia came to his side.

"I can give you a tour of the whole place tomorrow if that is okay with you," she said.

"That is fine," he returned. "Where do we sleep?"

Octavia pointed to a doorway near where they stood in the courtyard. "That was Festus's room. I was only summoned there if he..." She shuddered and trailed off. "I don't like to go in there."

Julius turned to face her and took her hands. "You never have to go in that room. Where is your room?"

She pointed to the opposite side of the atrium and said, "That room is mine."

"Well, let's go then," Julius responded as he dropped one of her hands and began leading her in that direction.

"Will we both stay in there?" She inquired urgently.

"I fully intend to sleep in the same room as my wife," Julius said gently as they reached the doorway.

He looked down at her, and she nodded at him meekly. He pulled open the curtain and discovered a room far grander than any he had ever been in before. The bed was large and adorned with many pillows. The floor had cushions for seating, and there was a small table with some sketches upon it.

"Do you draw?" he asked, pointing at the sketches.

Octavia blushed and nodded, "I know it's an uncommon hobby, but I enjoy it."

Julius turned toward her and looked at her intently, and then he brushed back some of her hair that had escaped from her elaborate hairstyle. Octavia made a quick inhale of air. He smiled at her and lowered his lips to meet hers in their first kiss as man and wife.

Esther stayed awake after the household fell asleep and prayed for her mistress. "God please keep her safe, and help Julius to be the blessing he appears to be."

Octavia woke up the next morning to the sounds of Esther bustling about her room and setting a tray upon her table. She reached across the bed and found that Julius had already risen. When Octavia sat up, Esther walked over to the bed and sat on the edge. She turned her concerned and questioning gaze over Octavia's face. "Did he hurt you?" she asked.

"No... he was actually quite kind. I didn't know that a Roman could be so caring to his wife. God has truly answered our prayers. I saw him at the market, silently reciting one of the songs of David, and when I asked, he admitted without hesitation to being a follower of the Way, in front of others!"

Esther smiled, "Praise Jesus! I was quite impressed with how he dealt with the other slaves yesterday, and he thanked the cook for breakfast this morning before heading to the market for more slaves."

"I am glad that he seems quite adept at running a home. He is bound to face scrutiny and interference from Festus's friends.

In fact, I'm surprised that they haven't tried to barge their way inside yet." Octavia replied.

Esther chuckled, "Julius told me that if anyone came by before he returned, I was to explain that the master of the house was out and that if they wanted to have an audience with him, they could attend dinner tonight.

"He told the cook that he would get him some help and that we should expect a crowd for dinner. So far, no one has come by to inquire, but they are not exactly a group of early risers, and they may not yet know about your turn of fortunes."

Octavia's eyes shone with both pleasure and trepidation at the idea of her new husband facing off against her old husband's cohorts. "We should be praying for Julius tonight," she suggested.

"I'm always praying for you, Mistress, and I will certainly add Julius to my prayers. But I do not think you have anything to fear. The master seems to have everything well in hand."

Octavia nodded in agreement and moved to the table to eat her breakfast while Esther left the room and went about her morning tasks. Once finished with her breakfast, Octavia picked up her papyrus and lead stylus and began to sketch Julius.

While sketching was not a popular pastime for nobility, and the papyrus was too expensive for the poor, she had always enjoyed it as an escape from her anxious thoughts and troubles of life. Festus had mocked her for her "ridiculous waste of resources," as he had called it, but he hadn't gone so far as to forbid her hobby. So, she was free to use the little money her mother had given her before she married to buy whatever she liked.

Festus had kept her well clothed so that she would not embarrass him at dinners, but he had not given her any other money in the five years they had been married. She wondered how Julius would handle Festus's money and estate, but it was out of passing curiosity and not genuine concern. Even if he spent all their money, and they had to downsize their lifestyle, she could still not imagine things being worse than they were even just two days prior. With that comforting thought, she used expert strokes of the stylus to capture the kindness in his eyes, and she smiled to herself.

Julius headed to the market, enjoying the sunshine and the feeling of once again being free. Before he left home, he had asked Esther for a list of necessary slaves for running the domus and had determined that instead of fifty, they could make do with about thirty-five as he became accustomed to managing everything.

Before he went to the market, he went to the nearest magistrate whom he had correctly predicted was the one handling Festus's affairs. The thin older man with a shiny bald head had changed in an instant from a professional government official into a flustered scatterbrain the moment Julius had explained the situation and asked to register his ownership of Festus's estate as specified in the late man's will.

While the magistrate glared at Julius and muttered under his breath, he completed the paperwork, and now Julius owned Festus's estate. Just in case that ill-willed magistrate did something foolish like "lose" the registration, Julius had asked for three copies. Then he had taken an essedum thirty minutes away and had given a second magistrate a copy before driving thirty minutes further to a third magistrate.

He also gave each of the magistrates a copy of his own will, specifying that Octavia would be the beneficiary of the entire estate should anything happen to Julius. He would make sure to somehow slip that into the conversation at dinner tonight, lest an ambitious enemy believe that getting Julius out of the way would put Octavia in the same or worse position than before.

That task had taken up much of the morning, but Julius was well aware of the corruption that was prevalent in Rome, and he would do everything he could to secure his and Octavia's future.

He had returned to the market near his domus and grabbed a quick bite of food. Now, he gazed at the slave marketplace, which was much larger and well-supplied than the one he had been sold from yesterday. Apparently, the slaves here were not considered a flight risk because they were unchained and only being monitored by their slavers. Julius also noticed that, unlike the other market, this one consisted mostly of slaves who were experienced at working in a grand domus. One of the first slaves he purchased, Isaiah, was a Jew who had been a household manager before his master had died.

Isaiah was very knowledgeable about running a large domus and helped Julius to select the other slaves for the home. Fortunately, he had known several of them and was able to give them good references. Julius now had a group of thirty-two slaves, and Isaiah was questioning a group of three women who would work to clean the home and serve food.

As Isaiah interviewed the women, Julius spotted a group of muscled men who were standing alertly in the shade of one of the booths. Immediately, he identified them as guards. He considered his enemies and the risk he was taking by inviting them to his home tonight and made his way over to interview a few of them.

"I am looking for several men to guard my domus and family," Julius informed the slaver nearest the guards.

"These men have all been extensively trained as guards and will make certain your domus is secure. Gaius has the most experience and training," the vendor answered as he gestured to a tall, tanned man.

Julius walked over to Gaius who stood motionless with his thickly corded arms crossed over his chest and a shrewd but not unfriendly expression on his face. Julius asked him several questions about his experience and training before hiring him to be the captain of his guards and using the captain's expertise to select six other protectors for Julius's household.

As he led his new household staff to their home, Julius smiled, quite pleased with his work for the day. He wondered what Octavia was doing and mused about the contentious dinner he was anticipating that evening. He had never been one to stand down from bullies, and part of him relished the thought of putting Festus's old friends in their place. Now that the paperwork was registered, there was nothing that anyone could do to oust him from his new role and inheritance.

CHAPTER 3

Sometime after eating her midday meal, Octavia was startled from working on her portrait by a roaring yell that she immediately recognized as coming from Marcus Valerii. He had been a friend of her father's and of Festus. When she had come of marrying age, she had overheard Marcus talking to her father one night at a dinner in her home about marrying her.

She was not sure why her father eventually chose Festus for her instead of Marcus, but she still saw Marcus at dinners and parties with Festus. She was always uncomfortable with the way he stared at her. He had been hovering around like a vulture since Festus's demise, always quick to remind her of her deadline and ask about her progress in finding a husband.

Meanwhile, she knew of his efforts to sabotage her, and she had been worried that he was waiting until close to the one-month deadline to swoop in and "rescue" her from the streets. In doing so, he would be able to keep her under his thumb for the rest of her life, all the while making her feel that he had saved her from a worse fate.

Octavia heard Esther's distressed voice joined by the new cook's as they attempted to pacify the enraged visitor, who was now clearly in the atrium.

"Octavia!" She heard his furious summons and stood with her hands clasped serenely in front of her. She walked steadily to the entrance of her bedroom and pushed back the heavy curtain.

She came face to face with a red-faced Marcus who, despite the cook and Esther's efforts, seemed determined to barge into her private quarters. Octavia gave her best diplomatic smile, released the curtain behind her, and answered sweetly, "Yes, how can I help you, Marcus?"

Marcus froze for a second, taken aback by Octavia's calm demeanor. He was not a very tall man, but he was stocky and stood perched up on the balls of his feet as if about to pounce upon her. After a momentary pause, he rested back onto his heels, squared his shoulders, and stared into her eyes as he began.

"The magistrate tells me that you are married! This cannot possibly be true! You have told me nothing of a suitor, and when I tried to visit yesterday, I was told by your slaves that you had disappeared!" He fairly shouted at her.

Octavia watched the sweat upon his forehead trickle past his salt and pepper hair and down his temple as she earnestly prayed in her mind, "Dear God, please help me. Give me the words to calm this man and keep him from sinning."

She put her hand to her chest and gushed, "Whatever is the matter, Marcus? Is someone injured? It isn't your mother, is it? I know she wasn't feeling well the last time we talked! Is she alright?"

Marcus lost some of the red in his cheeks and relaxed his hands, which he was clenching into fists at his sides. He let out the breath he was holding as confusion replaced the anger in his gaze.

"No, no one is injured, and my mother is much improved. I am merely concerned for you. There are many unscrupulous men in Rome, and as you know, I have always looked out for you, being a friend of your family since before you were born."

"Thank you for all of your concern, but as you can see, I am doing very well," Octavia replied. "In fact, my new husband is planning a dinner tonight for all my friends, and we would love for you to attend. It will definitely assuage your concerns that he might not be suitable for me."

She then arranged her face into an unnatural pout and continued as if wounded, "Honestly, I thought you should be happy for me. You did not want to see me out on the street, did you?"

Emotions warred for control over Marcus's face, and he began, "No, of course..." when he was interrupted by the sound of footsteps in the entry and a large number of people entering the atrium.

Octavia let out a relieved breath as she saw Julius separate himself from the crowd and stride toward her and Marcus, who now stood facing him. He walked around Marcus and put his arm around Octavia protectively before addressing the visitor. "I hope you are not here for dinner already. I have to say you are quite early. I am Julius, Octavia's husband, and as the new owner of this domus, I desire your company this evening for dinner. However, we do have quite a lot to get done before then."

Marcus still looked angry but also suitably chastised. "I am Marcus, and I have been looking out for Octavia, so I will be pleased to attend this evening and make sure that you are suitable for such a lovely wife."

Julius gave a smile and nodded with an almost predatory gleam in his eyes, "Of course. We will see you tonight, then."

Octavia held herself rigidly upright until she heard the front door close behind Marcus. Then she melted into her husband's side and exhaled a large sigh. "Thank you for showing up just then," she said in relief.

"I'm afraid that is more God's timing than mine, but are you alright? Did he hurt you at all?" He asked as he looked over her face.

"No, I thought for a moment he might, but I was able to deflect his anger enough until you got here. I had no idea how I was going to convince him to leave, though."

He pressed her tightly into his side. "I assume he is one of Festus's friends."

"And my father's."

"Well, it is promising to be an interesting evening. I acquired forty-two more slaves for the domus, including seven guards who are stationed around the outside of the home, so we will not have any more unexpected visitors, and Isaiah will be the new house manager. I already directed him to prepare for a feast tonight. Fortunately, the cook has been working on the meal since this morning when I left." Julius said.

Octavia looked up and noticed that the atrium was now empty except for them and heard their new staff busy at work in other parts of the house. Then she replied, "Well, I can't say that I am thrilled about having those people in my home again, but at least I will have the comfort of you being by my side."

"Of course. I will be right beside you all evening, and Lord-willing, we will never be forced to endure their company again." He paused for a moment, and after she nodded in acknowledgment, he added, "Also, I wanted you to know that I transferred the estate into my name, distributed that paperwork at several magistrate's offices, and named you my beneficiary in my will, just in case." He said as he looked down at her with a smile and a wink.

Octavia stared up into his face in awe. "You have shown more kindness to me in the last day than any man has ever shown me in my life. Thank you!" She stood upon her tiptoes and pressed her lips to his.

They pulled apart, and Julius stared intently back at his new bride. "You're very welcome... and thank you for choosing me. I think we will get along well together."

"I think so." Octavia smiled with grateful tears in her eyes.

Julius spent the rest of the day overseeing his new staff and making sure that everything was ready for the dinner. Esther informed him that five other "friends" had come to call upon him and Octavia and were now invited to join them for dinner.

Octavia had asked at one point if there was anything that she could do. He asked her if she would like to pick flowers from their gardens to adorn the dining area. The look of sheer delight she gave him had warmed him down to his bones.

He was delighted that pleasing his wife took so little effort while also despising the men who had made it so easy for him to sweep her off her feet. Part of him wished that he could make them regret how they had treated his wife, but then he recalled the words that his neighbors had told him about how God deals with his enemies. "Vengeance is mine, and recompense, for the time when their foot shall slip; for the day of their calamity is at hand, and their doom comes swiftly." Oh, how he trusted God's words during his captivity.

As he walked outside and into the estate's olive orchard, Julius passed by a guard who nodded at him before continuing his patrol around the house. Julius hiked for several minutes through a path in the olive trees to a small clearing where he sat upon a stone bench and looked at the gnarled trees surrounding him.

He then took a deep breath and prayed, "God, thank you for this new home and new start that you have given me. Thank you even for allowing my abduction, without which I would never have met or been able to free Octavia.

"Please help my anger not to burn about past injustices but help me to trust in you that you will one day make all things right. Guide my steps as I navigate this new role of master and husband. Help me to be gentle and understanding with my wife. Help me to not harm her through my words or actions.

"Please help the dinner tonight to resolve any lingering tensions from Festus's spite and disdain for Octavia, and please give me the words to say and the patience to endure through every trial. In the name of your son, Jesus of Nazareth, who died so that I can truly be free, I ask all these things."

As Julius finished his prayer, he was alerted to a presence out of the corner of his eye, and he whipped his head around to see who had overheard his conversation with God.

Esther stood meekly, holding a basket of flowers and looking terrified at his concerned look. "I'm sorry. I wasn't trying to spy on you. I just walked around the corner of the path as you were finishing."

"It's not a problem," Julius quickly reassured his concerned slave. "I was just pouring out my heart and didn't think about being overheard. I used to be able to sit and know that no one for miles around could hear me, but I guess I will have to adjust." He turned up his mouth into half a smile.

"What you were saying was beautiful." Esther sighed and shifted her basket. "God knew that we needed you here, and I'm so glad he sent you. I'm taking these to the domus and getting Octavia a fresh basket. I've never seen her this happy."

Julius smiled, "I'm glad too."

Octavia had never been excited for a dinner before, but she found herself smiling and humming as she arranged flowers in clay vases. She scattered flower petals over the elaborate floor mosaics, pleased to be covering the depictions of the false gods she used to worship in her ignorance.

She thought about how the flowers were supposed to prevent the diners from getting sick from the food. She wondered if God used flowers in such a way or if that was a superstition. Regardless, she and Esther had picked two basketfuls of flowers, and the dining room had never felt so festive to her.

Julius walked into the room and swept her up into a big hug. "The room looks excellent! You have done quite well."

"Thank you," Octavia said with a smile, unaccustomed to praise of any kind.

"You're welcome. We should go change now. Our guests should be arriving at any time," he informed her as he led her from the dining room.

Julius looked around the room at the men and women who Octavia had been surrounded by for years. Most of the men started drinking to excess immediately upon being seated, and it made Julius glad that they did not have any strong wines or drinks at the domus. The men were older, probably in their early fifties. They were mostly overweight and balding.

Those who had wives ignored them, and Julius had noticed that all the women were at least half the age of the men. The wives each stared down at their plates or at the frescos on the walls, studiously avoiding anyone's gaze and not participating in conversation.

Between courses and throughout the meal, he made it a point to smile at Octavia and squeeze her hand reassuringly. When his guests had arrived and all assembled in the dining room, he introduced himself as Octavia's husband and received looks that ranged from bored to undisguised hostility.

Marcus, who was the only unmarried man at the table, was clearly the most outraged. He bitterly ate his food with a vengeance, glaring at his host and hostess as if they were trying to poison him. Before the main course of roast pig was served, Julius took the opportunity to make a toast and address the issues that had been a concern for him all day. He stood and raised his glass.

"Hello, friends. It has been an honor to host this event with my stunning new bride. I know that you were all concerned about the conditions of her late husband's will, and although I know you were limited on what aid you could render her, given that most of you were already married, I want to thank you though for any attempts that you did make to help her in her time of need." At this, several of the men glanced at each other, and one of the women sat back slightly in surprise.

Julius continued his speech, maintaining his neutral expression, "It should therefore put your minds at ease that I have already recorded all the necessary paperwork with more than one magistrate to make sure she is never left in such a challenging position should anything happen to me. Now, Octavia and I will focus upon ensuring the upkeep of this beautiful home and forming lasting friendships. To my lovely wife and your hostess, Octavia!"

He watched as his wife blushed fetchingly, and everyone raised their glasses to drink their honey-sweetened wine. He didn't miss the fact that Marcus abstained from the toast and began furiously whispering to the man next to him.

By the time the roast pig was served, Octavia wanted this whole evening to be over. Julius and his attention were the only things keeping her from begging out of the room for not feeling well, as she had done at other exhausting dinner parties in the past. She had often endured such inane conversations about politics and rude jokes about women and animals, but this time, an added layer of awkwardness permeated every conversation.

Marcus looked as if he wanted to strangle her, and she was incredibly glad for her husband's foresight in acquiring guards for the home, one of whom was stationed in the dining room. Not one of the women would even look in her direction, even though in the past, they would all share glances when one of the men said something funny or ridiculous.

Gratitude for her husband and God for bringing him to her became her sole focus for the evening. She could not believe how expertly Julius had secured their position by making it clear that even his death would not undo what security their marriage had wrought. He had even implied that he was pleased with their efforts to help her when, in fact, he had been blatantly criticizing their sabotage and cruelty. In just a few sentences, he had made a lasting impression on all those men, making it quite unlikely they would ever return or try to foster a relationship with the newlyweds.

As soon as he was done eating his pork, Marcus stood abruptly, ground out through what sounded like clenched teeth, "Good evening," and stormed out. The rest of the men looked down at their plates and pretended not to notice his incredibly unceremonious exit. Fortunately, his departure seemed to bring an end to the festivities, and soon the couples were leaving.

Once they were alone, Octavia slid over to her husband and kissed him ardently. When she pulled back, he looked at her, a little startled and definitely pleased by her affections. "What was that for?"

"That, my dear husband, was for making me feel worthwhile and for ridding me of the worst friends a person could ever have."

He grinned at her. "Well, unfortunately, I think that ridding you of friends is a one-time thing, so I will have to find other ways to make you kiss me like that."

Octavia laughed and mused that she couldn't remember the last time she had really laughed.

CHAPTER 4

Over the next week, Octavia and Julius began to develop their routines together. Julius ran the domus by directing Isaiah, who was proving himself to be an excellent manager of the household. He appointed another slave, Linus, to be his personal secretary, who assisted him with business matters. Linus had previous experience as a secretary and was able to anticipate Julius's needs admirably. With his new aid's assistance, Julius began studying through Festus's records and found that his predecessor had owned many investment properties.

He discovered that in the city of Rome, he now owned five insulaes, large multi-level buildings, each of which contained many small apartments on the upper floors and shops on the ground floor. When he inspected the properties, he found everything in relatively good order except for one insulae in which the tenants were living in appalling conditions. He immediately went to work hiring laborers to rebuild areas of the insulae that were dilapidated and shoring up others.

Octavia kept herself busy directing her new slaves, who served her graciously and completed all of the upkeep of her sprawling domus. In her spare time, she worked on her portrait of Julius and looked forward to the times that they would eat together, times he would touch her for no reason, and times they would laugh together.

On the Lord's Day, they went with Esther to a believer's home for a time of worshiping the Lord. The three of them listened with the other believers as Peter recounted to them how he and his brother Andrew had been fishing when Jesus had approached them by the Sea of Galilee. They were enraptured with his account of how Jesus had said to the men, "Follow me, and I will make you fishers of men." Peter then read the words of Jesus that had been recorded as he sat upon a mountain and spoke to the people about blessings and how his followers should live.

Octavia and Julius were quite astonished when Peter read Jesus's words: "You have heard that it was said, 'You shall love your neighbor and hate your enemy.' But I say to you, Love your enemies and pray for those who persecute you, so that you may be sons of your Father who is in heaven. For he makes his sun rise on the evil and on the good, and sends rain on the just and on the unjust. For if you love those who love you, what reward do you have? Do not even the tax collectors do the same? And if you greet only your brothers, what more are you doing than others? Do not even the Gentiles do the same? You therefore must be perfect, as your heavenly Father is perfect."

Peter explained that this saying did not mean that they had to be perfect on their own but that they had to repent of their sins, and in so doing, they became perfected through the sacrifice Jesus made when he died on the cross. When they began to sing praises to their Lord, Octavia was enraptured with the depth and richness of Julius's voice, and she held his hand and sang with him. She also noticed when Esther glanced down at their clasped hands with a smile.

Back at home, Octavia considered all that she had heard Peter say. She ate her food and looked off into the distance until Julius looked at her with concern.

"What is it, Love?" he asked her attentively.

"I'm simply thinking about all that we heard today," she answered.

"Well, why don't we retire to our room and discuss it further as we prepare for bed?"

Octavia nodded in agreement and walked toward the room as Julius had a final conversation with Linus about the next day's schedule before joining her in their chambers.

As Julius strode through the curtain, Octavia gracefully sat upon a cushion in their room and pulled the pins out of her hair. "I just can't imagine how we can love our enemies! I do not love Marcus or the rest of Festus's friends."

Julius reclined back onto the cushion next to her and looked thoughtfully into space for a moment before answering, "I know what you mean, but the way that Jesus speaks about love seems to indicate that it is more of a choice than a feeling. If we choose to be kind to someone even if we do not like them, is that not showing them love?"

She ran her fingers through her hair, detangling her long locks as she considered this. "I suppose you are right. I had not thought of love being a choice and our actions being separate from our feelings in that regard."

He reached for her hand as she lowered it from her hair to her lap and said, "Perhaps the point is that because God chose us and saved us while we were still sinning against him and were his enemies, we should be looking for ways to show love to everyone, even if they hate us."

"I think you are right." Octavia smiled at him and leaned over to kiss him. As they retired for the evening, she thought to herself that she had never realized life could be this fulfilling and had never felt so secure in a relationship with another person before. It was remarkable, given the relatively short time she had known him.

The next day, Octavia went to the market with Esther and two of her other ladies. She had already purchased more ink to replace her dwindling supply and was admiring a soft wool mantle called a palla in a beautiful shade of green that she thought would complement her eyes. As she turned to ask for Esther's opinion, she observed Marcus marching through the market with Festus's old household manager, Julian. They were deep in conversation and did not notice her until they were only a few feet away.

A chill went up her spine as Marcus gave her a menacing grin. The look in his eyes was pure hatred, and Julian sneered at her from Marcus's side as they continued through the market without a backward glance.

Octavia prayed as she watched their progress, "God, please help them to turn to you. Please keep me from hating them. Show me how to love my enemies like you loved me."

Esther noticed her mistress's distress and put a hand upon her shoulder as the men turned and disappeared from view. She whispered, "God is in control of those men. They just don't know it yet."

Octavia smiled and turned toward Esther. "You are right, of course... Now, how do you like this palla?"

"It is the perfect shade of green to match your eyes, Mistress."

She nodded in agreement and made the purchase, but the brightness of the day had dimmed a bit for her after seeing her enemies, and she was ready to return to the domus.

When she walked up to the entrance, she observed two of the guards, Gaius and Felix, guarding the door. They nodded to her, and out of the corner of her eye, Octavia thought she saw Esther smile and duck her head slightly while looking at them.

Octavia and Esther went to her room to put away her purchases, and as Octavia let the heavy curtain door fall behind her, she noticed pieces of papyrus on the floor. She glanced at the windows in confusion, wondering if a breeze would have been strong enough to blow them off of her table. But as she approached, she realized with horror that it was her portrait of Julius. Someone had ripped it in two and written over both halves, "YOU MADE THE WRONG CHOICE!" The small amount of remaining ink in the clay pot on her table had been drizzled over the cushions on her floor in a random pattern to do the most damage possible.

"Oh, Mistress!" Esther exclaimed in shock and dismay as Octavia gasped.

Octavia barely registered that she had dropped her new palla. Then she ripped her eyes up from the destruction to glance around the room in concern. It occurred to her that the vandal might still be in the room, so she turned on her heel, grabbed Esther by the arm, and fled back to the guards. When they reached Felix and Gaius, the guards listened with concern to their tale, and the women stood with Gaius as Felix went to get more of the guards from their stations to search the domus for an intruder.

Julius and Linus returned home shortly after and were greeted by the sight of Octavia hugging Esther, who silently sobbed while Gaius swept his gaze around, angrily searching for threats.

Julius stepped toward Octavia. "What happened?" he inquired in grave concern.

She answered him with a slight hiccup in her voice. "Someone was in the domus, in our chambers! They tore one of my sketches and wrote a message on it. Some of the guards are inside searching for the intruder in case he is still here."

Julius commanded Linus to stay with the women and charged forward into the domus. As he was on the way to his room, two pairs of guards converged in the atrium. Felix was in one of the teams and looked at the other. "We did not find anyone," he reported.

A guard from the other group responded, "Neither did we."

Felix stepped toward Julius, "If it pleases you, Master, I will check for signs of how the intruder entered the domus while Atticus shows you the chambers. I will have the rest of the guards return to their patrols."

Julius nodded in agreement. "Proceed."

The guard named Atticus stepped forward as the others dispersed back to their posts. He led the way to the chambers, where Julius witnessed the room as Octavia had found it. He bent down and gazed at the portrait that Octavia must have been hiding as she worked on it. It was an incredible likeness to him, and the message was very clear. Someone was not over their disappointment that Octavia had married him. Julius had a pretty good guess as to who would have been responsible for such a petty prank.

He rose and dismissed Atticus back to his post before rejoining the group at the entrance to the domus. He noticed that Esther had stopped crying and was talking quietly to Gaius, who nodded as he continued to monitor his surroundings. Sitting on the bench by the door, Octavia looked off into the distance, petting the orange cat who lived in the gardens and often walked through the domus as if he were the master. As she noticed Julius, she stood, and he put his arms around her and pulled her close.

"Why would he do this? What purpose does it serve?" Octavia looked up at him beseechingly.

Julius sighed. "I don't know exactly. He might just be miserable and want us to be as well."

"I saw him in the market earlier, and he gave me this evil grin as if he had some mischief in mind." She shuddered in his arms.

Fury at the man who had caused this fear in his wife filled Julius as he held her, but he was prevented from answering by Felix walking back up to the group. "The bush right outside the window has a depression in it, and I believe that someone came from the street after the guard walked by on patrol. Then the intruder climbed in, did their damage, and when they were leaving, accidentally trampled the bush."

Julius looked between Felix and Gaius. "How many additional guards would be necessary to maintain a sentinel on every wall?"

Felix glanced at Gaius, who answered, "We would need four more men if you want two to remain on guard at the entrance."

Julius nodded and pulled away from Octavia. "Are you able to join Gaius and me at the market to acquire these new men? I don't feel comfortable leaving you without the entire domus defended."

Octavia squared her shoulders. "I am fine, really." She glanced at Esther, who nodded in silent agreement to join her.

Felix alerted the other guards, and soon, Gaius led the rest of the group on their mission. As they walked to the market, Julius was mulling over his options. Any direct confrontation would lead to Marcus pleading his innocence and get Julius nowhere. Ignoring the vandalism also had its risks, as no consequences might embolden their enemy to redouble his efforts at sabotage.

He recalled words from one of the scrolls that his neighbors had owned. King Solomon had written, "Unless the LORD builds the house, those who build it labor in vain. Unless the LORD watches over the city, the watchman stays awake in vain."

As he walked with Octavia's hand in his, he prayed to himself, "God, please watch over our house. Please keep us safe from our enemies and help us to be loving to our enemies while we also protect ourselves. I'm not even sure what that looks like. I cannot do this alone. Please keep Octavia safe. As King David also once prayed to you, 'Deliver me from my enemies, O my God; protect me from those who rise up against me.' "

CHAPTER 5

It had been three days since the break-in, and life had begun to regain its normalcy. Octavia still peeked inside each chamber before entering, but she did not jump at loud noises anymore. Julius had requested the destroyed portrait to be kept as evidence in case further threats were made, and Octavia had begun to work on a new portrait. Her husband had stayed home for the last few days working on records and sent Linus to monitor the workmen at the insulae.

He came and checked on her several times throughout the day and asked how she was doing as he ate meals with her. Often, when he walked through the room she occupied, he gave her reassuring hugs or squeezed her hand. He was quite impressed with her portrait and loved the way she was able to capture the smallest details in his eyes and expression.

Octavia was now sitting upon a stone bench in the courtyard garden and stroking the orange tabby cat she had lovingly given the moniker, Grumps. Julius had taken to calling him Emperor, given his propensity to go wherever he pleased. She was musing about her next project for the domus when Isaiah walked into the courtyard and handed her a missive.

"This arrived for you, Mistress."

Octavia nodded and took the note from his extended hand, "Thank you, Isaiah."

She opened the note with a slight tremble in her fingers as her insulated life had led to few friends who would write to her. She was greeted by her father's bold handwriting as it marched stalwartly across the papyrus. The fact that he had written this himself instead of having his aid do it spoke to the severity of his mood when he penned it.

She quickly scanned the note as Grumps, now indignant at being ignored, stood, stretched, and leapt down to saunter through his domain. Octavia's forehead pinched in dismay as she rose to find Julius.

As she walked into the tablinum, or office, that had once been Festus's, she barely noticed that Julius had removed all traces of his predecessor and made the room his own. He was perusing through scrolls and scribbling notes with a stylus when she entered the tablinum, but he paused as she entered. The smile that he had just for her faded as he took in her frazzled expression. He waved Linus from the room.

"What is it, Love?" he urgently inquired.

"My father sent a note," she responded in a monotone voice.

"I will assume from your expression that his intention was not to extend his congratulations for our new union?" Julius joked.

Octavia snorted out a half chuckle at the absurdity of that idea and said in a more bemused tone, "No... it is not."

Julius leaned back slightly, closed his eyes, and pinched the bridge of his nose. "Why don't you read it to me, and we can work through our response together," he suggested.

Octavia took a deep breath before beginning, "Dearest Daughter, I have heard from Marcus (who has the utmost concern for you and our family) that you have, through your poor decision-making, as a woman without a husband to direct her, now find yourself the subject of much gossip and disdain from your friends. I have been convinced that without regard for how this would reflect upon your family, you have married a low-class plebeian! Your mother and I are leaving our countryside villa to stay at our domus in Rome. We expect your hospitality for meals until we can resolve this situation. Your Father, Aurelius."

Julius lowered his hand and sat forward in his seat. "Well, that was direct."

He stood and walked to where Octavia stood with tears in her eyes. He hugged her and asked, "Did you write your father after our union?"

"I wrote a note saying that I had remarried and that the estate was secured according to Festus's will, but I did not mention your name or any details," she responded.

"So, your family knew you were about to be thrown onto the streets?" he clarified.

"Yes, I had written to my father three times after Festus died, begging him for help or for some kind of legal aid so that I would not be homeless, but he only replied to the first note with assurances that Marcus would take care of everything. Even my protestations that Marcus was doing nothing and that no offers to court me were forthcoming made no impact on him. He did not even acknowledge the second two notes I sent."

"Well, then he should be happy that his daughter is taken care of, but regardless, there isn't anything he can do to undo our marriage or the completed terms of the will," Julius reassured.

"But he is coming here! He will expect at least fifty slaves not including the guards and will look for any opportunity to undermine you and I with the slaves and the other publicans in the area," Octavia worried aloud.

"Well then, I must have a chat with him when he arrives," Julius said as he rubbed her back soothingly.

"We could leave and go to our country villa and just miss them!" she suggested.

"My dear, we can't avoid them forever, and the sooner we address this, the better."

"I suppose, but it will make life much more difficult for the duration of their stay," she responded.

"I would expect nothing less from anyone in your past. You were kind of a troublemaker, you know." He said in jest as he smiled down at her.

She smiled back at him and chuckled. "How do you always know what to say to make me feel better?"

"I'd like to think I'm getting to know you pretty well." He leaned down and kissed her.

Then he backed up and called for Linus, who was waiting outside the room faithfully. "Tell Isaiah that I need him immediately," he commanded the man.

Linus nodded and stepped out of the room before returning quickly with Isaiah.

Julius immediately launched into his request, "Isaiah, I need the domus prepared for Octavia's parents and their personal slaves to arrive at any time. They will expect to take meals with us. We only know that they are coming but not when. Tell the others to prepare for some hostility and that if they are questioned by any of the visitors, their response should only be: 'You would have to ask the Master.' I do not want any gossip from our staff."

"Yes, Master. I will ensure the utmost discretion from your household."

Julius nodded, "Thank you, Isaiah. Please let me know as you prepare if you feel we need to increase our staff to accommodate the extra guests. Linus, please assist Isaiah in any way until the guests arrive."

Isaiah and Linus both nodded and left the room to complete their duties, leaving Julius and Octavia alone together to pray that God would give them patience and strength to endure what was sure to be another trial.

Two days after the note was delivered, right before the midday meal, Octavia's parents arrived with five of their personal slaves to attend them. Julius, who was summoned to the entrance of the domus by Isaiah, stood holding Octavia's hand and observed as the man he assumed to be Aurelius strode up to the entry. His new father-in-law was a tall man with stark white hair and a matching, well-kept beard. He appeared to be in his late fifties and had permanent frown lines on his forehead and around his eyes.

As he entered the domus, he eyed the guards suspiciously, and his wife, Claudia, followed along meekly. She looked about twenty years his junior and was quite a beautiful woman with dark, almost black hair lightly streaked with a few white hairs. Julius could see the resemblance between his wife and her mother, who had Octavia's startling green eyes and delicate features.

Octavia released his hand and went to her mother who smiled and held her arms open for her. Aurelius surveyed the scene and gave a slight frown when he saw his wife and daughter embracing, as if witnessing joy further soured his mood. The frown turned to an angry scowl when he turned to Julius, who stood with an impassive expression as he regarded his uninvited guest.

"Hail, Aurelius. I am Julius, your new son-in-law."

"Julius, we have much to discuss," Aurelius glared as he replied.

Octavia and Claudia paused their reunion to glance at the men, and Julius addressed them. "Why don't you ladies go to the garden and enjoy the beautiful weather while we retire to the tablinum before our meal."

Octavia nodded and led her mother to the sunny garden while Julius led the way to the tablinum. The three women slaves who came with his in-laws followed their mistress while the two men and Linus followed Aurelius. Julius charged the slaves to remain outside as he invited his father-in-law into the room. He sat in a chair behind the table he used as his desk and motioned to another chair on the opposite side in which Aurelius sat stiffly.

Julius folded his hands in his lap. "I understand from your note that you may have something you want to discuss with me, and I assumed you would prefer privacy. Please address whatever issues are on your mind."

Aurelius blinked for a moment as if confused. "I was given the impression that you were an uneducated plebeian, but you seem quite well-educated to me."

Julius quickly responded, "I assume that you received a dismal report from Marcus who, without meaning to offend, I must report honestly that I have found to be quite malicious in his treatment of Octavia and I. Octavia had less than a week left before she was to be thrown out onto the street when I married her, and I assure you that she had no marriage offers other than mine. I do not know what Marcus's plan was, but he almost seems bitter that Octavia was not thrown out.

"I even invited him to our wedding feast the following day, and he quite rudely stormed out after my toast. Now, whenever we see him, he glares as if personally wronged. I, however, cannot see how he is possibly the wronged party in this situation. I assume, given your concern for your family's reputation, that you did not want your daughter out on the street?"

Aurelius stroked his beard as if deep in thought. "Of course not."

"Well then, I hope that you want the best for your daughter and will be able to keep an open mind despite a negative report by a biased and angry man," Julius said.

Aurelius gave him a piercing stare for a moment. "I have invited Marcus to dinner here tonight. I will judge between the two of you who is telling the truth then."

Julius swallowed down an angry retort and replied, "I understand your concern over a negative report, and therefore, I will, just this once, overlook your impudence at inviting an enemy of mine to my home without my foreknowledge, but you should know that your daughter and this estate are legally mine; and if you attempt to in any way undermine my position or do anything to hurt your daughter, you will never again be allowed into this house."

Aurelius's expression changed to one of begrudging respect. He stood and put out his hand over the table. "Agreed."

Julius stood and shook his hand.

Octavia looked around the dining room during the midday meal and smiled at her mother. The slaves bustled about serving them food while Julius and her father spoke together amicably. Once, she even saw her father laugh at a joke. For the first time in years, her mother smiled and looked closer to her age instead of ten years older. It appeared that seeing her daughter in a healthy and happy marriage raised her spirits.

Octavia observed Gaius, who was stationed just inside the dining room entrance, and Esther standing beside him with a sweet smile. The meal passed by pleasantly, and Octavia's parents retired to a spare room to rest while Julius and Octavia went to their chambers.

After seating themselves on the new cushions in their room, Julius began, "So your father invited Marcus here for dinner."

Octavia visibly blanched and stared at him with her mouth slightly agape. After a moment, she responded, "Why would he do that?"

"He believed Marcus when he wrote that I was an appalling choice for you, and I suspect that Marcus implied I had stolen you away from him."

"That's completely ridiculous!" she gushed angrily.

Julius put out his hands in a placating gesture and responded, "I know, and I think I have managed to convince your father to at least evaluate the evidence before he comes to any conclusions when judging between the benevolence of myself and Marcus. However, I did let him know in no uncertain terms you are my wife and that impositions such as this invitation would be permitted only this one time, and any future interference on his part will be met with outright estrangement. He seemed genuinely confused about Marcus not having courted you and the man's accusations that I was uneducated.

"So, we will see how dinner goes, but I will have Gaius and Felix in the dining room with us, and just to be on the safe side, we will arrange the seating with your parents between us and Marcus. That way, there will be no possibility of him slipping anything in our drinks."

"Well," said Octavia. "Thank you for handling that conversation, and as Jesus said in his sermon on the mountain top, we shouldn't be anxious."

"Exactly," replied Julius. "Let us pray for the dinner tonight and bring our cares to our Lord, who we know is in control."

They bowed their heads, and Julius began, "God, our Creator and Sustainer, please help us to endure all trials with grace and humility. Please protect us from evil, and please lead Octavia's parents and Marcus to repentance. Forgive us for our bitterness toward them, and help us to love them like you first loved us. Amen."

"Amen." She smiled at him and leaned forward to kiss him as he smiled back at her.

Later that afternoon, while Octavia and her mother walked through the olive fields together, her father and Julius regrouped in his tablinum to continue conversing. As they drank their watered-down wine, they discussed current politics and the annual olive harvest.

When the discussion turned to his new lifestyle, Julius smiled, "I have found your daughter to be incredibly helpful as I have been adjusting to the daily operations of the estate."

Aurelius threw back his head in an exaggerated laugh, "How could she possibly be helpful?! I love her, of course, but I have found that women are good for serving men and having babies and little else. I have always found it necessary to use a firm hand when guiding her and her mother. It's simply the way they were designed. The god Janus gave men brains and women wombs. What more can we expect of them?" He took a long drag from his wine goblet and chuckled to himself.

Julius clenched his jaw in disgust during his father-in-law's diatribe and took a deep breath as Aurelius waited expectantly for his agreement.

He spoke in a soft and measured tone when he replied, "I cannot adequately express how strongly I disagree with everything you believe about women. I think that if you talked with an open mind to a woman, you would find them to be quite intelligent and delightful beings. They are often quick to encourage, and I have found your daughter to be quite loving and loyal.

"According to the Word of Yahweh, who created all things, he created women as a helper to men. He did not desire them to be dominated by men but to be loved and cherished."

Aurelius looked stunned and then angry. "Yahweh! Are you a Roman Jew then, to blaspheme Janus and the gods of Rome?!"

"No, I am not a Jew, but I would love to tell you what I believe and why. I hope that we can continue a friendly discourse despite disagreeing," Julius implored with a calm challenge in his tone.

Aurelius studied him closely, and eventually, the anger in his gaze cooled, and he nodded in agreement with Julius's request for civility.

Julius began to tell him about his life, how he had been a Roman citizen since birth and a farmer by trade. "One day, my family had been infected by the plague; they were dying. For some reason, I was the only one who did not fall ill. I fasted and prayed to all the gods, and I went daily to the temples to offer prayer and sacrifices. But I received no answer to my pleas, and each of my family members died in turn, leaving me alone. I then turned to my work and stopped praying to the gods altogether. I felt that they had abandoned me in my time of need.

"One day, my neighbors, who were Jews, invited me to their home for a meal. I attended mostly out of curiosity because I had always been told that Jews never ate or socialized with Romans. After dinner, I spoke with the head of the household, Simon, who asked me what I thought was going to happen when I died. I replied that I would join my family in the underworld.

"He told me about the true God of all creation. One we could speak to and have a personal relationship with. I was skeptical, but I went to his home many times over several months to discuss this further. Simon told me of the God of all the universe, "I am that I am," or Yahweh. He created all the world, the animals, and the planets and stars. Then he created a man, Adam, and he took a rib bone from Adam with which he created the first woman, Eve, both created in the image of God.

"He only gave them one command, to never eat from the tree of the knowledge of good and evil. They were perfect and lived in the Garden of Eden, where they communed with God. But they became corrupted when they ate from the forbidden tree. From that point on, they were removed from the garden, and all their offspring were corrupted by evil. You see the evil in our world, right?"

Aurelius nodded skeptically.

Julius continued, "This evil is a result of humans breaking God's law. After they left captivity in Egypt, God gave the Jews ten commandments on tablets of stone, his law."

Julius used his fingers to count them out as he continued, "The commandments are that we should have no other gods but Yahweh, not take his name in vain or make carved images to worship, keep the Sabbath day as a day of rest, honor our father and mother, and not murder, commit adultery, steal, bear false witness, or covet our neighbor's wife or property. If we do any of these things, we have transgressed against a holy God and are worthy of judgment and death.

"But God promised that even though we are all guilty of breaking his law, he would make a way of salvation for all who took it. I realized that I had been sinning against this holy God who made me, and I was desperate for this salvation. Simon told me that in the past, the Jews had offered sacrifices of animals on

God's altar in order to atone for their sins while they waited for a Savior who God had promised would come and be the sacrifice for all who believe in Him.

"You see, God is three persons in one being: the Father, the Son, and the Holy Spirit. The Son is the Savior who was coming to the earth to save it. He made himself into the form of a man and lived a perfect life before being killed only a few years past."

Aurelius, who had been staring incredulously, widened his eyes in recognition as his mouth dropped open. "You are speaking of Jesus of Nazareth, the carpenter who was hung on a tree in Jerusalem! I have heard of this sect of Judaism. You follow the Way!"

Julius nodded, "I imagine you believe me to be a fool for believing, but I'm curious, do you ever feel guilt when you do something, even when you don't feel that you have done anything wrong and have not sinned against the Roman gods?"

"Yes... I suppose," he stammered.

"That is the conscience that God has put into all men. We have something inside ourselves that knows when we are sinning against the God who made us. In the past, with few exceptions, God saved only his chosen people, the Jews, but now, since his Savior took the punishment for the sins of all men and was raised from the dead on the third day, he has conquered sin and death, and all men, even Romans are able to receive the gift of grace and forgiveness of sins. All we have to do is ask God to forgive us from our sins, turn from them, and believe in Jesus as our Savior."

"You speak as if you were mad!" Aurelius bellowed in shock and consternation.

Now Julius chuckled, "I understand how you would believe that. I would have believed the same of a fellow Roman only two years ago, but I now have the assurance that when I die, I will not be punished for my sins in unquenchable fire but will be in paradise with my God for all of eternity."

Aurelius continued to stare in disbelief. "You truly believe all of this nonsense."

"I do believe, and I would like to challenge you to search out answers for yourself. As you believe that I am wrong, bring me proof that Jesus did not rise from the dead. You had to have heard that his tomb was found empty..."

Aurelius cut him off, "Of course! Because his disciples stole his body!"

"Or is that a lie that has been told to cover the truth? If you can prove that what I believe is a lie, I would love to see the proof, but if you cannot disprove my assertions, I urge you to consider your own eternity and relationship with the divine. If I am right, you are risking a lot by dismissing it out of hand."

"I suppose it wouldn't hurt anything to find you this proof. I have friends and a villa in Jerusalem that I have been meaning to return to and will plan a trip there next week. I'll bring you back your proof, because no son-in-law of mine should be blaspheming the gods in order to worship a dead man!" Aurelius asserted.

Julius smiled and raised his wine glass, "To the truth then."

Aurelius gave a half-menacing grin. "To the truth!"

Octavia had spent a blissful afternoon walking arm in arm with her mother among her olive trees. Because it had been several months since the pair had seen each other, Octavia told her mother all that had happened from Festus's death until the present, leaving out only the details of how she met Julius. She stuck to her abbreviated story of meeting him at the marketplace.

Claudia was thrilled that Octavia seemed so happy with her new husband. "I am so glad that you are married to him and not Marcus. Your father kept insisting that Marcus would take care of you, and I knew not to verbalize my opposition to the idea, but everything inside me was screaming in concern that he would not be a good husband. He is a widower, if you did not know."

"I was unaware," said Octavia.

Claudia went on to explain, "His dear wife fell ill and passed into the underworld about ten years ago, but during her marriage, she always seemed so sad, and I had observed bruises upon her wrists and arms on more than one occasion. I would not be at all surprised if he were responsible for your portrait being destroyed."

Octavia nodded in agreement, "It is our theory as well."

Claudia smiled at her and patted her hand, "Having a husband who listens to you and takes your thoughts into consideration is what I have always wanted for you. Life is long, and it can be very bitter when your husband views you as little more than an object."

Octavia felt tears well up in her eyes, "I am sorry, Mother. I pray for you often."

"So, you still believe in the Way, do you?" Claudia asked her daughter.

"Yes, Mother and I wish for you and Father to come to believe in Jesus as well."

Claudia smiled patronizingly and responded, "Like I said before, life is long. Who knows what might happen."

Octavia gave her a smile, but sadness filled her eyes at the thought of her parents' lives after death and the idea that they might be separated from God and from her forever.

There was a comfortable silence for a few moments as they made their way back to the domus to prepare for dinner. She soon shook off her melancholy and prayed for her parents' salvation.

53

CHAPTER 6

As the sun began to descend, Isaiah entered the dining room and announced Marcus's arrival moments before the man strode into the room. He narrowed his eyes as he looked around the dining area, noting the two guards and the seating arrangement that placed him far from Octavia and Julius.

Aurelius stood from where he had been lounging on a couch. He grasped Marcus's forearm, and the other man returned the greeting. "Hail, Marcus. I hope you are doing well."

"Hail, Aurelius. I am well. I have missed you around Rome. You know that no one brings as much insight to the counsel as you do when you are in town."

Aurelius laughed and indicated that Marcus should take his position on the couch. As both men reclined, Julius nodded to Isaiah to begin serving their first course.

The dinner progressed amicably with no arguments or raised voices, but Julius did not miss the way that his father-in-law watched everything and how he frowned slightly when he observed Marcus casting disparaging looks toward Octavia. Marcus did not initiate any conversations but spoke politely when

Aurelius engaged him. Julius drew Octavia into the conversation by asking her to explain the new fresco she had commissioned for one wall of the dining room upon which the current plaster was starting to peel. She smiled at him and proceeded to explain her vision of a painted scene of a man and a woman holding hands in a garden with the sun shining down on them and the birds singing in the olive trees. Julius smiled at her encouragingly even as Marcus and her father looked incredulously at her as if she should not have her own ideas for a home.

At the end of the meal, Aurelius asked if he could use the tablinum to have a conversation with Julius and Marcus.

Julius nodded and extended his arm toward the room. "Of course."

Marcus stood and looked almost nervous as the group of men went into the tablinum.

Aurelius wasted no time but turned to the other men where they stood. "Marcus, I have been told that you did not, in fact, ask my daughter for her hand as I had assumed was your intention. Is this true?"

Marcus fidgeted and fingered a fold of his toga. "Well, I hadn't quite yet, but you must know that I was planning to. I just hadn't found the right time yet. She was still grieving..." He trailed off.

Aurelius flushed angrily, "My daughter was less than a week from being cast out of her home and into the streets. I had already expressed to you my outrage at Festus's idiotic will. I married off my daughter so that she would be cared for, not treated as a common slave! You, in turn, assured me that you would take care of her! Then you implied in your letter to me that an interloper who could barely read had stolen her from you! How can you possibly reconcile these conflicting narratives?"

Marcus sputtered and glanced at Julius in embarrassment before returning his gaze to the glaring older man. "I...I was going to take care of it, and I suppose I wrote hastily in my anger. I thought that Octavia knew I was going to take care of her, and it seemed to me that her choosing a stranger was a direct slight against me."

Aurelius puffed out his chest and continued sternly, "Well, you asked me to come here and resolve this, and I have judged that there is nothing to resolve. You, through your own inaction, lost the chance to marry my daughter, and while I do not agree with everything that Julius believes, I know that he is an honorable man and will take care of Octavia, which is more than I can say for you. You will not interfere with my daughter anymore. You had your chance, and I no longer need you to look out for her. Do I make myself clear?"

"Yes, of course," Marcus ground out before he turned on his heel and strode from the room.

"If you'll excuse me. I need to ensure he leaves peaceably," Julius said over his shoulder as he hastily followed Marcus.

Aurelius trailed just behind his son-in-law, and the two men stood in the entrance of the atrium watching as Marcus stormed out of the house, past the guards, and into the street.

"I want to thank you for what you said in there. I will take care of your daughter," Julius said when Marcus had disappeared.

Aurelius sighed, "I know you will. I just wish I had listened to my daughter's letters instead of trusting Marcus to marry her."

"Well, I have to say that I am happy he didn't marry her." Julius quipped with a smile.

Aurelius chuckled as they walked back to the dining room to rejoin the women. "I'm still going to prove you wrong about Jesus."

"I look forward to seeing your evidence."

Over the course of the next week, Octavia and Julius hosted her parents for their evening meals. They had lively conversations about many aspects of Roman life and world events. Julius often drew Claudia and Octavia into the conversations and was amused at Aurelius' shocked expressions when his wife or daughter said something witty. It was as if the man was still so blinded by his prejudice that his mind just couldn't comprehend what he was hearing.

After the week was over and her parents had left for Jerusalem to find evidence that Jesus was simply a dead carpenter, Octavia sat with Julius in their room. She cuddled close to his side. "Thank you for all that you have done this week. I have always felt invisible to my father until now. He actually listened to what I said. I do hope he continues to talk to my mother. She has often complained that he treats her more like a clay pot than a living person."

"Why don't we pray for them?" Julius suggested.

Octavia nodded, and Julius began, "Our Father, thank you for allowing us to see a new side of Aurelius this week. Please help him to treat Claudia well and help him to come to realize the truth about you as he seeks to disprove you. Amen."

"Amen," she echoed.

Julius kissed her. "Are you comfortable if I start to go out to work on the insulae again?"

"Yes, we haven't had any incidents in weeks, and hopefully the talk with my father will prevent Marcus from taking further actions against us. My father is powerful in the local government and would be a bad enemy to make," she said.

"Very true," responded Julius. "Well, since you are comfortable, I will go tomorrow and see how everything goes."

Octavia nodded sleepily against his shoulder, and Julius picked her up and carried her to bed.

The next day, after working at the insulae, Julius returned home with Linus to find that no incidents had occurred in his absence. After conferring with Octavia and Isaiah about the day, he was sitting in his tablinum, looking at a scroll about a piece of land he now owned in the countryside far to the north that had no apparent purpose. He mused to himself about why Festus would have wanted this particular property that from all he could see was bringing in no money and was simply sitting idle. He raised his head to ask Linus for his opinion when he saw Gaius enter through the curtain.

"Master, might I have a moment of your time to make a request?" asked the captain of the guards.

Julius nodded, "Speak."

"The guards and I have been working in shifts for weeks with little breaks, and I was hoping to make a plan with you that would allow for us to take periodic days off one at a time so that you will never be unguarded."

"Yes, of course; I am sorry that I had not considered that. Please write up a calendar of your days off and submit it to me for approval," Julius easily acquiesced.

Gaius relaxed his shoulders a bit but still stood as if at attention until Julius dismissed him.

Three days later, on the Lord's Day, Julius led Octavia and Esther down the streets on the poorer side of Rome to the home that the believers would be meeting in this week. As they were greeted and entered the home, they observed Peter speaking with a tall, muscled man whose back faced them. As the man turned, Esther gasped slightly, and her two companions followed her gaze to see Gaius shaking Peter's hand and smiling cheerily.

As he continued to turn and find a seat, Gaius's gaze rested upon the trio, who now stood about five feet away staring at him. The smile faded from his lips, and his long stride ate up the ground between them.

"Hail, Master, Mistress, Esther." He nodded at each in turn. "Did you come seeking me because of a problem?"

Julius managed to regain his composure first and answered the man, "No, we did not know that you were going to be here."

Gaius's eyebrows raised. "So, you are also believers in the Way?"

Octavia and Esther wore matching smiles of delight as Julius replied, "Yes, we are, and we are so glad to know that you are a brother in Christ."

Gaius smiled again and directed his arm toward some cushions on the floor. "Would you care to sit together then?"

"Of course," they responded.

Julius and Octavia sat down beside each other with Esther on Octavia's right and Gaius seated by Esther. Octavia noticed the sly glances that Esther kept shooting toward Gaius as they worshiped and prayed with the believers.

Peter spoke of God's provision for his people and how he had witnessed on two different occasions Jesus taking only a small amount of food, and after he blessed it, the food multiplied until it was able to feed huge crowds of people. The believers listened with spellbound attention as Peter talked about all that he had heard and seen on those days.

When the service was over and the group of four made their way back toward the domus, Julius smiled and said, "What an incredible God we serve." The others echoed their agreement. As they approached the marketplace, Gaius said that he had some items he needed to purchase and asked if anyone needed him for anything.

Esther timidly spoke up. "If you don't mind, I have a couple things that I would like to purchase, and I could join you."

"I would be happy to escort you to the market and back home." He put out his arm for her to take as they left the other pair and walked on.

Octavia smiled as she watched them go. "I knew that Esther was interested in Gaius and have seen them speak often. I am pleased to know that they share a common faith."

Julius nodded in agreement. "We will pray for God to work his will in their lives."

The couple strolled back home and did no work for the rest of the day, in obedience to their God's command to rest on the Sabbath.

Gaius smiled to himself as he walked along with Esther. What an incredible stroke of providence that his master and mistress were believers in the Way! He was also thrilled that he had this opportunity to spend time with the beautiful, demure Esther, the woman he was always trying to catch a glimpse of as he guarded the domus. He suppressed a regretful sigh, wishing that he was in a position to get married.

Another month passed by, and Julius and Octavia went about their daily lives, learning more about each other and how to run their household together. The artist Octavia had hired came and completed the new fresco in their dining room. They went with Gaius and Esther to fellowship with the believers every Lord's Day.

At one church assembly, they had witnessed Peter preaching, and were surprised when he paused as he noticed a blind man sitting in the group. Then he told the blind man that in the name of the Lord Jesus Christ, he was healed. To everyone's amazement, the man's eyes, which had been a cloudy white, were now clear, and he jumped up, shouting that he could see! They also witnessed Peter healing two other people from their maladies on separate occasions, and the whole congregation praised God for His blessings.

They formed several friendships with other believers from the church and had Peter and these believers over to their home for dinners most days of the week. Octavia had never felt such a feeling of belonging and love as she did at this point in her life.

One day, while Julius was out working on the insulae, Esther hurried into the atrium where Octavia was sitting and drawing her reflection in the impluvium. Octavia glanced up and noticed that her servant looked terrified. Esther moved at a most awkward and rapid pace toward her with a piece of papyrus clutched in her pale hand.

Octavia looked at her with concern. "What is wrong, Dear?!"

Esther held out her hand with the papyrus and shakily said, "One of the guards found this on the side of the domus. It was pinned with a bloody dagger in a crack between two stones."

As Octavia took the papyrus, she noticed that it contained no words, only a crude drawing of a man and a woman hanging from crucifixes. There was bright red blood dripped over the sheet, and in her shock, she thrust the distressing message away and watched as it fluttered to the ground at her feet. Her hands shook, and she wished that Julius was home.

Gaius then entered the atrium. "Mistress, the orange cat that roams around the property is dead. We just found him, and it appears that is where the blood on the dagger and drawing originated. We are on high alert, and you do not need to fear. Isaiah has gone to fetch the master, and I will stand guard over you until he returns and gives us orders."

Octavia nodded at Gaius and took a deep breath. "God, please protect us," she whispered, and she noticed that Gaius nodded before standing at attention with his face studiously trained at the entrances to the atrium.

Octavia turned to Esther. "He killed Grumps! There was no need to do that. What could he possibly stand to gain by escalating his violence against us?!"

"I do not know, Mistress. Would you like me to pray for us?" her slave answered her.

"Yes, please do."

The women bowed their heads as Esther began, "Our great God, we do not know why this is happening, but please protect us from our enemies. Help the master to choose his next move carefully. Help the responsible party to be revealed for the evil man that he is. Please comfort Octavia and help us not to have a spirit of fear but one of peace, knowing that you are in control of all."

About an hour later, Julius ran into the atrium, and Octavia launched herself into his arms. He inspected the note and dagger and commanded Gaius to go to the nearest centurion and relay to him their plight.

"It is time to involve the authorities, and hopefully, they can put an end to this madness," Julius declared.

CHAPTER 7

A short time later, the centurion who was charged with keeping order in this section of Rome arrived with a company of five of his soldiers. He introduced himself as Cato, and Julius launched into an explanation of their situation. Then, the newlyweds watched as the soldiers collected the note, dagger, and torn portrait.

"Do you have any idea who would be angry with the two of you," Cato asked.

Julius and Octavia shared a look before Julius launched into the story of the will, their marriage, and the less-than-enthusiastic reception they had received from Marcus. The centurion glanced between them and listened carefully.

He asked a few clarifying questions before declaring, "I think we have enough here. We will speak to Marcus Valerii about his whereabouts and will follow up with you. In the meantime, keep up your guard. I will station five of my men outside your home to assist your guards as we search for answers."

Julius looked relieved as he nodded at Cato and held Octavia's hand while the soldiers dispersed themselves around the domus. Then he looked down at her and said, "I will write a letter to your father detailing present events. He may have more insight into this situation than we do."

Octavia nodded and felt a little bereft when he left her to go to his tablinum and pen the letter. She rubbed her arms and decided to sit in the garden and pray while she waited for the midday meal. She hoped that some food would soothe her stomach, which had been sour throughout the day.

After Julius was finished with his letter, he rejoined Octavia in the courtyard and sighed. "Hopefully, we will hear from Cato soon."

He looked at her in concern, "Are you alright?"

A tear rolled down her cheek. "I know it may seem foolish, but I am really going to miss Grumps. He was a comfort to me over the years that I was married to Festus. Now I feel like I lost a good friend."

He pulled her close and kissed the top of her head. "It doesn't seem foolish at all. I often think of my animals, especially the ones that I had raised from birth. I suppose I will never know what happened to them, but I imagine most if not all of them have been killed by now."

She looked up at him with tears now streaming down her face. "I'm sorry. I hadn't even considered the fate of your animals."

He patted her hand as they shared a moment of sad reflection on their losses.

Soon, they walked to the dining room and began their meal. Despite Octavia's hunger, she did not feel well enough to eat more than a few bites of cheese and bread.

Julius looked at her with concern, "Do you need to lie down, Love?"

"Yes, I think the excitement of the day has just been too much for me, and I will lie down for a while," Octavia responded.

Octavia woke from her nap several hours later. Her stomach had still not settled, and she hoped that a drink might make her feel better. She walked from the room to ask Esther for a drink when she heard a commotion at the door. Just then, Julius and Isaiah hurried from the tablinum toward the noise.

Octavia followed behind them, and from her position behind the men, she was able to witness an enraged Marcus being restrained by two domus guards and a soldier.

"How dare you accuse me of killing a cat! Why would I do something so, so stupid?!" He yelled ferociously at the master of the house.

Julius maintained his calm demeanor as he replied, "I did no such thing. We have had some threats and vandalism here in the last few weeks, and that included someone coming onto our property today and killing my wife's cat. I did not accuse anyone but told the centurion about the enemies we have. Your name came up for obvious reasons."

Marcus looked incredulously at the guards, soldiers, and Julius. Then he backed up slightly, shook off the guards who were lightly clasping his arms, and straightened his toga. He glared at Julius. "I may not like you and think that you are a no-good plebeian who is not worthy of Octavia or the great Festus's estate, but I would never waste my time or resources on a lost cause! I was away on business all week and arrived home from my villa this evening, so you will not be able to pin your misfortunes upon me."

He leveled one more glare at the guards and left in a huff. Julius took a moment to thank the guards before returning to the entrance of the home and noticing Octavia.

"Are you feeling any better now?" he asked her.

"Not really, but I was just going to get a drink."

Esther, who had appeared from another room, said, "I will get you one now."

Octavia nodded and looked back at Julius. "Do you believe him?"

He sighed. "I don't know what to believe. I highly doubt that any of Festus's other friends are behind these events. He is clearly the one who had the most to lose from you marrying me, and he undoubtably still carries a grudge."

Esther returned with a goblet of watered-down wine for Octavia, who felt a bit refreshed after her drink.

Two more days went by before they heard from Cato. He returned around midday, and Octavia saw him join Julius in the tablinum before leaving a short time later. Esther informed her that she witnessed him leaving with three of the five soldiers who were guarding the house.

Julius exited the tablinum shortly after Cato left and reclined with Octavia in the dining room. Her appetite had still not returned since the day Grumps was killed, and her stomach turned over in anxiety at the thought of what Cato had said to her husband.

Julius did not make her wait long before launching into his retelling of the centurion's visit. "Cato said that Marcus could not have possibly killed Grumps or left the note. He was indeed out of town as he claimed. He could have hired someone to do it, but Cato and I both agreed that it seems unlikely given the passionate nature of the crime."

Octavia nodded in silent concern, and he continued his narrative, "Cato believes that whoever did this probably meant to leave the note inside the home like last time but, upon finding the domus well-guarded, was forced to wait in the olive orchard where he came across Grumps and decided to seize the opportunity to cause us more pain. Then he waited until the guard on that wall turned his back, slipped through the trees, and tacked up the sheet before running off. The guard heard a sound and turned to see the message and dagger, but no sign of the perpetrator. Cato is convinced that our home is well enough guarded that the man cannot come into the house, so he took back three of his guards and will only keep two on the property for now.

"I believe we will be safe with all the guards that remain." He paused for a moment. "I notice that you still haven't been eating much. Are you sure you're alright?"

Octavia looked at the food in slight disgust. "I don't know. I think I might be ill. I have been so tired and sick to my stomach ever since the incident the other day."

Julius watched as she picked at a piece of bread. "I'm sorry you don't feel well. I plan to stay in the domus with you for a few days, and I was thinking that we could go out to our countryside villa for a few weeks and get away from the threats here. I think it is unlikely that whoever is bothering us will follow us all the way out there."

Octavia smiled and nodded. "That sounds nice."

Later that afternoon, Esther helped Octavia to prepare for her nap.

"Mistress, I hope that you will not think me rude, but I had noticed your indigestion for the last several days, and it made me consider. Have you had your womanly cycle since you married Julius?"

Octavia froze for a moment, taken back by the abruptness of the question. She looked to the side in concentration as she thought back. Then she gasped in shock, "No, I haven't. Do you think...?"

"I think I should ask for a midwife to come check you and confirm," responded Esther quickly.

"Yes, of course, you are right. No need to get too excited when we don't know anything yet."

Esther propped up a pillow behind Octavia and smiled. "I think it is fine to be excited for the possibility of a little one."

Octavia smiled back. "Go fetch the midwife quickly and try to avoid telling Julius if possible. I don't want to falsely elevate his hopes."

Esther nodded and rushed from the room.

She returned about an hour later with a midwife who checked Octavia and confirmed that she was indeed expecting. Octavia thanked and paid the midwife, who left just as Julius was entering their room carrying a small box.

"Who was that?" he asked.

"That, my dear husband, was a midwife."

"Why? Wait? Are you saying that...?" Julius's eyes widened as he waited for her response.

Octavia beamed at him as she nodded yes.

He wore a stunned expression as he walked over to where she sat upon the bed and settled next to her, positioning the box next to himself. She stared at him as his face slowly altered into a wide grin.

"I'm going to be a father!" He exclaimed as he gently ran his fingers down her face.

"Yes, the midwife said that he or she should be here in around 7 or 8 months."

"Wow, what a blessing!" Julius closed his eyes. "Thank you, God!"

He looked at her again. "Do you still want to travel to the villa, or should we stay here?"

"I think I would like to go to the villa. I will feel safer there."

"Okay, I will tell Isaiah to prepare. How did Festus's country slaves treat you? Should I hire more slaves to take with us?"

"No, Festus rarely took me there. He went to the villa when life here with me was tiring or boring. I have only been there once, and it was a brief stay," she answered.

Julius looked pleased and said, "Great. Well, we will assess them when we get there then. Oh, I almost forgot, I had Linus pick you up something from the market."

He took the box from his side and handed it to her. As she opened it, she was startled to see a little orange head pop out of the box.

"Oh!" she exclaimed.

"I know he isn't Grumps, but I thought that with very little training, he could become just as good at strolling about as if he were the master of the house," he grinned.

Octavia snickered as she pulled the little kitten out of the box and cuddled him to her chest. "Of course he can."

Preparations for the coming journey went smoothly, and Octavia sat most of the time, watching the commotion around her and trying not to think about how bad she felt. She endeavored to remain upright and not expel the contents of her stomach. She always felt as if she needed to but never actually did. Esther was constantly bringing her small morsels to nibble on in order to sustain herself. How could such a little baby cause so much nausea?

On her last visit, her mother had warned her that if she was blessed with a child, she would likely feel quite ill, but she had not expected this never-ending nausea and the exhaustion that seemed to seep into even her bones. Julius was torn between his joy at having a child and his sympathy for his wife's condition.

CHAPTER 8

At last, it was time to head to the villa, which was located in the countryside, far from the heat and the noise of the city. Octavia clutched her husband's hand as they boarded their carpentum, the four-wheeled carriage with a wooden arched roof that was only owned and used by the most elite of Roman society. She had silently believed it to be frivolous and unnecessary when Festus had excitedly brought it home. She had rarely been inside it, and Julius preferred less ostentatious modes of travel. However, the trip to the villa was a lengthy one, and the carpentum was the most comfortable means to get there.

While the couple was accompanied in the carpentum by Esther and Gaius, they had employed the use of a larger raeda cart to follow them and transport their luggage, a few essential members of their household staff, and three more of their guards: Felix, Apollos, and Atticus. The other guards remained at the domus to watch over it during their trip.

Octavia was relieved to be in the comfort of the carpentum which had a much smoother ride than other forms of transportation available. She still laid her head against the cushioned back and closed her eyes in an attempt to quell the constant nausea brought on by her condition. She fell into a restless slumber while Julius observed the countryside as they flew down the stone road. Esther and Gaius spoke together in hushed tones so as to not disturb their mistress.

After several hours of travel, their carpentum pulled to a stop in front of a sprawling villa. Julius looked over at Octavia, who appeared relieved to have arrived, and he assisted her from the vehicle. The couple observed the resplendent exterior of the home and entered with Esther and Gaius.

Julius felt almost stunned at this extravagant display of wealth. The villa was by far larger than the domus in Rome. The central courtyard contained a grove of orange trees and looked about twice the size of the atrium to which he was only barely accustomed. A slave immediately came out to meet them. He nodded politely at Octavia and leveled a scrutinizing but not unkind gaze at Julius.

"How can I help you?" asked the slave.

Julius looked intently back at the man. "I have married Octavia and am your new master. Did you receive the missive I sent you?"

"Very good, Master. I did receive your message, and all has been prepared for your coming. I am Demas, the household manager for your villa."

"Excellent," responded Julius. "I am bringing guards and some essential staff from our domus. They should arrive shortly. Please show them to their quarters when they arrive."

Demas nodded in agreement. "Just call if you need me, Master." He gave a short bow before bustling off toward another part of the house.

The group of four travelers strolled through the magnificent home. Julius gazed upon an opulence he could scarcely have imagined. He walked up to a window and touched the glass panes. He had heard of such luxuries but had never anticipated owning a property with them. The home included a giant library, much larger than the one at the domus, two baths, and a gymnasium.

Throughout the entire villa, the floors were covered with colorful mosaics and were heated from underneath by a system of pipes that circulated hot air from the furnace. All rooms were covered with frescoes, and Julius counted over a dozen richly decorated bedrooms on the first and second floors, not including the slave quarters.

After about thirty minutes of exploring, the group returned to the courtyard. Julius looked around at the orange trees and the system of watering troughs that would hold rainwater and use gravity to disperse it to each tree.

Octavia sat with Esther upon a stone bench while Gaius stood at attention near the front entrance. At that moment, Julius was alerted by a noise and saw Gaius stride outside. He returned momentarily with Felix. Several slaves came to unload Octavia and Julius's possessions while Linus entered the villa. Julius watched as his eyes widened at the sight of the majestic interior. Then, Linus focused his attention upon his master and made his way over.

"Hail, Master. Do you need anything from me?"

"Thank you, Linus. I hope your trip was well. I do not require anything this evening. Tomorrow morning, after breakfast, we will begin to examine the scrolls in the tablinum. Demas is the house manager here and will show you and the rest where to stay."

"Very good, Master." He nodded and walked away to assist with the luggage and receive his room assignment.

Julius moved over to where Octavia sat, "I believe we should go to the dining room for our dinner. Do you feel up to eating anything?"

"I am sure that I can find something to nibble on." She smiled at him weakly and stood.

He offered his arm, which she accepted as they walked to the dining room. The slaves had arranged flowers over the floors and in vases on the tables. As they entered and reclined on their couches, the slaves who were in the room left to fetch their dinner.

Julius watched his wife carefully. He knew that she did not appreciate too much scrutiny, but he was concerned about her and the baby. He would have to find a midwife nearby to check on her. He could tell she had already lost weight, and he wasn't sure how much she could afford to lose.

The food was superb, and he enjoyed the courses of cheese and breads, and a variety of seafoods. His favorite was the large prawns fished from the Mediterranean. This cook might be even better than their incredible cook at home. Festus had clearly not spared any expense. That thought made his brow wrinkle in concentration.

"What are you thinking so hard about over there?" Octavia questioned him with a smile.

Julius looked up at her and said, "I was just thinking that I am hoping to find quite a few scrolls about Festus's business ventures in his tablinum here. I noticed in his records at the domus, there are mentions of various money-making ventures that are only referred to by initials. I am sure that it was just his shorthand, but Linus and I are struggling to decipher it all."

She nodded in sympathy. "I wish that I could help you, but Festus never even mentioned business affairs in front of me. He was similar to my father in that he thought women were too stupid to understand business or money."

"Well, if you are interested in knowing about our finances, all you have to do is ask. Once I figure it all out myself, I will write out a list of our ventures for you. It would be good for you to know and understand in case something ever was to happen to me," he said.

"Thank you."

"You are welcome, my Love." He paused for a moment. "Did you have a preference on which chambers you would like us to employ while here? I was considering the room right by the tablinum. What are your thoughts?"

"It is a lovely room. Honestly, I cannot even remember which quarters I stayed in the one time I was here. The room next to the tablinum seems to be as good as any other," she answered.

"Perfect." He waved over one of the slaves standing in the corner of the dining room. "Please inform Demas that we will be staying in the bedchamber next to the tablinum."

With a quick "Yes, Master," the slave hurried from the room.

After dinner, Julius and Octavia retired to their quarters for the evening, but he found himself unable to sleep. After a long day of travel, he expected to be fast asleep instantly, but the hours ticked by, and for some reason, he could not seem to keep his eyes closed for more than a few minutes at a time. He finally decided that he would go through some of the scrolls in the tablinum. That should be sufficiently boring to help put him to sleep.

He rose from his bed and upon seeing Octavia sleeping peacefully, he picked up his lamp and slipped from the room. He heard one of the slaves or guards walking quickly over the mosaics, but he did not see anyone as he lit his lamp with a torch that was mounted on the wall in the corridor. He walked toward the tablinum when he noticed an acrid smell of smoke that was out of place in the large domicile.

Just then, he observed the faintest tendrils of smoke pouring from around the edges of the curtain in front of the tablinum. Julius nearly dropped his lamp in his haste to reach the room. As he pulled back the curtain, he observed that a candle had fallen upon the desk and was now burning the scrolls there.

When he saw the fire, he leapt into action. He raised the alarm of "Fire!" and set his own lamp out of the way to prevent adding fuel to the flames. Then he rushed to the curtain door and ripped it down just as two slaves ran into the room. These recruits helped their master to lift the heavy curtain and use it to smother out the blaze.

While they worked, Linus and Demas, along with several other slaves ran to the tablinum. It only took a few minutes to extinguish the fire, and Julius left the room for a deep breath of untainted air while some of the other slaves assessed the damage.

"It seems as if only two scrolls were burned, Master."

"Well, that is a blessing, but who was in my tablinum?" Julius questioned firmly. He took in the faces of all the staff surrounding him and noticed Octavia standing on the edge of the crowd with Esther.

"Someone left a candle burning in this tablinum and either through intent or negligence knocked it over. I do not need to tell you that the tablinum is private, and without permission, slaves should not enter, much less be reading private scrolls," he said as he continued to scan their faces. He observed expressions of concern, confusion, and outraged indignation at the idea of a fellow slave who would be so presumptuous.

"Was anyone in this corridor in the last thirty minutes? If so, you might have seen or heard someone." He waited for a response, and when he received none, continued, "From now on,

I will always have a guard posted here between my chambers and my tablinum. It is my sincerest hope that this was nothing but a foolish bit of negligent curiosity, but I will protect my family and business by any means necessary."

He directed a stern glare upon each of them in turn. As he looked at them, all but his guards, who nodded at him, cast their eyes down rather than meet his gaze and risk being viewed as defiant or responsible.

He turned to Gaius, "Please open the window to air out the room and stand guard here the rest of the night."

Gaius nodded in response and moved into the tablinum with purpose.

After he had dismissed the rest of the staff, Julius turned to Octavia, who was shaking slightly with shock or exhaustion. He wrapped her in a hug before taking her by the hand and leading her back into their bedroom. Fortunately, the curtain had prevented the smoke from permeating into their quarters.

"Do you really think that this was intentional? Who raised the alarm?" she inquired.

"I found the fire and raised the alarm. I heard someone scurrying down the corridor when I was coming out of our room. The fire had just started to burn the scrolls when I discovered it, so I am sure the person hurrying away was responsible. Whether they were malicious or just nosy and clumsy, I am not sure. It is possible that they heard me moving around in our room and got spooked so that they knocked over their candle in a rush to avoid being caught snooping, or they could have been unaware of my restlessness and thought that they would cause much more damage before the fire was discovered.

"Either way, it was almost definitely a member of the staff since the guards did not alert us to any outsiders entering the villa. I instructed Demas that he was to set up some of the existing staff to act as guards to supplement the sentinels we brought from

Rome. And it was most likely a member we brought with us. Someone who lived here all the time would have to have a very strong motive for snooping around while we are here instead of simply waiting for us to leave again."

Octavia nodded in agreement. "Did you hear something that roused you?"

"No, I simply couldn't sleep and thought that I would get an early start on tomorrow's reading in the tablinum," he answered.

Octavia wore a relieved expression as she responded, "Well, fortunately, God did not allow you to sleep tonight. All the records and possibly even our lives could have been lost if not for your insomnia."

"Very true." Julius gazed upwards at the ceiling. "Thank you, God, for protecting us this night. Thank you that the damage was so minimal. If this was an intentional act of sabotage or worse, please help us to discover the guilty party. Either way, please continue to keep us safe and help me to understand Festus's records. Amen."

"Amen," she repeated after him in strong agreement.

An hour later, while Octavia slept in his arms, Julius was finally able to drift into a restful slumber.

Julius woke early the next morning with a feeling of urgency. He gently extricated himself from the bed without waking Octavia and did his morning ablutions before walking to the dining room for his breakfast. The staff quickly brought him a meal of fish, fruit, and a loaf of bread that he dipped into honey. After he finished, he sent for Linus and a guard to relieve Gaius and made his way to the tablinum. The guard and Demas met him outside the room, where the faint smell of smoke still leached into the hallway.

Julius sent Gaius away to rest as the new guard took his place. Then he looked at Demas. "Please arrange for a new curtain to be hung here today. That will be all for now."

"Yes, Master," he said before turning to leave.

Julius then turned to Linus. "Let's see if we can't make sense of these records."

Three hours later, Julius felt as if his eyes were crossing. He had never seen such confusing annotations on scrolls before. He had learned that in addition to this villa, Festus had owned three more across the empire, but he was not yet sure how Festus had paid for them or where the funds were coming from now to continue paying for their staff and upkeep. Also, Julius was perplexed by the names of the properties that Festus had owned. It seemed as if he was hiding his acquisitions, but Julius could not think of any reason he would have been obscuring his ownership of his investments.

He had discovered through persistent research that the ventures listed as T.L.P. and O.L.T. were a winery and a sawmill, respectively. However, there were still six other initials about which he had not been able to find any information.

He looked over at Linus. "Have you found any mention of a business named P.P.E.?"

Linus glanced over some of the scrolls on his smaller desk and looked up. "I have seen it mentioned three times on these scrolls, but only with monetary amounts that seem to make no sense. There is no additional information on what the letters mean, or where this venture is located, or even what it is." He looked up and shrugged in vexation.

"Well, I'm sure we will find the information on that business and the others eventually. We still have quite a few scrolls to look through," Julius assured the other man.

He let his eyes wander over the piles of scrolls unceremoniously stacked in cubbies and the dozens resting in heaps on the floor. Festus had clearly not been much for organization.

"Let us break for our midday meal," Julius told his relieved secretary.

Julius found Octavia in the dining room. He described to her what he had found as he watched her nibble her food. She still looked a little green and sat straight up when she ate instead of fully reclining, but he noticed that she ate more this afternoon than yesterday. He was pleased with her increased appetite and thought a little prayer of protection for her and the baby.

"Oh, I almost forgot to mention that I did hear back from your father, who has no ideas about the vandalism at the domus. He is concerned for our wellbeing, and I have replied to let him know we are here for the time being."

"I wonder how his quest for answers about Jesus is coming," Octavia mused.

Julius smiled at her over his glass, "I am sure it is going to be quite enlightening."

She smiled back at him with a hopeful gleam in her eyes.

CHAPTER 9

Two more weeks passed at the villa, and Octavia still felt as if all the energy was being sapped from her body. She had written to her mother with her news, and Claudia wrote back to assure her that this was normal and would likely pass some time in the next month.

Octavia loved the villa and spent many hours in the courtyard and gardens sketching the orange trees and other plants. She also chose several scrolls from the library to read. The new selection was quite a treat since she had long finished reading through those that interested her in the library back home. Julius still checked on her occasionally, but she did miss his attentiveness as he was busy studying through her late husband's records.

One afternoon, on a day she was feeling a little better, she was sitting in the baths enjoying the rejuvenating effect of the cool water when she felt a small flutter inside her. She started in astonishment and grinned as she held her midsection in awe. "Thank you, God, for this baby, and please keep him safe."

After dressing and joining Julius for their evening meal, she excitedly told him her news.

"That is wonderful, Love! You also seem to be feeling a little better today."

"Yes, I felt terrible in the morning but after the midday meal, I have had almost no nausea."

"That is great." He paused as he took in her beaming face. "I have some good news as well. I have deciphered the information for all but one of Festus's investments. However, there seems to be a link between that business and a property that I had noticed months ago. Interestingly, the property itself does not seem to generate an income. It is a puzzle that I cannot seem to solve. I would just travel to the property, but it is weeks away, and I do not wish to have you travel or leave you for such an extended time in this condition. It does not seem to be a pressing concern at present, so I plan to leave it be until after the baby is born."

"Thank you for considering me in your business decisions." She smiled at him a bit shyly.

"You say that as if it is out of my character, dear Wife. Be careful lest you offend me, and I decide to take my trip early." He teased her with a grin and a laugh.

She laughed with him and playfully smacked his bicep with her palm.

"And now you're going to make me spill my drink! The impudence!" He made an exaggerated face and gently tickled her side as she collapsed against him in a fit of giggling.

Later that night, as Octavia fell asleep next to her love, she thanked God again for her life.

Several hours later, Octavia woke in the middle of the night with a dull pain in her abdomen. She sat up quickly with a gasp. Julius, alerted by her movement, sat up with bleary eyes and took a second to orient himself before uttering, "What is it?!"

Octavia did not answer for a moment. She no longer felt any pain and thought that she must have dreamed it until she felt it again. She grimaced as she held her stomach.

"Something is wrong," she whispered through the pain.

"What do you need me to do?"

"Get Esther."

He hastily donned his tunic and ran into the corridor, where he yelled for the guard to fetch Esther. He returned to Octavia's side as she sat with fear in her eyes and tears streaming down her face.

Esther arrived, and a messenger was dispatched with instructions to return in haste with a midwife.

Julius could do nothing but hold his wife's hand and pray as the hours moved past. Her pain intensified, and when the midwife finally arrived, she gave the news they were all anticipating with dread. The baby was coming far too soon. He wished that he could reach Peter in time and ask him to heal the baby, but the apostle had left to travel to Jerusalem a few weeks prior. There was nothing they could do except pray for the lives of the baby and Octavia.

The midwife was adamant that Julius should leave the room, but his will was stronger than hers, and in the end, the midwife gave up her prodding with a huff and continued helping Octavia while Julius held his wife's hand. Esther wiped the sweat from Octavia's brow as she labored for another thirty minutes or so. Then, the tiniest little baby arrived still.

Several days passed in which Octavia did not have the physical or mental fortitude to leave her bed. She didn't want anyone near her. She drank what Esther brought to her but refused to eat more than a little cheese and bread. She ignored the midwife who came to check on her. When Julius came to talk to her, she turned away to face the wall. He had stopped sleeping in the room with her after that night, noting her obvious desire for solitude.

Every night, she cried so vigorously that she wondered if she shouldn't perish with her son for the sorrow of losing him. But every morning, as if summoned back to this life by the sun or by God himself, she woke with swollen eyes and resumed her mourning.

She knew deep inside that she should pray to God, but she felt abandoned and betrayed. "How could He let this happen?! He must not be such a good God after all," she thought in despair.

On the sixth morning of her self-imposed isolation, Julius walked into her room. She could tell from his look of determination that she would not be permitted to ignore him this time. She watched as he advanced to the bed and sat upon the edge. She didn't bother turning away.

"You must get up now. Lucius is gone, but God still has us here for a purpose. You will rise and meet me in the dining room for breakfast in half an hour," he commanded her.

Then he abruptly rose and strode out of the room as Octavia watched his back with her mouth agape and her eyes wide.

Esther joined her in her room, having apparently been summoned by Julius. She helped Octavia to wash up and prepare for breakfast. As Octavia allowed herself to be dressed, she seethed with anger at her husband. She was used to being commanded around by Festus, but she had not believed Julius capable of such cruelty toward her.

When she left the room, she observed Atticus guarding the hallway. She ignored him and held her head stiffly upright. She arranged her face into the bored, neutral expression that she had used in her previous marriage to guard herself and marched silently to the dining room.

When she arrived, Julius was already reclining on his couch with a scroll next to him on the table. Instead of taking the place next to him as was her habit, she sat on the other side of the table and looked down at the food that had been arranged exquisitely.

She heard Julius sigh. "I am sorry if you think me too harsh, but your isolation is not good for you. Right now, you need me to guide you because you are unwilling or unable to make reasonable decisions for yourself."

She looked up at him defiantly. "How can you act as if nothing has happened?! How can you go on as if Lucius never existed?"

Julius looked at her with a mix of sympathy and anger. He took a deep breath before answering. "You are mistaken if you believe that you are the only one in pain, but I know that I cannot change anything by refusing to live. I need you to learn that as well."

Octavia swallowed an angry, sinful retort and glared back down at the food in front of her.

"You must eat now." He commanded her in a firm but also gentle tone.

She bitterly picked up the food, barely noticing what it was before beginning to eat it. They ate in silence until they were both satisfied. Then Octavia sat with her hands folded in front of her, waiting to be dismissed. Instead, Julius began speaking to her again.

"I wish to read something to you. It is a scroll from the Israelite writings. Have you heard of a follower of Yahweh named Job?" he asked her.

Octavia did not raise her eyes as she shook her head no.

"He was a servant of the Most High long before Israel was a nation. This book was written about him, and I think that you will find it most applicable to our current circumstances."

He began to read to her, "There was a man in the land of Uz whose name was Job, and that man was blameless and upright, one who feared God and turned away from evil. There were born to him seven sons and three daughters..."

As he continued, Octavia listened attentively and then silently wept while listening to the narrative of Job's children perishing.

"Then Job arose and tore his robe and shaved his head and fell on the ground and worshiped. And he said, 'Naked I came from my mother's womb, and naked shall I return. The Lord gave, and the Lord has taken away; blessed be the name of the Lord.' In all this Job did not sin or charge God with wrong.'"

Julius laid the scroll to the side and studied his wife as her shoulders heaved and tears ran down her cheeks. He stood and made his way to her side. Hesitantly, as if afraid she would push him away, he put his arms around her, and when he sensed no opposition, he held her tightly.

Octavia felt his tears falling on the top of her head as they finally grieved together.

After Octavia had returned to her room to rest, Julius slipped from the villa into the countryside. For the past several days, he had thrown himself into his work and read countless scrolls to take his mind from his grief. That was how he had found, tucked away in a corner of the vast library, the scroll of Job. God only knew why Festus had it. Likely, he had acquired so many scrolls he didn't even know what most of them were.

Now, Julius hiked along the hills, barely taking in his surroundings, and when he was tired, slumped down onto his knees under a beech tree. He stared off into the distance and let out a guttural yell until he had no breath left in his lungs. Then he sat back against the tree trunk and wept. He wept for his son, for Octavia, and for the life he had just a week prior. He was wise enough to know that life could never be exactly as it was before.

"God, I am such a hypocrite. How can I expect my wife not to blame you when I myself do?!" Immediately, the horror of his sin filled him with shame and sorrow. "Please forgive me, God! Help me to bless you even in this. Please give me wisdom. Help me to understand!"

When he had finished pouring out the grief of his soul to God, he felt a little calmer, and he rose and walked back to the villa. When he neared the domicile, he heard a crunching coming from that direction. He looked up to see one of his guards, Apollos, rounding a tree and heading in his direction.

"Hail, Master. You have been gone for quite some time, and as darkness was fast approaching, we decided to send out a few men to search for you. I am glad to see you."

Just then, Felix came from behind Julius.

"Hail, Master. Hail, Apollos. I heard your voices and am pleased that the search was successful."

Apollos looked slightly confused. "I didn't realize you were part of the search. I had searched for you to ask you to join but couldn't find you."

"Ah yes, one of the others found me and alerted me," Felix answered.

Julius broke in, "Well, as you can see, I am back and in good health."

Apollos nodded and blew his horn in two short bursts to alert the other searchers that their missing master had been recovered. Then, the three men returned to the villa as darkness began to fall.

For the next few days, Octavia joined Julius for meals, and after each meal, he read aloud the story of Job. They learned together how the bereaved Job handled his grief as they worked hard to deal with their own.

One evening after dinner, the couple were holding hands when Octavia looked at Julius with tears in her eyes, "Do you think that I did something wrong, and that's why the baby died? Maybe the cold bath that I took, or maybe I sinned against God."

Julius started in surprise. "Of course not! God was not punishing Job when his children died, and you did not do anything to cause a miscarriage. Cool baths are a part of life. Pregnant women have been taking them for centuries."

He sighed and rubbed his thumb over her fingers. "Babies die because we live in a sinful and broken world, and God holds the numbers of all our days. He had chosen a smaller number for Lucius than we would have liked, but He is good regardless. We just have to believe that even when our human experiences seem to contradict it."

Octavia nodded, "So you don't blame me?"

"Of course not. It is no more your fault than it is mine. Do you blame me?"

"No, of course not." She looked beseechingly into his eyes. "I am having a hard time sleeping without you in the bed. Will you return to our room?"

He smiled at her, "I would love to."

CHAPTER 10

After three more weeks went by, Julius woke with the sunshine streaming through the curtains in his room. He decided that he had gleaned as much as he possibly could from the scrolls in this tablinum, and he was ready to leave this place and its memories far behind. He rolled to his side and saw that Octavia was beginning to stir. He watched as her eyes moved beneath her eyelids and realized once again how lovely she was. Then her eyes opened, and she smiled at him. It was one of the first real smiles he had seen from her in weeks, and it was like a balm to his battered heart.

"Are you ready to leave this villa, my dear Wife? I think I am ready to explore our investments and head to another villa." He looked at her questioningly.

Octavia blinked for a moment. "That sounds lovely. Where will we go?"

"I thought maybe we could travel around Italia checking on our investments and then take a mostly sea voyage to reach our villa outside of Jerusalem. We can catch up with your parents and see how their search for truth is going. Your father said they planned to stay there for the rest of the year. What do you think?" he asked.

"I did not realize that we owned a villa outside of Jerusalem. How long will it take us to get there?"

"It should take several weeks. Are you prepared to take such a long trip?"

"I think it sounds like a grand adventure," Octavia said as she smiled.

"Perfect."

Julius sent ahead a letter to alert the staff of the Jerusalem villa of Julius and Octavia's journey. The preparations to leave took three days. Esther and Gaius once again rode with them in the carpentum, while the rest of their guards and Linus rode on horses. The four in the carriage discussed the words of Jesus as they rode. The topic then turned to the Torah, the five books of Moses. Octavia was delighted to learn how educated Esther was about these books.

"My parents taught me all they knew about the Law and the Prophets. I am from the Levitical line or the line of priests. They were the ones responsible for keeping the book of the law, completing the sacrifices, interceding to God on behalf of the people, and the keeping of the temple," Esther said.

Octavia nodded, and she noticed that Gaius's eyes never left Esther's face.

Octavia responded to Esther. "Did your parents tell you why God allowed his people to be conquered by Rome?"

Esther's face fell in sorrow as she answered. "Yes, they did. God was very clear with his people when he led them into the land he had promised to them. He told them to purge all the evil nations from the land and conquer it to be their own. He told them that if they did not put to the sword these wicked nations that they would lead the Israelites into idolatry."

She looked up at her companions and noticed their shocked expressions. "I know that may not sound kind of him, but you have to understand that these nations were completely depraved. They were sacrificing their own children in fire to their pagan gods."

Octavia gasped in revulsion.

Esther continued, "We must trust that God is always right even when we would be wrong if we made the same decision. As Creator, he is allowed to do all that he wants, and because he is good, everything he does is good. Therefore, he made a covenant with the Israelites that if they worshiped him alone and held to his law and teachings, he would root them into that land and bless them forever. But my people sinned against God by not obeying and devoting those nations to destruction. Instead, they married into the foreign nations and worshiped their detestable gods.

"They were wicked in the sight of God and men, so God allowed them to be conquered several times by different nations — first the Assyrians, then the Babylonians. Then, after the people repented, he brought a remnant of the people back into the land. Now Rome has conquered, but during this time of captivity for my people, God's son has come into the world and opened a way of salvation for Gentiles as well as Jews. Therefore, I do not know what will happen to Israel.

"I feel deeply for my people, but even my own parents have denied Christ as Lord and cling to their belief that a conquering savior is still to come. I do not know if Israel will ever be restored as a nation or will ever collectively accept that our human idea of the savior who was going to bring us earthy freedom from our enemies was flawed. Instead, Jesus came to free us from our spiritual bondage."

As she paused, Gaius asked, "What made you believe that Christ was the Savior?"

"I was told about Jesus by a believer in my last home. She told me how Jesus fulfilled all of the prophets' prophecies, and I was astonished to realize that she was correct."

After a long pause, Julius jumped in, "I am excited to meet with more of the disciples in Jerusalem when we arrive. Although, I have heard that the persecution by the Jews is rather severe there, so we may have a difficult time finding them."

The others nodded in grim agreement, and they shared a prayer for their fellow believers in Jerusalem, Rome, and abroad.

The next day as they continued to ride along, Julius asked Gaius how he had become a slave.

Gaius looked stoic as he began his tale. "I am sure that you have heard of the Roman practice of leaving unwanted babies or young children in refuse heaps."

At their sad nods of assent, he continued, "My family abandoned me. Slavers often search those areas for abandoned children that they can raise as inventory to sell. I was picked up by a slaver who raised me and sold me when I was seven. I worked for several different masters, and as I grew, one of my masters recognized me as a good candidate for becoming a guard. He had me trained to fight and defend my master and his property.

"He was a believer in the Way and led me to the Lord after I had been his guard for a few years. When he experienced a change in his fortunes, he was forced to downsize and sold me back to the market. He was very apologetic, but he had unavoidable legal obligations. Three days later, I was standing in the market when you approached me with this position."

Julius leaned forward and clapped his guard on the arm. "Well, while I wish that your early years had been different, I am very happy to have you on my staff."

That afternoon, they arrived at one of their vineyards, and Julius and Octavia were pleased to see how well it was managed. The owners and their staff all relaxed and enjoyed some of the wine.

The conversations over the next week continued to draw the four closer together in their friendship, and they each shared their own knowledge of God with the others. They traveled in the carpentum to the different properties during the days and lodged in inns at night. Octavia found the constant companionship and changing scenery to be an effective distraction from her grief, and she thought that Julius was also slowly healing from their heartbreak. The pain still hit her like a punch to her core at times, but these episodes came with decreased regularity.

One evening, the women had retired to their quarters at the inn, but Julius, Felix, and Gaius remained in the dining area, talking in front of the fire. Felix soon excused himself to his quarters to rest. When Julius and Gaius were the only ones still in the room, Julius thought again how much he enjoyed Gaius's friendly banter and their deep, thoughtful conversations.

Soon, there came a natural lull in the conversation, and Gaius turned from where he was watching the flames dancing and lapping up the wood. He fixed his gaze upon Julius.

Julius noted that Gaius almost looked nervous, and he waited, puzzled at what the man might have to say.

"You know that I have always been a slave?" Gaius began.

Julius nodded, unsure where this conversation was headed.

He continued, "I have never thought about marriage as a possibility for me because I know of the uncertainty of a master's whims. If I marry, my wife or I could be sold and separated at any time. Any children we bore would be the property of our master. I have been saving my pay for many years, but I still have a few years before I will have enough money to buy my freedom."

"You are interested in marrying Esther," Julius said with certainty.

Gaius exhaled a deep breath. "Yes, I suppose I have not exactly hidden my interest."

Julius smiled at him. "I believe you to be a trustworthy man and would like to think that we have become friends."

Gaius looked a little stunned at this admission. "I would like to agree with you," he said with a slow grin.

"I will agree to free both you and Esther with the agreement that you will work for us for your normal wages for the duration of your current committed years of service or until you have paid for your freedom. However, during that time, you will be technically free and unable to be sold. Your children would be yours, and if something happened to Octavia and me, you would be free and safe."

Gaius looked shocked. "You would do that for us?"

"I think it is how God would want me to behave toward a brother and sister in Christ, and it is how I would want to be treated if I were in your position. Have you talked to Esther about your interest?"

"No, I didn't want to get her hopes up, but I have noticed her glances, and she seems to be interested in me as well."

"Octavia mentioned to me that she thought she had noticed something between the two of you. I would be happy to free you and witness your marriage anytime you two are ready."

"I cannot tell you how much I appreciate this," Gaius said, with a jubilant expression on his face.

"I can imagine." Julius grasped Gaius's forearm and pulled him into a hug.

Esther woke up the next morning in her slave quarters and walked toward her mistress's room to help her get ready for another day of travel. When she turned a corner, she stopped short and almost ran into a large body that was barreling toward her. Strong hands grasped her forearms, and as she looked up, she blushed when she saw Gaius staring down at her with his charming hazel eyes.

"Excuse me, I wasn't looking where I was going." She attempted to walk around his bulky frame, but his hands did not release her arms, and he stood firmly in place. She looked back up at him questioningly.

Gaius rushed to speak, "Esther, I must tell you that from the first time I saw you at the domus, I was captivated by you. You are beautiful and kind, and you worship Christ with an incredible faith. I talked to the master yesterday about the possibility of our marriage. If you have no interest in me, I understand and will never bring this up again. We can forget this conversation ever happened..."

Esther opened her mouth in surprise and pleasure. She cut off his rambling. "Of course, I am interested. What did the master say?"

"He said that as long as we work for him for the rest of our time or until his death, he would free us now to be married so we cannot be separated or lose our children."

"What a generous offer!" Esther exclaimed.

He fidgeted nervously, "So my question is, would you agree to marry me and work toward our freedom together?"

Esther beamed up at him, "I would love to."

He dropped her arms and pulled her into a hug. "Thank you. He said we can proceed whenever we would like. There is a magistrate in this town. Would you want to be freed and get married today?"

"That sounds like a dream! Of course, I do," she answered with excitement.

Esther took his offered hand, and they headed upstairs to talk over details with their master and mistress.

The other slaves were given the day off to go to the market while the four traveling companions walked in pairs to the magistrate's office. First, Julius freed the couple, and then he and Octavia witnessed their union.

Octavia smiled at her loyal servant and prayed that Gaius would be as kind a husband as Julius had proven himself to be. She looked up at her husband and grinned as she thought about the deal that had led to their marriage and the commensurate deal that was resulting in the marriage of two of their slaves-turned-friends.

Octavia and Julius walked around the town of Neapolis while Gaius and Esther returned to the inn.

"Are we planning to visit the mysterious property on this trip?" she asked her husband.

Julius replied, "No, I had considered it, but when Linus and I were planning the route, we realized that it would have to be its own trip. It is the only property we own in Raetia. We have been heading south from Rome toward the Mediterranean, where we will board a merchant ship and sail to Jerusalem. Raetia is in the mountains far to the north. After this adventure, I think we should travel up that direction toward our villa in Britannia. It will be a long journey, and I hope to learn more from the scrolls at the villa in Jerusalem before we go."

Octavia nodded in agreement.

The trip took two more weeks as they leisurely traveled the countryside and inspected more of their properties. They stopped at mansiones or rest areas whenever they tired, and Octavia loved seeing more of the empire she had been born into.

As they came within a few days of the coastal city of Tarentum, Julius sent Linus and Apollos to ride ahead and secure passage for the travelers on a merchant ship. When the rest of the group reached Tarentum, they viewed a vast olive grove they owned. As the ladies tired of walking the fields, they returned with Atticus and Gaius to the carpentum. Felix accompanied Julius who walked the perimeter with the manager of the field.

Julius observed with curiosity an area on the edge of the field that had mounds of dirt but no olive trees. He counted six mounds, all about the same size, roughly six feet long and three feet high.

"What are those mounds?" he asked the manager.

The manager looked back at him blankly, "I am honestly not sure. When I was hired to look over these fields, Festus told me that this area was never to be disturbed. I found this to be an unusual command, but who am I to question the will of the master? I have not allowed any workers near that area the entire time I have worked here."

Julius squinted his eyes and stared in concentration. "Something about the arrangement and size of those makes me think of gr...."

Felix cut off his sentence. "Pardon me, Master, but I have worked at an olive orchard before and have seen mounds such as these. Sometimes, the master wants to age barrels of wine in their olive orchard. It is believed to bring luck and blessing to the wine, causing a preferable flavor. It appears to me that he is aging several barrels and did not wish them to be disturbed. He may have worried they would be stolen if he told the manager about them."

Julius cocked his head to the side and listened with interest. "I have never heard of this."

Before Felix could respond, Linus rode up on a horse. He looked at the company of men and saw the mounds of earth before sliding to the ground and addressing Julius.

"Hail Master, we were able to secure passage on a ship to Jerusalem, but it leaves tomorrow morning. The next one isn't for three more weeks. We arranged to pay our fare when we arrive in the morning in case you were delayed and missed the ship, but if you want to leave on that ship, we should hurry to procure supplies."

Julius nodded quickly. "Yes, of course. You and Apollos get us rooms at the inn where you have been lodging and give our driver the location. We will join you there and then go out for the supplies we will need for our journey."

Linus remounted his horse and rode away as Julius turned to thank the manager and briskly walked back to the carpentum with Felix.

The rest of the day was spent buying provisions, storing them on the ship, and boarding their horses and carpentum. Julius met and was pleased with the captain of the ship and fell asleep that night eagerly awaiting their impending sea voyage.

Their trip across the Mediterranean was blessed with blue skies and favorable winds. The ship's captain remarked that the gods must be with them on this journey. Julius responded that his God was always with him. The captain laughed good-naturedly and ended the conversation by responding, "Whatever you say," before walking to his quarters.

Julius found that the sea air agreed with him, and he was grateful when Octavia became used to the rocking of the ship. They walked the deck together and talked of the future. Octavia wanted to travel to each of their villas before returning to Rome. She asked him about the different areas of the empire she had never visited. They talked about everything except children. Julius knew that it distressed Octavia every time she began her cycle again. He held her as she cried and did his best to comfort her. After a few days, she would return to her normal state of only grieving occasionally over their loss.

CHAPTER 11

When they reached Jerusalem, they immediately set out for Aurelius and Claudia's villa in Bezetha, which was closer to the coast than their own villa near the Mount of Olives. Julius noted that his in-law's villa was quite beautiful but not as grand as the one they had left to take this journey. As soon as they arrived, Claudia rushed from the home to embrace her daughter, who promptly burst into tears.

Aurelius emerged at a more dignified and measured pace. He grasped Julius by the forearm, which he reciprocated. "Hail, Julius. I have been sorry to hear of your misfortunes. How are you holding up?"

"It has been difficult." He looked toward his wife, who was being gently escorted into the villa by Esther and Claudia.

"I can see that. Do come in. Let's go to my tablinum and catch up." Aurelius invited.

Julius nodded and followed his father-in-law. When they reached the tablinum, slaves brought them goblets of honey wine, and the men relaxed into their chairs.

"Have you learned any more about the vandalism at the domus or the fire at the villa?" asked Aurelius.

Julius sighed in exasperation and responded, "No, and honestly, I'm not sure if the troubles at the two locations are even related. Also, in all our travels around Italia and to here, we have had no afflictions whatsoever."

Aurelius looked at him perplexed. "It is certainly a strange business. How is my daughter doing?"

"She is fine with the vandalism, but losing the baby has been quite heart-wrenching for her," Julius shook his head in grief. "And me," he added.

Aurelius nodded sadly. "We lost two babies, and I was convinced that Claudia would never stop crying. When we had Octavia, my wife was more joyous than I had ever seen her. I was, of course, hoping for a boy, but the gods don't always give us what we ask for, do they?"

"I can only answer that about my God, and the answer is no, he does not always give what we ask for, but we have faith that he always gives us what we need," Julius answered.

Both men stared at their drinks for a moment in silent contemplation. Then, Julius talked about their pilgrimage around Italia. Aurelius looked curiously at him when he mentioned the mounds in the olive orchard.

"I have never heard of such a thing, but I have never owned an olive orchard either. I also didn't know that Festus had a villa in Jerusalem," said Aurelius.

Julius nodded in agreement and looked searchingly at the older man. "So, have you found any evidence to refute the claims that Jesus was raised from the dead and is the Son of God?"

Aurelius shook his head with a laugh. "I knew you would come along to that sooner rather than later." He paused. "I have not found anything definitive yet."

"What have you found?" Julius queried with piqued interest.

Aurelius took a deep breath before beginning his tale. "I interviewed two of the sentries who were on duty at the tomb. They both agreed that they had fallen asleep, and the disciples must have taken the body. I was perplexed, though, to find that their stories didn't quite line up when I asked for details about that night. One even asked me if I had talked to the leaders of the synagogue. He seemed to think that I was grilling him to get him into trouble, and he let it slip that the Jews would vouch for him that he did nothing wrong. I found that curious because I wondered what dealings Roman sentries would have with Jewish religious leaders.

"I went from there to speak with the aforementioned Jewish leaders. I had a hunch and asked them how much they had paid the guards to lie about what they had seen. The faces of the leaders revealed that my hunch was correct even though they denied my accusation fiercely. It was obvious to me that they were hiding their part in the whole affair and, for some reason, were covering up for the soldiers. They were extremely tightlipped about any other inquiries I made.

"So, in conclusion, on the point of the supposed resurrection, I do believe there is a conspiracy to suppress the truth about the body's disappearance. I do not have enough evidence, however, to conclude that it was raised from the dead."

Julius wore a satisfied smile on his face as he listened. Aurelius smirked back at him, "Don't look so smug. I am not done looking into the matter, so don't think you've won just yet.

"On the point of him being the 'Son of God' as you claim, I have found several witnesses. A few have even been willing to speak to me once I assured them that I was not there to prosecute them. They tell scores of stories about miraculous events that they attribute directly to Jesus, and those stories, unlike the sentries', are remarkably consistent.

"Currently, I have my cohorts searching for a man who was supposedly blind from birth and was cured by Jesus. This whole matter is taking more time to research than I had anticipated, given the Jews' fear of talking to authority figures, especially Romans. However, I needed something to do in my old age, and a mystery is always good fun. Isn't it?"

"It surely is." Julius smiled.

"We named him Lucius because he was a light in our lives," Octavia said sorrowfully.

Claudia looked at her daughter in concern. Octavia was sure her mother noticed the weight that she had lost and the puffiness around her eyes. She had served her daughter some grapes and wine and now sat with her in the gardens. Octavia gave her a shell-shocked look and lowered her eyes to the grass.

"Do you still believe in your God, Dear?" Claudia asked in concern.

Octavia looked up quickly. "Yes, of course. Without my faith and Julius, I don't know where I would be."

Claudia nodded and took her hand. "I haven't told you this, but before you, I lost two babies as well. A little boy and another little girl. I thought that I would die. I was absolutely hopeless before I became pregnant with you. I had even determined in my heart that if you died, I was going to travel to the coast and throw myself off the cliffs."

Octavia looked at her in shock as she continued.

"I could not see a future for myself without children, but I have come to learn that life is long, and maybe your God will bring you a child sooner than you think. He grants wishes, right?"

"No, Mother, he gives us what we need even if it is not what we wish, even if we dread it and cannot understand how it could possibly be good. We trust him that it is good. We also trust that He has a reason for us to be living even when we don't know what it is." Octavia answered.

Her mother nodded and continued to drink her wine. "I am not sure I have ever heard of a God like that. In fact, I'm certain that I haven't."

Octavia drank and ate and spent the next hour explaining her faith in Christ to her mother. As she did so, she felt a contentment in her current circumstances.

By dinner time, Octavia was feeling less of the grief that had threatened to overwhelm her the moment she had seen her mother. Dinner was enjoyable, with good food and pleasant company. Her father even asked her some questions about her opinions on their travels and properties.

That night, as she drifted to sleep in the protective embrace of her husband, she whispered, "Thank you, God."

Aurelius invited the travelers to stay and rest an extra few days before making the day-long journey to their villa. Julius used the opportunity afforded by the delay to send a message to the household manager and let him know when they would arrive. A thought made him pause as he wrote. Then he directed that three guards should be hired and should alternate watching over the tablinum where Festus stored his records. He hoped this extra precaution was unnecessary, and he did not want to think that a member of his party might tamper with the scrolls, but he could not take that chance.

On the second day at Aurelius's villa, while their wives wandered through the gardens, Julius and Aurelius again conferred in the tablinum. They were having a lively debate about the new emperor, Gaius Caesar Augustus Germanicus, who some liked to call Caligula, meaning "Little Boots." He had acquired the nickname from his childhood days when he would wear his complete child-size soldier's uniform and follow his military father around.

Julius and his father-in-law were arguing over whether Caligula's expansion of the emperor's powers was beneficial for the empire or could lead to a harsh dictatorship. While there were rumors that Caligula had murdered his predecessor by smothering him with a pillow, both Julius and his father-in-law agreed that there was no evidence of foul play and that the much-loathed former emperor had almost certainly died of natural causes.

In the middle of their discourse, a messenger entered hastily into the tablinum. The men looked up, startled as the messenger began, "Master, the Jews you hired have found the man who was blind, and additionally, they found a friend who was with him and claims to have been lame for thirty-eight years before Jesus healed him."

Aurelius and Julius were on their feet in a moment. Aurelius quickly addressed the servant as if any delay might cause the men to disappear. "Have the hired men confirmed with their families that these men did in fact have these deformities?"

"Yes, Master, they thoroughly interviewed the neighbors and families so as not to waste your time."

"Well, where are they, and when can we meet?" Aurelius asked swiftly.

"The men will meet you tonight an hour before dusk at the sycamore tree just outside of the old Fish Gate. They believe you are Jews who have been converted to the Way and want to interview them for an account you are writing. They do not wish to be referred to by name, claiming that they want all the glory to go to their healer."

Julius frowned at this deception. "They will be concerned that we wish them harm when they see we are Romans."

Aurelius looked at him with a smirk. "Good thing we're bringing a believer with us then to convince them otherwise."

Julius grunted but didn't agree.

Aurelius, Julius, and Gaius left the villa in time to reach the Fish Gate at the appointed hour. The gate itself had been mostly destroyed during the Roman conquest, but it was still a well-known entrance to the city. When they arrived, they decided to wait from a distance until they saw two men walk through the gate and stand watchfully under the sycamore tree.

As they approached the men, one of the Jews nudged the other and nodded in their direction, clearly having noticed their approach. Both strangers stiffened in concern as the Romans advanced.

Julius reached them first, "Peace, friends! We mean you no harm. My friend and I are believers in the Way. I have challenged my father-in-law here to find evidence to disprove my assertions that Jesus is the Son of God and raised from the dead. He had been in Jerusalem researching the life of Jesus when he learned about you. I did not know about the deception that led you here until this afternoon, and I apologize. However, I can assure you that we only want to hear your testimonies, and you have nothing to fear from us."

The Jews looked at each other, and one nodded. Then the other man proceeded to speak, "We wish to remain anonymous, but we will tell you our stories. I was born blind, and one day, I was in the city when I heard a crowd approaching. As I hurried to move out of their way, I heard some men speaking at the front of the group. People often used to speak about me in my presence, as if I were deaf, in addition to being blind.

"One man asked a second if my parents or I had sinned so that I was blind. The second man answered that my blindness was not a result of sin but was designed by God to bring glory to His name. I was stunned by these perplexing words. Then I heard the man spit upon the ground. He came over to me and rubbed something that I learned later was his saliva mixed with the dirt from the ground onto my eyelids. He then told me, 'Go, wash in the Pool of Siloam,' so I did. As soon as I washed my face, I opened my eyes and could see! For the first time in my life, I perceived more than just darkness.

"When I went home, some of my neighbors didn't even recognize me but assumed I was someone with similar features, not the same man. I assured them I was the same man who was born blind. When the leaders of the synagogue heard the commotion, they came out to investigate. They asked me what had happened, and when I told them, they even asked my parents to verify my former blindness. They asked many questions about the man who healed me, which I could not answer. Then, they grew angry with me and excommunicated me from the synagogue, making me an outcast once again.

"Later, the healer, who I believed to be a prophet, found me alone and now exiled. He asked me, 'Do you believe in the Son of Man?' I responded, 'And who is he, sir, that I may believe in him?' He said, 'You have seen him, and it is he who is speaking to you.'

"Then I said, 'Lord, I believe,' and I worshiped him. The man, Jesus, then said, 'For judgment I came into this world, that those who do not see may see, and those who see may become blind.' 'Some of the Pharisees near him heard these things, and said to him, "Are we also blind?" Jesus said, "If you were blind, you would have no guilt; but now that you say, 'We see,' your guilt remains."'"

The narrator spoke animatedly as he recounted his tale to the astonished Romans. "I then followed Jesus as he preached around Jerusalem. At the Festival of Dedication, Jesus was in the temple courts, and the Jews asked him, 'How long will you keep us in suspense? If you are the Christ, tell us plainly.'

" 'Jesus answered, "I told you, and you do not believe. The works that I do in my Father's name bear witness about me, but you do not believe because you are not among my sheep. My sheep hear my voice, and I know them, and they follow me. I give them eternal life, and they will never perish, and no one will snatch them out of my hand. My Father, who has given them to me, is greater than all, and no one is able to snatch them out of the Father's hand. I and the Father are one." '

"Then the Jews picked up stones to try to stone him! I was afraid that they were going to kill all of us! But he miraculously slipped away from them, and neither the Jews nor I could find him. Later, I heard that he had come into Jerusalem again, but before I could rejoin him, I was informed that the Jews had crucified him.

"I did see him twice more after that, though. I was gathered in a group of his disciples and followers when he appeared in our midst. He showed us his wounds from the nails and the spear that was thrust into his side. I touched him and knew that he lived again.

"Then on another day, I witnessed as he seemed to float back up into the clouds of heaven. As I was standing there, astonished by the sight, two men in white robes appeared in front of us. They said to us, 'Men of Galilee, why do you stand looking into heaven? This Jesus, who was taken up from you into heaven, will come in the same way as you saw him go into heaven.' "

Aurelius stood with his mouth open and his eyes fairly bulging with shock as he heard this narrative. Julius and Gaius stood in enraptured pleasure at hearing this eye-witness account of their Lord.

When the first Jew stopped speaking, the second entered into the conversation. "I fear that my story, while no less astonishing, is much more tragic than my friend's. I was lame for thirty-eight years. Every day, I would go to the pool of Bethesda near the Sheep Gate, where there was a legend that an angel would periodically swirl the waters of the pool. It was said that whoever got into the water first after the water moved would receive healing. I, being lame, was never able to get into the pool quickly, and so believed that I should never receive healing.

"One day, a man walked up to me and asked, 'Do you want to be healed?' I explained how I could not reach the pool in time, but he told me, 'Get up, take up your bed, and walk!' Immediately, I leapt to my feet, rolled up my mat, and started on my way home, thrilled with my good fortune! However, the Jewish leaders were quick to correct me for carrying my mat on the Sabbath.

"I wanted to defend myself from their censure, so I told them that the man who healed me had told me to do so. They asked me who the man was, but I didn't know because he had rejoined the crowd. After that, the healer came up to me again in the temple. He said to me, 'See, you are well! Sin no more, that nothing worse may happen to you.' I asked one of his followers who the man was, and to my shame, I then found the Jewish leaders and told them that it was Jesus who healed me and told me to pick up my mat on the Sabbath."

The man hung his head in remorse. Then he raised it once again. "I believe he has forgiven me even for this. I was there when he was crucified. I had been at the marketplace on the way to Golgotha early in the morning when I saw Jesus, my healer, bloody and bruised, wearing a crown of thorns upon his head. The soldiers had another man carrying his cross because Jesus could barely stand."

He took a deep, shuddering breath and continued his story, "I felt compelled to follow and witness what I knew was to be his execution. I will skip the details of his suffering, as I'm sure you are all aware of the horrors of crucifixion. I was transfixed, staring for hours at the man who had saved me from my misery. The sky was dark even though it was day, and there was no storm. I saw him look down at me, and when he did, the words that he spoke to me came back into my mind with complete clarity. Then I heard him cry out, 'Father, into your hands I commit my spirit,' and he died.

"I left the gruesome scene and started walking home in a fog of grief and confusion. As I passed a nearby cemetery, I noticed that some of the graves were open. I was curious at the sight because graves are usually only open during a burial. Then I saw three men wearing burial shrouds walking toward the city. When I saw them, I ran in terror all the way back home. I spent several days in my home, not eating, barely drinking, praying to God, and wondering what all these things meant. When I finally emerged, I heard of the disappearance of the body of Jesus, and I was certain that he had been raised from the dead just like the men in the cemetery.

"I prayed to Jesus for the first time and said that I knew I had sinned, but I begged him to forgive me for my sins and for revealing him to the Jewish leaders. I felt responsible for his death and thought that if I hadn't pointed him out to the leaders, they might not have been able to secure a conviction. However, when I began to meet with other believers, they helped me to realize that it was God's plan for Jesus to die and be raised as the final sacrifice for our sins. I am sorry for the part that I may have played in his death, but I am forever grateful for him coming to earth to die for me.

"When gathering at a believer's home, I met my friend," he said as he gestured to the other Jew. "We found that together, as eyewitnesses to his healing powers, death, and resurrection, we made a good team for telling others about our Savior."

The man stopped speaking, and the Jews stared at the Romans as if unsure what reaction they should expect. Julius and Gaius beamed at them while Aurelius looked flummoxed and unhappy.

After a beat of silence, Julius responded. "Thank you for telling us your reports. It is marvelous to hear from more witnesses of our Lord's life, death, and resurrection."

Dusk was beginning to fall when the men stopped conversing. Julius nodded discreetly to Gaius, signaling him to turn and lead Aurelius back to their vehicle.

Julius paused until his compatriots were out of hearing before re-engaging the Jews, "I know that you must be cautious, but Gaius, our wives, and I greatly desire to fellowship with the believers on the Lord's Day. We will be staying near the Mount of Olives and are hoping that we can attend a service."

The men looked at each other and nodded once again in apparent agreement. "Meet us at the Valley Gate two hours past sunrise, and we will lead you there."

Aurelius was eerily silent all the way back to the villa, and he waved Julius off when he asked if Aurelius would like to speak more on the topic.

He remained quiet about what they had witnessed for the duration of Julius and Octavia's stay at the villa. They could do nothing but pray for him and hope that God opened his eyes to the truth.

CHAPTER 12

On the day of their departure, as Julius, Octavia, and their staff set out on their half-day journey to their villa, they saw the remains of the old wall around Jerusalem. Esther seemed enraptured by the view of the city of her ancestors. She stared through the window of their raeda long after the city was obscured by villas and trees. Tears slowly trailed down her face as Gaius held her protectively against his side with one arm around her shoulders and his hand holding hers. Octavia reached forward and patted her friend's knee to comfort her over what must have been an agonizing sight.

Soon, they reached their villa outside of the city near the Mount of Olives. They introduced themselves to their household manager, Dido, who met them at the door with a bow.

"Hail, Master, Mistress." He addressed them each, then turned to Julius. "I have done as you instructed."

"Thank you, Dido. Please show the staff we brought where they should stay."

"Very good, Master." He nodded to the other staff and led them inside toward the slave quarters.

Julius held his arm out to Octavia with some anticipation. "Are you ready to explore another villa?"

She smiled at him. "Most definitely."

They entered to find a villa about the size of the Roman domus. It had a beautiful courtyard with two rows, each containing three pomegranate trees that were fairly dripping with beautiful pink fruits. Octavia walked to the closest tree and plucked a fruit from it, amazed by the sight. Esther, who had returned to the courtyard and anticipated her mistress's needs, left and returned with a knife. Octavia didn't think she had ever tasted anything as sweet as that fruit.

After touring yet another villa, the pair ate dinner and went to rest in their room, the one nearest the tablinum. One of the guards that Dido hired stood outside in the hallway, and the couple slept soundly, knowing that they and the records were safe.

The next morning was the Lord's Day, and most of the staff received the day off to go to the market while Julius, Octavia, Gaius, and Esther met the believers at the Valley Gate at the appointed time. They were led into the city and to a believer's home. Initially, most of the church members kept their distance and gazed at the Romans with trepidation. However, when Peter turned and saw them, he threw his arms around the visitors in joyous recognition. The apostle turned and introduced them as fellow believers, after which the Romans were enthusiastically welcomed by the rest of the assembly.

Peter then introduced them to James and John, two more of Christ's disciples. When it was time for the sermon, they took turns speaking to the congregation about Christ's resurrection and ascension to heaven.

Another disciple, Matthias, stood with a scroll and addressed the assembly, "I am here to tell you of the man named Saul who previously persecuted the church here in Jerusalem. Most of you have probably heard of him and his conversion, but for those of you who haven't, I will give a brief summary and an update on his current doings.

"A few years ago, Saul was traveling to Damascus to hunt down more believers and bring them back here for prosecution when he was blinded by a bright light from heaven."

Matthias then looked at the scroll as he read, "Jesus spoke to him saying 'Saul, Saul, why are you persecuting me? It is hard for you to kick against the goads.'

"Saul replied, 'Who are you, Lord?'

"And the Lord said, 'I am Jesus whom you are persecuting. But rise and stand upon your feet, for I have appeared to you for this purpose, to appoint you as a servant and witness to the things in which you have seen me and to those in which I will appear to you, delivering you from your people and from the Gentiles—to whom I am sending you to open their eyes, so that they may turn from darkness to light and from the power of Satan to God, that they may receive forgiveness of sins and a place among those who are sanctified by faith in me.'

"God instructed a believer named Ananias to heal Saul's blindness and baptize him. Now Saul uses the name Paul and is beginning to travel and preach the gospel to both Jews and Gentiles!"

The congregation rejoiced at this powerful work of their Savior, and they all sang hymns and ate their midday meal together. Julius privately gave a significant sum to the disciples to aid in the ministry and help those church members who were suffering from the persecution of the Jewish leaders. He also gave a separate but significant amount to be sent to the apostle Paul to aid in his ministry.

After the service, Julius and Octavia approached Peter, who once again embraced the couple. Julius began to explain the loss of their baby as Peter listened sorrowfully before answering:

"God has a plan for you and for Lucius, and while it is true that God has given some of us the ability to heal, that does not mean that we can change God's plan. Even if I had been there, I would not have been able to keep your son alive when God did not wish it. Your prayers alone were sufficient to bring about his healing if God had so willed.

"It has been difficult to explain this concept to many of the believers because their friends and family members are still dying at times, and we have to explain to them that we are not God. We cannot decide who lives or dies. That duty lies with God alone," Peter explained lovingly and with great sympathy. Then he prayed for them that they would be comforted and brought closer to their Lord through their trials and grief.

They spent another hour talking to the believers and listening with wonder and amazement to James tell the story of Jesus healing a demon-possessed man by sending the demons into a herd of pigs, causing the swine to jump into the sea and drown. When the rest of the believers began to disperse and head to their homes, Julius's party gathered their belongings and left.

As they walked back toward the city gate, where their vehicle was waiting to take them back to the villa, Julius noticed Gaius stiffening and swinging his gaze around. Julius looked around to see if he could detect what his guard did. However, he only noticed that they were in an abandoned street between two buildings with bits of trash scattered about and haphazardly blowing in the wind.

"What is it?" Julius asked in concern.

"I am not sure, Master, but I have a bad feeling." Then he shifted his stance and loudly commanded, "Everyone, move to that wall!"

He pointed to the wall of a large building next to the road they had been traversing, and while Julius and the women hurried over to where he indicated, Gaius stood between them and an alleyway. After escorting the women out of the way and into an alcove in the wall, Julius turned to see three rough-looking men pour out of the alley. The leader had dark, glittering eyes and wore the slightly tattered clothes of a bandit. He and another of the men brandished daggers that glinted menacingly in the sun, while the third man was armed with a large club. All three men wore turbans over their heads and around their lower faces so as to obscure their features.

Gaius pulled his long sword from his belt and took a defensive position between his foes and his friends. The first man lunged forward to distract him while the club-wielding man tried to circle around behind him. The third stood back, waiting for his opening. Gaius easily parried the leader's dagger away with his sword. Then, so quickly that Julius almost couldn't make sense of it, he twisted the sword to ram the butt of the handle into the man's temple.

While that man dropped, the second man raised his club. No one had time to utter a word of warning before Gaius whirled around and stabbed the man through his midsection. As the women gasped in revulsion, the third man, who had waited until Gaius's back was turned, now charged toward him. Gaius whipped back around, using his momentum to swing his bloody sword into the man's arm as the dagger thrust forward into the spot Gaius had just vacated. The man fell with an ear-splitting shriek.

When the action was over, one man was dead, one was bleeding profusely, and the last was unconscious. Gaius stood at the ready in case another attacker lurked in the shadows. However, when no more ruffians appeared, he yelled for soldiers.

While Julius held Octavia so that her face was pointed away from the gruesome sight in front of them, Esther ran and clung to Gaius's arm and looked him over.

"I am okay. I'm trained to fight," he reassured her.

"I know, but I was still terrified."

He kissed the top of her head and straightened back to attention as a group of soldiers appeared on the scene and interviewed the victims of the attempted violence before releasing them to return home.

Upon reaching the villa, Julius took Gaius into the tablinum. "Do you have any ideas about what happened today?"

"I think those men were waiting for someone to come by. Whether they were waiting for us specifically or we just happened into their trap, I cannot say for sure. However, I can speculate and find it quite odd that they attacked our guarded group instead of a group without a guard."

Julius knotted his brow in concentration, "I was also concerned about that. I don't like this turn of events. What do you recommend for us going forward?"

"I think that you should always have at least two guards with you and that Octavia should stay inside the villa unless you and the guards accompany her. Also, you should always carry a dagger with you," Gaius suggested.

"I agree. I will need to hire more guards. Can you go with Dido tomorrow to hire the guards we require?" Julius asked the guard.

"Yes, we will go to the market after the first morning shift change."

Julius nodded and smiled, "And thank you, my friend, you were certainly impressive in action."

Gaius smiled ruefully, "I need to practice. I'm getting slow."

On the following day, Julius ate breakfast with Octavia and was about to head to the tablinum to look over Festus's records when Dido rushed into the dining room.

"Master, a wild beast has gotten into the paddock of donkeys. One is torn to shreds, and another is gravely wounded."

Julius quickly stood and rushed past Octavia, where she sat up on the couch with a look of horror. "Stay inside!" he commanded her.

Then he collected his guards, Apollos and Gaius, and they went to check on the donkeys. As Julius approached with Gaius on his right and Apollos on his left, they witnessed a small group of slaves standing grimly outside the paddock, which was built into a cave in the hillside. Stones had been used to build a fence around the front of the cave and a small wooden door formed the entrance. The trio was drawing near when Julius stumbled slightly before righting himself. As he bent down to check on the item that had tripped him, he detected a low whizzing sound over his head. Just then, he heard Gaius yell, "Get down!"

Julius, who was now crouching on the ground, was still not completely sure what happened when Gaius told him, "We are too exposed. Keep your head down."

Then, he had no choice but to run with his head ducked down as Gaius pulled him to the cover afforded by the paddock. At one point, he thought he saw a blur to his left, but he kept running until he reached the cave. As he entered through the gate, he nearly tripped over the mangled remains of one of his donkeys. When he was safely inside with the rest of the slaves, he turned and was shocked to see Apollos lying in the field with an arrow protruding from his chest. As Julius stared, he could not detect any movement from the man, so he said a quick prayer that his guard still lived.

Gaius looked at the group that now crowded into the paddock, trying to avoid the donkey carcass as flies buzzed around them noisily. He went to the two donkeys that remained unharmed and bleating in urgent agitation. As he untethered them and led them to the entrance of the cave, he spoke to Julius.

"I will set these loose to graze and give you more space in here. I need to go out and investigate where the archer was positioned. I imagine that our assassin has realized his failure and retreated to avoid the possibility of more guards joining in the hunt, but remain in this shelter until I or one of the other guards return with news of the archer's defeat or retreat. Do you have your dagger?

Julius nodded to him and pulled his recently sharpened blade from its sheath at his side.

"Be on your guard," Gaius commanded as he left.

Gaius snuck out of the cave, keeping himself compressed against the hillside for cover. As he moved to where he had seen the archer, he prayed for God to protect him, Julius, and the rest of the men in the cave. He knew that Apollos was dead. He had seen his glazed eyes before pulling his master into the cave. There was nothing that could be done about it right now. Later, he would mourn his friend and fellow guard.

Now, Gaius used the tall grass, stones, and trees as cover to move silently into position while carefully listening to be certain that no man or beast would pass him and head to the paddock. It would take too long to circle around the side of the large hill, so anyone who decided to attack the paddock from the archer's former position would have to pass him.

When he arrived at the location where he had seen the archer, he examined the empty place behind a small boulder. The tamped-down grass showed him where the enemy had obviously been sitting and waiting for Julius to arrive. As he inspected the area, he detected a few drops of blood on one side of the boulder. In his mind's eye, he could see the man wiping down the blade of the weapon he had used to slaughter the donkeys as a ruse to expose Julius.

Gaius crouched down low as he heard the almost imperceptible sound of someone walking carefully through the tall grass. When the sounds came close enough, he jumped up and wrapped the tall man into a headlock. The man struggled for a second before whispering out of his compressed throat, "Gaius?"

Gaius eased back on the pressure for a second. "Felix?"

The man nodded furiously. "Yes, it's me."

Gaius released him and looked at him closely. "Where did you come from?"

"Atticus had just relieved me from guarding the front door of the villa when one of the slaves told me about the donkeys, and I decided to come check on the situation. I immediately discovered Apollos—may he rest in Hades—and I sent for Atticus, who went to the paddock, while I chose to inspect this area myself. This boulder seemed like the perfect vantage point for our shooter," Felix expeditiously explained.

"Well, it was, but I think he is long gone now. Let us see if we can track him," Gaius replied.

The two men were able to follow the tracks of the archer for another two hundred yards until they reached a road that doubtlessly held the archer's means of escape.

When Julius arrived back at the villa, he felt numb. While he had not been particularly close to Apollos, he had liked the guard and felt responsible for him. As he entered the courtyard, he saw Octavia sitting on a stone bench with her head down and eyes closed. Immediately, she raised her head and looked up at him with a mixture of fear and relief in her eyes. She jumped up and clung to him.

"What happened!?" she questioned in a rush.

Julius explained to her the series of events culminating in Gaius and Felix returning to the paddock and assuring him and the slaves of their ability to return to the villa safely.

Octavia wept at the thought of losing her husband and the loss of their guard, and Julius held her tight. He sat with her and prayed. "God, please keep us safe and show us who is responsible for all these events. Thank you for protecting us today and helping us as we grieve the loss of Apollos."

Soon, Dido announced the arrival of the local centurion. Julius had the guards show him where the events of the day occurred. Then he spent the next hour in his tablinum explaining to the centurion the unfortunate events that had been plaguing them since Rome. The man, unfortunately, had no insight into these happenings and advised him to arrange more guards and be careful. Then Julius spent the rest of the day planning for Apollos's burial while Dido and Gaius traveled to the market for more guards.

Julius had a difficult time sleeping that night, with the events of the day running constantly through his mind. He knew he was missing some crucial bit of information, but he could not think of any possible motivation for or connection between these incidents. He could feel Octavia next to him shifting often in her sleep as if plagued by nightmares. Finally, as dawn neared, he slipped into a restless slumber.

Octavia tossed and turned, sometimes falling into a light sleep and other times turning over to check that Julius was safely beside her. The events of yesterday and today had brought back to her mind the persistent danger that dogged them wherever they went.

She could not recall any such incidents of violence in her life before Julius, and she could not help but feel partially responsible for somehow bringing trouble to him. She could not understand what was happening. Were these incidents a result of something Festus had done? Did someone still hold a grudge against her for marrying Julius?

As the thoughts swirled in her head, she felt her anxiety like a beast clawing at her insides. She struggled to control her breathing as her chest remained tight.

So she prayed, "God, please help me to trust you even in these perplexing times. I know you are in control, but I cannot seem to trust my entire future into your hands. Thank you that Julius was unharmed, and please keep us safe."

The tightness in her chest did not fully ease after her prayer, but she was able to control her breathing by taking deep breaths and reminding herself over and over that God had protected Julius.

CHAPTER 13

In the several weeks following Apollos's murder, Julius found himself too distracted to delve into the mountain of scrolls in the tablinum. Aurelius and Claudia had arrived to support their daughter and son-in-law in the aftermath of the assassination attempt and were staying with the couple.

Octavia found the weeks a bit lonely. She spent some time with her mother, but the older woman came down with an illness and took to her bed the second week. Octavia felt that she hardly saw Julius at all and felt trapped as she was sequestered in the villa because of the danger lurking outside. She missed having fellowship with other believers and having the freedom to leave her home.

Julius used the time he had with Aurelius to learn more about his predecessor and often ate or drank between meals with his father-in-law.

"What did you know about Festus's business ventures?" Julius queried one afternoon.

Aurelius looked up from his drink, "I really didn't know specifics. He was quite tightlipped about his investments. I knew about the insulaes in Rome, and although I suspected he had many other diversified interests, I could never confirm it. I just knew that he had a very stable income. To my knowledge, he did not have any creditors or any previous children who would leave Octavia destitute when he passed away. I thought he would be a good husband for my daughter, but it seems I did not know him very well at all."

"Who was his personal secretary? I don't recall meeting one when I married Octavia." Julius mused.

"Julian was his household manager and secretary," the older man answered.

"How could he manage both the home and the business affairs?" Julius inquired.

"From my understanding, he would delegate the household to a different slave when he was gone on business. He was actually a rather persnickety man for a slave, and I never liked him. For some reason, Festus found him invaluable, but I never understood why."

Julius sighed, "Well, I was hoping I could ask his secretary to help me understand his records, as they have proven to be more complicated than I would have expected. Did you know that he owned several properties under different names, including this villa? Is that common?"

Aurelius looked up sharply, "No, I didn't. That is highly unusual. It definitely indicates that he was hiding something, but I'm not sure why anyone would want to hide a villa. If you want me to look at any of the records with you, I would be willing to help."

"Thank you, Aurelius. I will look into them soon and let you know. Also, I was wondering how your quest for evidence is coming."

Aurelius took a moment before he carefully responded, "Yes, I suppose you would be curious. I am beyond perplexed. Every bit of evidence I find leads to the conclusion that Jesus miraculously healed ordinary people and even raised a friend of his named Lazarus from the dead. I met with Lazarus and his sisters, and my servants interviewed about a dozen mourners who all say they saw Lazarus come out of his grave days after he was buried! The Jews have been trying to re-kill Lazarus, I assume, to prevent him from spreading the word about his miraculous resurrection.

"I could even believe at this point that Jesus is the son of a Roman god, but I am having a hard time grappling with the claims that Yahweh is the only God and that Jesus is his son but still technically part of him. How could all the gods of Rome be fictitious? How could a father and a son be one being?"

He paused and let out a long sigh. "I have even begun to pray that if Jesus is God that he would reveal this knowledge to me."

Julius responded, "Some of the details of God's nature are a mystery that can only be explained by the fact that he is greater than us, so we cannot possibly understand fully. But Jesus did say, 'Ask, and it will be given to you; seek, and you will find; knock, and it will be opened to you. For everyone who asks receives, and the one who seeks finds, and to the one who knocks it will be opened.' "

"Yes, well, I am seeking answers," his father-in-law responded.

"Octavia and I are praying that you find the truth," Julius replied encouragingly.

Aurelius looked as if he were about to respond when Dido rushed into the dining room where the men were sitting.

"Master, the sentinel outside your tablinum just frightened away an intruder!"

Aurelius and Julius jumped to their feet and rushed through the courtyard. When they arrived, they observed one of the new guards standing at the entrance to the tablinum, using his hulking frame to keep the curtain door open. His eyes fixed upon his master, and the sentinel immediately began his report as the men approached him.

"Master, I heard something inside your tablinum, and when I opened the curtain, I observed a man holding a scroll. He was perched upon your desk and had his head and shoulders through the window. I yelled at him to halt, but he did not even pause as he kicked off from the desk and threw the rest of his body through the window. I then called for one of the other guards, who followed the intruder only a couple of moments behind him. I stayed to guard the tablinum."

Julius and his father-in-law listened with rapt attention, and as the guard concluded his anecdote, Julius hoisted himself onto the desk and looked through the window. This villa did not have the luxurious glass windows of the last villa. Instead, the windows were only covered with curtains. As he peered through the large, high window, he only observed trees and boulders with no signs of movement.

Then he turned as he heard hurried footsteps on the courtyard stones. He alighted from the desk and led Aurelius back into the courtyard. There, he took in the sight of Gaius and one of his new guards holding the arms of a scrappy young man who could not have been more than eighteen. The guards pulled the man forward as he glared and struggled weakly against the trained men. Gaius held a scroll in his hand, and the group abruptly stopped when they reached Julius.

"Master," Gaius began, "we caught this man trying to escape the property with one of your scrolls."

Julius inspected the young man who now had his angry eyes cast toward the floor.

"Are you the one who killed my guard, Apollos?" Julius demanded furiously.

The young man looked up quickly with surprise. "No sir, of course not. I have never killed anyone."

Julius saw the fear in his eyes that he was trying to cover with his angry glare. He took in the man's shabby clothes, scrawny frame, and dirty face.

"Let's retire to the dining room." He turned to Dido, who was standing at the ready. "Bring food for a meal."

Everyone in the courtyard looked shocked at Julius's command. To dine with a man in this part of the world was to declare him a friend.

Julius looked expectantly at Dido until the man stuttered, "Of...of course, Master."

Julius led the way to the dining room, where he and Aurelius reclined on couches. At his signal, the guards deposited the intruder onto a couch on the other side of the table. The young man held himself stiffly upright, and the guards stood behind his couch within touching distance. Julius continued to stare at the man while they waited a few minutes for food to be brought.

When his servants arranged the food on the table, Julius observed the man stare at it and swallow longingly.

"Please eat," Julius suggested firmly as he gestured toward the feast of lamb, fresh bread, and pomegranates.

The man looked at Julius momentarily, apparently weighing his options, before he dove into the food as if he hadn't eaten in days.

Julius and Aurelius watched him but didn't eat. After a few minutes, the man finished and looked up abashedly.

Julius met his gaze and began, "I find that it is difficult to think clearly when one is deprived of food. I need you to have all of your wits about you as you answer my questions. First, I will tell you what I know... I know that you were paid by someone to go into my office and steal a scroll. What I don't know is how deeply involved you are with the plot to kill me."

The man swallowed and his eyes rounded with fear of the Roman death sentence that possibly awaited him. He nearly tripped over his words in a rush to justify himself. "Sir, I had nothing to do with any plot to kill anyone. I was only given some money to sneak into your tablinum and find that scroll. I need the money because my parents died last year, and I am struggling to care for my three younger siblings.

"I have been sneaking into your tablinum every day for three days. I was told that a guard was posted outside the door, so I would have to be silent. The first two days, I didn't find anything, but I finally did today. Unfortunately for me, I accidentally knocked another scroll off the desk onto the floor as I was leaving and so alerted your guards."

Julius continued to study him. "Was there not a guard on that wall for the last three days?"

"No sir, I was pleased to find that while the other walls were attended, that one was unguarded."

"Hmm," Julius hummed as he rubbed his chin in thought. "Who hired you?"

"I don't know; the man wore a turban wrapped around his head. He met me in the city and gave me the instructions and a portion of the money. He met me every evening at dusk at the Brook Kidron to check on my progress. He promised to give me the rest of the money when I brought him the scroll."

"What scroll were you looking for?" Julius asked in a placid voice so as to not betray the urgency of this information.

"He told me to find one that had details about a property in Raetia."

Julius glanced over at Aurelius, who met his gaze and maintained a blank expression on his face. Then they looked back at the thief. "What is your name?" Julius inquired.

"I am Onan."

"Onan, I need to confirm your story about your family. Then I will decide what is to be done with you."

The man hung his head in resignation and nodded. "Yes, sir."

Julius then stood and turned his gaze to Gaius, signaling the guard to follow him from the room.

"Who was supposed to be guarding that wall during the day?" he asked when they stood alone in the courtyard.

"Felix was, Master."

"Bring him to me and get two more guards. After I determine the cause of this lapse in security, we will go into the city with Onan to find his family and confirm his story. I want to bring Esther with us to assure his younger siblings we mean them no harm."

Gaius nodded his assent and turned to find Felix. Then Julius returned to the dining room. He looked at the remaining guard and commanded, "Tie his hands together and hold him in the courtyard until we are ready to leave."

Julius and Aurelius waited in the dining room until Felix was brought into the room. The guard looked very disheveled and slightly chagrined, and Gaius said by way of explanation, "I found him in the slave quarters with one of Claudia's maids."

Aurelius burst out, "How dare you touch one of my slaves!"

Felix stood tall and made his face like granite.

Julius stood slowly and squared his shoulders. "Are you responsible for Apollos's death?"

Felix's hard face turned to one of shock and dismay. "Of course not, Master. All I am guilty of is falling in love with a slave from another master."

"You were assigned to the wall outside the tablinum for the last three days, were you not?" Julius interrogated.

Felix looked perplexed at this. "I was originally given that duty, but I asked Atticus to switch shifts with me, so I took the night shift, and he was to cover the daytime."

Julius looked at Dido, "Summon Atticus to me."

"Yes, Master."

The four men remaining in the dining room stared at each other in tense silence until Dido arrived with Atticus, and Julius began to question the new arrival.

"Did Felix ask you to switch shifts with him and watch the wall outside the tablinum during the day while he watches it at night?"

Atticus looked surprised and glanced at Felix before answering, "No, Master, while it is true that my original assignment was to watch the tablinum wall at night, I thought that Felix asked me to watch the GARDEN wall during the day, not the tablinum wall. I have been watching the garden wall with another guard. I assumed that we had two guards placed there to protect the mistress and her mother since they spend most of the day in the garden. I didn't realize I was guarding the wrong location."

Felix's features changed to reflect his consternation and regret. "I am sorry, Master! It seems this was my fault. I thought I was clear about my assignment, but I guess I was not."

Julius felt such irritation with the slave as he could not recall experiencing in recent memory. "Explain your relationship with his slave!" he ordered as he pointed to Aurelius.

"I have been conducting a relationship with Aelia ever since your in-laws first came to visit at the domus in Rome. Atticus is the only one who knew, and he has been changing shifts with me so that I could meet with her. She is with child, Master."

Julius bowed his head and sighed in frustration, and for a moment, he allowed envy for the couple and bitterness over the loss of his legitimate child to burn inside his heart. Then he mentally shook himself. "God forgive me for my envy!" he prayed silently.

He looked back up at Felix and Atticus. "For now, Felix, you are to stay in your quarters until your shift watching the TABLINUM wall. Atticus, you go guard the tablinum wall until Felix relieves you. No one will be switching shifts without Gaius's permission. He is the captain of my guard to prevent foolish mistakes such as these! You are both fortunate that this intruder was not seeking a life! I will decide what to do with you later."

He dismissed all the guards with a wave and sat forward with his head in his hands for a moment after they left the room. He heard Aurelius ask, "Why didn't you have them beaten immediately?"

Julius raised his head, "Please tell me that you are not going to have that pregnant slave girl beaten."

Aurelius sighed, "In the past, I probably would have, but I think your gentler nature is rubbing off on me. I will not have her beaten, but I will likely sell her. I cannot tolerate this kind of rebellion and immorality in my staff."

"Perhaps, I will buy her from you. I do not like to see families separated," Julius said.

Aurelius blinked at him in shock. "So, you will reward your slave's impudence?"

"No, I will find a suitable punishment, but I do not believe that anyone is benefitted by the child being bereft of a father."

Aurelius stared at him, considering his comments and responded, "You know, when I first heard about you, I really thought I was going to find you to be a dull, vacuous presence in my life, but the more I get to know you, the more you challenge my core beliefs. I find that things are never dull when you are around."

"I will take that as a compliment." Julius smiled back at the man.

Aurelius went to join his wife and daughter in the gardens while the group consisting of Julius, Gaius, Esther, and three other guards took a cart into the city. A restrained Onan directed them through the streets that became increasingly narrower. When they reached a road too tight to fit the cart, they left the driver and the cart and traveled by foot. In the ruins of the city, they discovered that many poor families were living in squalor among the toppled stones and charred wood left by the Roman siege. These members of society's undesirables had used old rugs and curtains to hovel together makeshift roofs and homes in an effort to shelter themselves from the elements.

The streets were lined with refuse, and the stench of death and unwashed bodies made Julius's eyes water. He was wondering about the wisdom of coming here, even so well guarded, when Onan, who was walking in front with a guard gripping his rope, pointed ahead. "That is our home there."

He pointed at a brown rug that was covering a little indent in the toppled stones. The area inside was smaller than the space inside the cart they had ridden, and Julius was moved to pity by the three small faces that poked out of the hovel to investigate when they heard their brother's voice.

A girl who must have been ten or less came forward out of the space and looked at her brother. She motioned for the other two to stay inside, and she looked at the group with naked fear in her face.

Julius nodded to Esther, who barely moved toward the girl. "Hello, what is your name?"

"I am Tavi. Why do you have my brother tied?" the girl responded piteously.

Julius spoke then, "Your brother broke into my home today."

The little girl darted her eyes back and forth to her smaller siblings as if looking for a way to escape with them.

Julius put his hands forward in a gesture of peace. "I am not here to hurt you. Only to confirm that his story is true. Is Onan a good brother?"

Tavi nodded vigorously. "He is the best brother! He always feeds us before he has eaten, and he has taken good care of us since our parents died."

Julius turned to Onan, "I see that you were telling the truth, and I want to make you an offer. Instead of turning you over to the Roman authorities for stealing, if you will agree to be my slave, I will allow your family to come live with you in the slave quarters. You will be paid the normal wages of a slave minus the cost of your sibling's food. If any of them choose to work for us, they will receive just wages. You can one day purchase your freedom for 1,500 denarii. That is the going rate for a slave with no previous qualifications, and I believe, a more than fair rate for a man who was caught stealing from me."

Onan asked timidly, "But my siblings would be free?"

"Yes, your siblings would be free."

Onan let out a relieved sigh. "Yes, thank you, Master. I will gladly become your slave to pay back my debt to you."

"Excellent. I will draw up the paperwork after we return to the villa, and we will register it with the local magistrate tomorrow. I will have you get settled with your siblings for a few days, and then I will give you your assignment." Julius instructed.

Onan then addressed Tavi, "We are going to live in a large villa with these people. Get Benjamin and Ephron and our things."

Tavi rushed into the burrow and emerged with two filthy little boys who were obviously twins and a small, stained brown bag slung over her shoulder. The boys appeared to be about three years old, and they clutched their sister's skirts tightly with fear. Esther sympathetically walked near them, talking to the three children, and easing their troubled minds as they returned to the cart.

Once the group reached the vehicle, Julius had Onan explain to two of the guards where the man had met him near the Brook Kidron every evening. He then dispatched the guards to surveil that location and try to catch the man responsible for hiring Onan while the remaining group rode to the villa.

Julius watched the children's awestruck faces as they caught the first glimpse of their new home. Even though the fast-approaching darkness of evening was obscuring some of the grandeur of the villa, the children did not seem any less impressed. When they arrived and walked inside, the three younger ones swept their heads around in an awe-inspired stupor while Onan looked at the faces of the people with whom he would now be employed.

Dido and Linus stepped forward to greet their master. Dido sported the carefully schooled expression of a servant who had long since ceased to be surprised by a master's whims, while Linus froze and took in the ragtag group of street children with a dropped jaw and a gasp.

Octavia and her parents then joined them in the courtyard, and Julius explained how Onan was a new member of the staff and that the other children would be assigned a room in the slave quarters. Dido led them away while Linus, who quickly recovered his calm, asked if Julius would like him to draw up the paperwork for Onan.

Julius nodded and entered the dining room. As he did so, Gaius held out a hand, and when Julius paused, he pulled out the scroll that Onan had stolen earlier and offered it to his master.

"I have kept this in my tunic all afternoon to prevent it from disappearing in the confusion."

"Thank you, Friend. I had forgotten all about it, but I am sure I would have been worrying over its location tonight when I had a chance to lie down and think over the day. Before you retire, please check that all the guards are at their assignments." Julius requested.

"Yes, Master." Gaius nodded and went to join the other slaves for their evening meal.

The two guards who had been sent to do surveillance returned and reported that no one had come to the meeting place at the brook. Somehow, the man who hired Onan had known that he wouldn't show up. Julius didn't believe it was a coincidence. Somehow, an enemy was getting information about his actions, and he suspected it was a staff member who was betraying his confidence. He just wasn't sure how to find the responsible party.

CHAPTER 14

That night, Octavia sat in her room waiting for Julius to join her after going over the schedule for the next day with Linus. She sat on the edge of the bed and held herself. Thoughts swirled in her mind like bees around their hive. Why would Julius bring small children into her home without even consulting her first? Did her thoughts and feelings mean so little to him?

She had felt that he was pulling away from her since they had arrived in Jerusalem. The time that he had been spending with her previously, now suddenly, he was spending with her father. She wondered if she was easily replaceable. Was she really as worthless to Julius as she had been to Festus?

Even in the evenings, he was exhausted and didn't want to talk to her or hold her. He used to ask her opinion before making decisions for them. Now, he just took counsel with Aurelius. Even during meals, he did not include her as much as he used to. He didn't touch her on the shoulder or give her hugs or kisses for no reason anymore.

She blinked back tears and took several deep breaths as she waited. Finally, Julius pulled back the curtain only to pause in the entrance when he viewed the distressed posture of his wife.

"What's wrong?" He glanced around the room as if the answer might be found in their surroundings.

"Why did you invite small children to live with us? Why would you think I would want that or be okay with it?!" Her voice, which had begun at a normal talking level, swelled in a crescendo until it reached a near yell by the time she was finished.

Julius opened his eyes wide with shock and let the frustrations of his day flow through him until he was nearly vibrating with anger. "How dare you speak to me that way!"

His raised voice broke through the dam of Octavia's tears, and she began to sob uncontrollably.

Julius took a steadying breath that did nothing to stop his arms from shaking. He lowered his voice to a controlled tone, "I need some space tonight. I will sleep in one of the other rooms. Good night!"

He strode angrily into the courtyard and saw the guard staring studiously into the rows of pomegranate trees as if he had not heard the loud exchange. Julius huffed and retreated into his tablinum. There, he lit his lamp and pulled the stolen scroll from his tunic. He might as well read it now because he was definitely not going to sleep any time soon.

He looked over the scroll, and what he read confused him all the more. The top of the scroll had the location and geographic specifications of the mysterious Raetia property. Under that header were written three columns. The first column was a list of names, and the next two columns showed amounts of money. On the left of the scroll, some of the names had Xs next to them. He decided to ask Aurelius about the scroll tomorrow to see if he understood it.

Julius sat back in his chair and rubbed his eyes. He started to think about his conversation with Octavia. As he thought back, he realized that he definitely wasn't as patient with her as he could have been. He tried to think through the last month from her perspective, but he still could not reconcile the series of events with her yelling at him as she had.

He sighed and picked up the scroll, which he had planned to keep with him for the foreseeable future. While he could not see the value in it yet, he knew it was the key to at least a part of this mystery, or someone wouldn't have gone to such lengths to acquire it.

Julius prayed, "Please, God, forgive me for how I talked to Octavia, and please help me to love her as I should."

Octavia lay on her bed and felt as if she had cried all the tears she had.

"So stupid, so so stupid." She repeated to herself as she tapped her temples with her fists.

Suddenly, she heard a sound at her door and saw the light of a lamp. She sat up quickly, afraid that it might be an enemy, but she was relieved and partially terrified to see Julius's face in the lamplight.

Octavia wiped at her eyes and quickly choked out, "I'm so sorry for yelling at you."

Julius stared for a moment and walked over to the bed, leaving the lamp on the bedside table as he climbed up and sat next to his wife.

She continued in a rush, "I've been feeling as if you don't want to be around me. You don't talk with me as much or touch me, or spend time with me. I feel trapped in the villa and can't even go to church. Then you invited these children to live with us while I'm still struggling with our loss, and it just felt like you didn't care about me."

Julius sighed and brushed her hair back from her face, "I am sorry that it came across that way, and you are right that I haven't been spending enough time with you. I didn't realize the effect that staying in the villa was having on you."

He then explained Onan and his siblings' situation to her with eyes begging her to understand and affirm his decision. "If I turned him in for stealing, he would have been beaten, killed, or enslaved, and his family would have starved. If I didn't turn him in, he would have likely continued into a life of crime for lack of employment options and would have eventually been caught.

"I really don't think he's a bad young man, just one in a desperate position. I couldn't see another way to protect him and his innocent siblings. I really didn't think about them affecting you because they will be in the slave quarters."

He began massaging his temples as he finished his explanation.

Octavia nodded slowly as she considered all the options. "I think that you made a reasonable decision with the circumstances presented. However, I wish you had consulted me before you left to meet his family. I don't think you have considered the needs of small children. They can't be simply confined to a room in the slave quarters with only a ten-year-old sister watching them until they are old enough to work."

Julius mulled this over for a moment. "You're right. I should've consulted you. Maybe together we could've come up with a better plan. Why don't we assemble a large guard on the Lord's Day? We will leave most of the guards a safe distance from the home where we will meet so that they will not know the exact location, and Gaius will escort us the rest of the way as long as he believes he can keep us safe.

"Then we will consult with the other believers and see if anyone, perhaps a widow, can come to the villa to watch and help raise the three children. If we can attend services with no danger, we will plan to attend more in the future."

He paused and looked at her deeply. "I will also make more of an effort to spend time with you again. I've had so many things on my mind with the assassination attempts and your father being here, and business concerns that I am afraid I have let our relationship suffer. I will work on that immediately."

Octavia smiled, "Thank you. I love you, and I think that hiring a nursemaid is a fantastic idea."

As Julius pulled her into his arms, he said, "Excellent! And tomorrow morning over breakfast, you can give me advice about how we should handle our guards."

Octavia smiled in relief and kissed her husband.

The following morning, Julius arranged for the servants to bring breakfast into their room so they could spend time together privately. He also sent word to his in-laws that he and Octavia would be spending the day relaxing together after the excitement of the day before.

Before they began their conversation, Julius prayed that they would have wisdom, and then he spent the next hour explaining to Octavia the concerns he had with someone passing messages to their enemy and the options he had for dealing with Felix and Atticus.

"So," Octavia began thoughtfully, "if we assume that reports to our enemy, whoever that is, have been passed along from the time we were in Rome all the way until now, the only conclusion we can draw is that the culprit is one of the people we have had with us the whole time. That means the only possibilities are Gaius, Esther, Linus, Felix, Atticus, and Apollos. However, it is unlikely that it was Apollos since he was murdered, and someone still sent word that Onan was captured. Also, I cannot possibly believe it was Gaius or Esther. That leaves just Linus, Felix, and Atticus."

Julius nodded at her encouragingly as he chewed his food, so she continued. "Also, if it isn't Felix, and we sell him, we will be separating him from his unborn child. But if we keep him and buy his lover from my father, they could marry and be a family. Then, if he is guilty, and we sold them, we would be separating a husband, wife, and child. And, if we sold Atticus and, or Linus, it would just be as a result of unconfirmed suspicions, and we would have to live with the idea that they may go to cruel masters."

Julius swallowed his food and responded. "We also must consider the fact that to maintain order in our home, we need to in some way punish Felix and Atticus for abdicating their responsibilities and ignoring Gaius's orders. My idea is to add money to the price of their freedom. More money for Felix than for Atticus because he instigated the disobedience."

"That seems like a fair and reasonable solution. How much do you think we can trust our new guards?" she asked.

Julius sighed and responded, "I think that most anyone can be bought for a price. None of their lives are their own, and if they think someone will pay them the money for their freedom, I doubt there is much they wouldn't do for it. We have made loyal allies in Gaius and Esther, but that is by far an anomaly. I think that I may have purchased Onan's loyalty by saving him from punishment and sheltering his family."

"Could you train him to be a secretary and have Linus work on things that are not of critical importance?" Octavia suggested.

"I could do that, and I can tell the staff that no letters will be sent from the villa without being inspected. However, it will be difficult to prevent someone from using their day off to go send a message or meet with a contact, and it would tip our hand and put our traitor more on guard."

Octavia paused her eating for a moment as she thought. "What if, instead, we have Gaius and two of the new guards watch our suspects when they leave the villa? The villain is bound to slip up eventually."

Julius smiled at his clever wife. "That is a good idea. I am thinking that we should purchase Felix's girl from Aurelius, provided he plans to marry her. Then if Felix has sent messages to our enemy, it is possible this will buy his loyalty back to us, and we will not be responsible for breaking apart a family. Also, we add the money to what Felix and Atticus owe, alert Gaius of the mole, order that the suspects be watched, and keep Linus from any sensitive information."

"I think that sounds like a good plan, dear Husband, and we will trust God with the results." She smiled and leaned forward to kiss him.

The next day, Julius found Linus waiting just outside his chambers. "Linus, I will assign you a new room to use, and I want you to use your notes from our travels to begin compiling a comprehensive list of all the properties that we visited in Italia with their specifics: who ran them, how many people worked there, etcetera. I will bring you additional scrolls you need, but I am trying to organize the scrolls by subject and location and believe we can better coordinate if we spread them all between two rooms."

Linus showed no emotion as he nodded, "Yes, Master."

Julius then spent the early morning setting up Linus in a room near the slave quarters and brought him the scrolls he would need to begin his task.

Later that morning, Julius called Gaius to his tablinum and revealed to him all aspects of the strategy to smoke out their spy and the corrective actions he planned to take for Felix and Atticus.

Gaius nodded in agreement. "That sounds like a good plan. If I could make one suggestion, I would put both those guards on duty only in areas that require multiple guards, like the front entrance to the villa. Therefore, they cannot leave an area unguarded if their potential benefactor asks them to."

"Perfect. Thank you, Gaius. Please send in Felix."

In a short while, Felix entered the tablinum with a stoic countenance. He stood at attention in front of the desk with his eyes focused upon the far wall past Julius and waited for his punishment to be declared.

"Felix, before I talk of punishment, I want to ask you something. If you had the opportunity to marry and live in the same household with Aelia, would you do so?"

Felix looked quickly down at his master and in a resolute voice, declared, "I would."

Julius studied him for a moment and then began his proposal. "I then have a plan that I think would work for everyone. I am not a proponent of physical punishments; instead, I plan to increase the amount that you owe for your freedom by 300 denarii. I will also buy Aelia from my father-in-law, so you will be married and be able to raise your child together.

"I will not separate or sell either of you unless it becomes absolutely necessary, as in the case of a betrayal or intended harm toward myself or my household. And I will do everything in my power to keep your children with you and Aelia always. Do you understand?"

Surprise and hope warred for control on Felix's previously impassive face. "I understand and would never do anything to harm or betray you, Master. You are most generous with your servant. May the gods bless you."

Julius replied, "My God has already blessed me, and I thank you for your dedicated service to me through the last several months. I will speak to Aurelius about Aelia today, and hopefully, we can have you married by the end of the week. I will have new paperwork for you to sign soon. Please send Atticus in."

Felix nodded, and Julius didn't miss the twinkle of joy in the man's eyes as he turned to leave the room.

Atticus also maintained an impassive expression until Julius told him that in lieu of a beating, he would owe Julius 100 extra denarii to buy his freedom. Then, his face lit with a smile of relief as he thanked his master.

After the midday meal that Julius shared with his wife and in-laws, the ladies left so he could speak to Aurelius privately.

Julius began, "First, I want to have you look at the scroll that Onan was attempting to steal yesterday."

He handed the older man the scroll and drank as he watched Aurelius's expression change from one of interest to grave concern.

"I am not sure about the tender amounts in these columns, but I recognize a few of the names. The very concerning thing is that these three with Xs next to them have all either died or disappeared in the last five years or so. Some of them were my friends, and I have been concerned about this man in particular." He pointed to one of the names with a big X by it.

"One day, about a year ago, he was just gone. He told his family that he was meeting with someone and would return within a week. His family hasn't heard from him, and no one seems to know where he went."

Julius looked back at the list and noticed that twelve of the twenty-five names had Xs beside them. "That is deeply troubling. I think that I will need to go to the Raetia property and see what is happening there, but it may not be safe to take Octavia, and the weather will prohibit me from going until next spring."

"Octavia can stay with Claudia, and I will go with you. We will make sure to take plenty of guards with us," Aurelius committed.

"You don't need to trouble yourself," Julius replied in surprise.

"Julius, I was not diligent enough when I betrothed my daughter to Festus. Evidently, he was not the man I believed him to be, so at least part of your troubles is a result of my negligence, and I will certainly not leave you to clean up my mess without my help."

Julius leaned forward to grasp his father-in-law's forearm and pull him into a hug. "Thank you."

The men sat in silence for a little while, and Julius put the scroll back into his toga. "I have worked out my punishments with the slaves and am planning to buy Aelia from you. Have you talked to your wife about losing her?"

"Yes, and she agreed that we would have to sell her. Is Felix going to marry her?"

"Yes, he is."

"Good." He paused for a beat. "It's odd. I never thought I would care about a slave or their child, but for some reason, I have started to care about other people, even slaves."

"That's a good thing. Are you still praying for answers about God?" Julius inquired.

"Yes, and Octavia has been discussing the gospel and her faith with Claudia, who now says she believes in Yahweh. Now I'm wondering what we must do to be saved. You talk of your Jesus saving you from your sins, but how does it work?"

Julius replied, "All you must do is repent from your sins and believe in the gospel message that God sent his son Jesus to live the perfect life you were supposed to live but didn't. Then He died the death that you deserved, taking your place and creating a way for you to have communion and an eternity with God in heaven. You must turn your back on your old sinful life and strive toward a life of obedience to God. You will still fail and sin, but when you do, you repent and know that your sin is covered by the blood of Jesus."

"I do believe. I have found the preponderance of evidence to be overwhelming that Jesus was the son of God and that he rose from the dead and ascended to heaven. I have spent months searching out witnesses, and I have been entirely convinced. I have found that I do not want to do the things that I used to do," said Aurelius.

"That is great!" Julius joyfully exclaimed.

"I suppose I should pray that God would forgive me of my former sins and keep me from sin," Aurelius suggested.

"Most definitely. Can I pray with you?"

"I would like that, thank you."

CHAPTER 15

The sun shone brightly upon the stones surrounding the Pool of Siloam as the believers gathered on this Lord's Day to witness the baptisms of Aurelius and Claudia. Julius and Octavia held hands and smiled at one another. It had been an incredible blessing for Octavia to attend services with her parents for the last two weeks, and now, as they witnessed this outward expression of their new faith in God, Octavia's heart swelled with gratitude for her Savior.

She thought about all the blessings in her life. They had experienced no new incidents in the weeks following the attempted theft. They had hired a nursemaid from the church to watch over Onan's siblings and teach them. To her surprise, Octavia had found that playing with them in the garden had become an amusing pastime for her.

As the winter gradually crept over the empire, she realized that the icy pain that had banded itself around her heart when Lucius had died was beginning to thaw. She no longer felt the devastating pain of her loss with as much frequency. Julius had been making a concerted effort to spend time with her and talked with her often.

Aurelius and Claudia shook the hands of their fellow believers and beamed the smiles of those who had finally found peace in their lives.

Later at the villa, Octavia felt nauseous at the evening meal and jolted upright with the realization that her womanly cycle was late. She thought back and realized that she was likely as far along as she had been when she found out she was pregnant with Lucius. She saw Julius look at her questioningly, but she did not want to say anything in front of her parents, and she gave him a placid smile while reclining once again.

After the meal, she excused herself to find Esther and asked her to call for a midwife tomorrow.

The three remaining members of the party stayed in the dining room conversing when Aurelius turned his thoughtful gaze to Julius. "I received a note today from an old friend, Brutus, who has been traveling in the empire and plans to winter here. My curiosity was immediately piqued when I realized that his name was one of the names on the scroll, without an X beside it, of course."

Julius sat up in concentration. "Would you like to invite him here so we can ask why his name was on the list?"

Aurelius nodded, "That is what I had been contemplating. You can invite him to stay for a few days while we are here, and we can ask him about it. Maybe we can glean more information before our trip. I will send him an invitation tomorrow."

Julius smiled at the prospect of solving this mystery.

Octavia woke the next morning and spent the next few hours in hopeful anxiety. The midwife arrived right before the midday meal, and Esther escorted her through the empty courtyard to her mistress. Octavia instantly recognized the midwife, Baracha, as a believer from church with whom Octavia had conversed several times before, and she was immediately comfortable with the woman. The midwife checked her and confirmed that she was pregnant. She also gave her dried raspberry leaves to steep in hot water and drink every day.

Octavia walked with the woman from her room back through the courtyard and just passed the tablinum door when Julius and Aurelius stepped out and came to a sudden stop. Julius looked at the woman and nodded. "Hail, Baracha. How is your family?"

The woman glanced at Octavia before answering, "Hail, Julius. My family is well. I was only here for a quick visit. God bless you and your family."

Then she rushed through the courtyard with Esther as Octavia looked at Julius with a concerned glance.

Julius looked at his father-in-law, "Please start the midday meal with Claudia. We will join you soon."

Then, as Aurelius walked away, he gently grasped Octavia's arm and led her into their quarters. "Isn't Baracha a midwife?"

Octavia nodded with some trepidation. "I just started to suspect yesterday and wanted to confirm before mentioning it."

"So, you are with child?!" he asked excitedly.

"Yes, I am," she answered in a measured tone.

Julius sat on the edge of the bed. "How do you feel about that?"

Octavia sat next to him and sighed. "I honestly thought I would be more excited, but I kind of feel... numb. I am excited but also worried that we will lose this baby too."

"I understand, Love, but we will choose to live in the moment and the knowledge that God has given us. And what we know is that he has blessed us with another child," he reassured her.

Then he took her hands and bowed his head. "God, please keep Octavia and this baby safe. Please, if it is your will, help this baby to be born healthy. Please help us not to be anxious about the things we cannot control and to trust you even in the things that we are afraid of. In the name of Jesus, Amen."

"Amen." Octavia paused for a moment before adding, "I would like to keep this between us for now."

Julius nodded in assent, and they joined her parents in the dining hall.

A week later, Aurelius's old friend, Brutus, arrived at the villa. As the visitor greeted Aurelius with a handshake, Julius took a moment to study the man. He was dressed in a most extravagant fashion with a scarlet mantle over his toga. Gold rings with impressive stones covered every finger and glittered in the light of the courtyard as he greeted Aurelius animatedly. He brought an impressive retinue of slaves, and Julius immediately bristled at the demeaning way in which he spoke to them.

For the next two days, Julius suffered through the boorish man's presence at the villa, choosing to spend much of his time in the tablinum or with Octavia. On the second day, Aurelius slipped into his tablinum and collapsed into the chair on the other side of Julius's desk.

"Please tell me I was never as insufferable as that man is!"

Julius smiled and wisely kept his mouth closed.

Aurelius continued, "He has gone into the city for the afternoon, and I think we should ask him about the scroll this evening after the women have retired. You have doubtless noticed that he drinks to excess whenever the opportunity presents itself, and his sensibilities are dull after dinner. It would be the perfect time to pry the truth from him."

Julius nodded in agreement. "Hopefully, he will be on his way soon after."

Aurelius groaned in frustration. "Looking at his life and manner is so strange to me now. I used to be him. I wanted everyone to regard me as a wealthy and wise man, but I was so blinded to how I actually treated people. It's astounding!"

"God has done a great work in you. Have you told Brutus about your new faith?" Julius asked.

"Yes, but he laughed and changed the subject to his latest women conquests."

"All we can do then is pray for his soul," Julius responded in calm acceptance.

After dinner that night, when Brutus was merrily drinking and laughing at every story, Aurelius nodded to Julius, who produced the scroll that never left his possession.

"My friend, my son-in-law, found this in Festus's records and was perplexed by it. When he showed it to me, I noticed your name on it. We were wondering if you could help us to understand what the scroll is referencing.

Brutus chortled and nearly spilled his glass as he set it upon the table to take the scroll from Aurelius. He took a moment to focus his eyes on the heading. While he read over the list, the smile fell from his features, and his face paled in the lamplight.

"What is this?!" he demanded, suddenly angry.

"That is what we are asking you, Friend. Neither of our names are on the list, and I am sure that you could not have missed the names with Xs by them. I haven't heard from Plinius for about a year now, have you?"

Brutus's hand was shaking as he dropped the scroll upon the table and shuffled away from it. His manner betrayed his words as he began, "It is nothing. I did some business with Festus several years ago. He asked me to invest in a property—said that he was running a business that would double my investment. That number in the column right next to my name is the amount I invested. The amount in the next column is the amount he paid me back. As you can see, it was over double my initial investment. He told me that it was nothing illegal and I believed him."

The inebriated man pursed his lips closed as if trying to prevent more information from escaping while Julius and Aurelius exchanged glances.

"And the Xs, do you know to what they refer?" Aurelius continued his inquest.

"Of course not," Brutus exclaimed belligerently.

Julius began to apply more pressure to the quivering man. "I have been in contact with the local centurion since I have had two attempts on my life in recent months. Because you cannot shed light on this baffling scroll, perhaps I will turn it over to him to investigate further."

The other man blanched and struggled to catch his breath.

"I will, of course, let the centurion know that you are in town. Perhaps you will remember more while he is interrogating you," Julius continued threateningly.

The man threw his hands out in front of himself and grasped the edge of the table until his knuckles turned white. "Please don't do that. I will tell you, okay! Just don't involve the military."

Julius relaxed his posture and gestured to the man to continue his story.

"Festus told me that it was legal, but he also made me agree not to keep any records of the investment and not to speak of it to anyone else. I was blinded by the amount of money I would be getting and didn't want to look into the matter further. I gave him my investment and received the profits only four months later."

He looked at Aurelius. "As you know, that is an incredibly fast return. I was thrilled and asked if I could continue investing. Festus just grinned at me and told me it was a one-time deal. Then he reminded me to keep my silence, and I went about my life and forgot about it.

"Over a year ago, about a month before his disappearance, Plinius came to visit me and asked me about investing with Festus. He told me that he had invested a large sum six months prior but that Festus was now being enigmatic about when he would get his money back. I assured Plinius that I had made a similar deal and that I had promptly received a large sum back from him, so he had no need to worry. This seemed to quell Plinius's concerns, and we went about our lives.

"Then, a week or so later, I was dining with Festus and had imbibed too much wine when I jovially mentioned, 'By the way, I thought the investment I made with you was a one-time opportunity.'

"He glared at me sharply and asked what I meant by that. I recounted that I had heard from Plinius about his contribution, which hadn't been returned. In spite of my inebriated state, I was quite aware of the displeasure of my comrade, and I was quick to reassure him that I had assuaged the other investor's fears.

"However, if anything, this only seemed to further enrage Festus. He screamed at me, 'You were charged to keep silent about the whole arrangement! Obviously, you are a buffoon who cannot be trusted!'

"I had never seen the man so furious, and I leapt up from my seat as if completely sober and ran from his presence.

"Two days later, I was in the market when a man lunged out the alleyway with a knife and attempted to stab me. Fortunately for me, at that moment, a thief ran into the alley to escape capture from pursuing soldiers. In his haste, the thief jostled the assassin, preventing his blow from reaching me, and the resulting commotion and presence of the authorities allowed me the opportunity to escape. My secretary, who had been with me, tried to convince me that the man was only seeking my money and not my blood, but I knew from the moment our eyes met that the man was determined to end my life.

"The next day, my cup-bearer fell down dead from a poisonous dose of cyanide in my drink. I saw then the harbinger of my impending doom, so I retreated to Alexandria and hired myself a new staff. I was correct that the distance had thrown off my pursuers, but I heard about Plinius disappearing. I have held out hope that Plinius had escaped like me; however, the X beside his name on the scroll seems to indicate otherwise.

"I finally felt safe to leave Alexandria since I heard of Festus's death, but if someone is still trying to kill to hide this information, there must be another man involved."

Julius and Aurelius listened silently during the man's story and assured him that they would continue to be silent about his part in this business unless they needed him to testify against the culprit in the future. When Julius returned to his chambers that evening, he recounted the conversation to Octavia, and they prayed for continued safety and wisdom.

The next day, Brutus left early without the exuberance he had exhibited upon his arrival. Julius suspected that the man would leave town immediately and resume his hiding.

Two days after Brutus left, Gaius was spending his morning following Atticus into Jerusalem on his day off. It had been difficult to spy on his fellow guards without them noticing. So far, Felix seemed enthralled with his new wife and spent every moment of free time with her. Linus appeared perpetually bored, and Gaius often wondered if the man had any pleasures or desires in life at all. Atticus acted like a typical guard. He went about his duties as commanded, never complained, and never fell asleep on duty. Gaius understood the master's reasoning when determining who could be a mole in the household, but it was difficult for him to picture any of these men in that role.

As Atticus traversed through the winding streets of the city, Gaius followed at a safe distance and let his mind wander to his wife and how much joy she had brought to his life in the last several months. She was so kind in a world that had been so hostile to him since childhood. Sometimes he had to remind himself to be gentle with her as he was accustomed to being abrupt in speech as well as in his actions.

He jerked himself to a jarring halt as he saw Atticus stop in a market square in front of another man. Gaius hid himself behind a wall and watched as Atticus spoke to the other man while glancing around surreptitiously. Then he handed the man a folded note and took off in the other direction from Gaius across the square. Gaius watched the other man while tracking Atticus out of the corner of his eye. The contact slid the note into his bag while the guard disappeared back into the maze of streets.

Gaius stepped forward and headed toward the note holder as the man began walking leisurely away from where Atticus had retreated. The guard followed the contact until they were on a smaller street, where he intentionally bumped into the man and knocked him onto the ground hard.

Gaius deliberately slurred his words as if inebriated and reached for the man's bag, which had fallen beside him. "I am... so ssssorry siiir."

As he helped the angry man to his feet, he slipped the note out of the bag and handed the bag back.

"You fool! You could have hurt me," the man began as he brushed off his tunic. However, when the man glanced up and observed Gaius, who stood a foot taller than he did, he stuttered an assurance that no harm was done, and he scurried away, clutching his bag.

Gaius stared after the man and carefully began to follow him once again. He took his time cautiously blending into the streets, hoping to uncover who hired this man to carry the missive. However, after entering another city square, the contact jumped into a cart and was carried off down the street. Gaius looked around and spotted another cart for rent. He jumped in and instructed the driver to follow his target. He never took his eyes from the other cart as they moved as rapidly as possible through the crowded streets.

Suddenly, a group of children ran out into the street blocking Gaius's cart, and in spite of the driver yelling at the children to move, they continued angrily tussling with each other. It took several minutes, and their father emerging from their home to yell at them before they cleared the street. By the time his cart was free from obstacles once again, Gaius's target had disappeared.

He sighed in frustration before looking down and unfolding the note which read: "Brutus Adrianus came and spoke to the master who has the scroll with him at all times."

When Gaius showed the note to Julius, he let out a shuddering breath of disappointment in Atticus but was also relieved that the mole was discovered. Then, he stationed a welcoming party to be prepared for the return of the traitor.

When Atticus returned to the villa, he entered the courtyard, coming face to face with Gaius and Julius, who was holding the offending note. Atticus turned to glance over his shoulder and found that two guards stood on either side of the door he had just entered through and blocked his retreat. Gaius stood with an angry scowl on his face and his arms crossed while Julius assessed the betrayer through narrowed eyes.

Atticus lowered his shoulders in an apparent posture of one who knows they are caught. Then he gave a half grin and said, "Hail, Master. How can I help you?"

"Are you responsible for the murder of Apollos?" Julius hastily began.

His face remained bemused as he answered calmly. "No, all I did was send out some information. I did not know anything about the assassination attempts."

"Who hired you?"

But Atticus just stood with the same half grin and refused to answer.

Just then, Aurelius entered the home behind him with the local centurion and two soldiers. Julius quickly explained the situation and gave the officer the note. He left out the information about what was contained on the scroll or anything that Brutus told him.

"We will take him to question him. Do not fear. We will learn the extent of his involvement in the attempts on your life and to whom he was passing messages."

CHAPTER 16

The winter passed slowly for Octavia. Her mother was very helpful while she felt as miserable in her early pregnancy as she had been with Lucius. Some days, she felt like her anxiety for the baby was going to swallow her whole, but on those days, she was surrounded by her friends and family who prayed with her. The believers at her church also prayed with the family, and Baracha came for frequent visits to check on her and Felix's wife.

Julius spent much time just holding her and supporting her. She leaned into his strength and thanked God every night for her husband's love and care. She knew that Julius was frustrated by the lack of answers about who Atticus was communicating with, but the former guard would not speak to the soldiers and remained imprisoned for his part in the crimes.

One day, when she first felt the baby move inside her, she burst into tears, remembering how she had just felt Lucius move the day he died. Julius held her and reminded her that this baby was in God's hands alone and encouraged her not to mourn over a baby who was still living. She still held so much fear as the weeks crept along, but the baby continued to grow inside of her despite her fears. As her belly grew, she also grew in her faith, constantly turning to the Lord in prayer that his will would be done.

She continued to play with Onan's siblings in the garden on some days and began sketching again. She found that she craved pomegranates and was grateful for the trees full of them in the courtyard. She was still not able to leave the villa without Julius and the guards, but she found that she felt safer inside.

Her constant nausea and exhaustion eventually faded away, and she only rarely suffered from bouts of the sickness. She and Julius accepted her parents' offer to stay with them and support them through the pregnancy. Octavia enjoyed seeing her parents grow in their knowledge of their Savior. She smiled every time she saw her father show her mother affection, something that he never would have done previously.

One morning, as the spring air smelled sweetly of new growth, the garden was alive with crimson poppies blooming in abundance, and pink blossoms dotted over the almond trees, Octavia walked from the garden into the courtyard where she saw Baracha entering the home.

"Hail, Baracha. Are you here to check on me today?"

"No, actually, Aelia is having her baby," the midwife answered.

"Oh, should I come to help?" Octavia asked cheerily.

"No, dear Friend, it is not good for pregnant women to be around laboring women. I will let you know the news when all is complete."

Octavia nodded and joined her mother in the gardens as she waited for the news. Her mother was writing out a hymn on a piece of parchment. The women talked and laughed together about a silly argument they had witnessed in town on the way home from church service.

Hours later, when it was almost time for dinner, Baracha found Octavia in the gardens and gave her the news that Aelia had delivered a healthy baby boy whom they had named Cassius. Octavia smiled and thanked the midwife for the news. As the woman left, Octavia's smile faded, and she looked down at the ground in thought. When she felt her mother's comforting hand on her knee, she looked up at Claudia.

"How are you doing, Daughter?"

"Sometimes, I find it hard to understand why God allows some babies to live and others to die. Not that I wanted anything bad to happen to Aelia or her baby, of course," she rushed to explain.

Claudia looked at her with eyes full of compassion and understanding. "I know, Dear One. I don't have the answers to those questions. I think we must just trust that God's plan is best even if we don't understand it. I did enjoy hearing in church about David's son and how after he died, David took comfort knowing that he would be with his son again one day."

Octavia smiled at her mother. "Thank you. That is encouraging, and thank you for all of your support over the past several months. This pregnancy has been more difficult for me emotionally than I had anticipated."

"I understand. I remember being a nervous wreck when I was expecting you as well. I thought that at any moment the gods were going to come and pull you to Hades with my other babies. I am gladdened now to think about them being in heaven with God instead."

Octavia leaned over and pulled her mother into a hug.

As the winter faded into spring, Julius offered God a prayer of thanksgiving that their baby was growing well, that Felix's baby was healthy, and that there had been no further actions from their unknown assailant. He had originally planned with Aurelius to travel to Festus's mysterious property in the spring. However, he knew he could not leave Octavia until well after the baby was born and the child proved to be healthy and stable.

Linus had finished writing up a comprehensive guide to his investment properties and businesses, and Julius had allowed him back into the tablinum after the spy was captured. Now, the two men, sometimes with Aurelius, went through Festus's records while Onan took notes. They found three more businesses that Festus had owned in Jerusalem.

When Octavia was doing well and was not anxious about him leaving for the day, he, Linus, Onan, and some guards took short trips to view these businesses. One was a textile mill that produced beautiful fabrics and was efficiently managed. Another was a stone quarry that provided building materials for the city. He found that the supervisor of the quarry was abusing his employees, so he spent a few days finding a suitable replacement. The final business was a pomegranate orchard that sold its produce in the marketplace.

When walking around the pomegranate field, Julius halted in surprise as he observed four mounds identical to the ones he had seen at the olive grove in Italia. He stared in stunned amazement and turned to Linus. "Do you remember the similar mounds at the olive orchard in Tarentum?"

The secretary responded, "Yes, I wonder if Festus had wine aged here as well."

Julius looked curiously at the orchard manager, who said that Festus had instructed him to leave them alone and had not elaborated about their contents. Julius felt an odd sense of déjà vu. "Bring a shovel," he commanded the manager.

The manager turned to leave, when suddenly, Julius heard a loud scream from behind him. He spun around to see Linus doubled over and holding his foot off the ground while hopping wildly on his other foot. The other men searched around desperately for the source of his agony, when one of the guards yelled, "Scorpions!"

Julius observed a group of several scorpions writhing on the ground where Linus was bouncing animatedly. He yelled, "Everyone move back!"

As he yelled, he ran forward and grasped Linus by the shoulders, pulling him away from the dangerous creatures. "Help me get him to the cart," he yelled to one of the guards.

On the way home, Linus's foot continued to swell, and sweat dripped down his face. He moaned whenever the cart jostled, and Julius poured some water on the sting in an effort to ease his suffering.

At the villa, one of the slaves was instructed to make a poultice for the unfortunate man, and Linus was carried to his quarters, where some of his fellow slaves used cool compresses on his face and the sting. Julius dutifully checked in on his servant every hour during that day and the next until the man began to recover.

When Julius told Aurelius of that day's events, they both puzzled over the mounds.

"When Linus is better, I will go with you to look into it... Odd that the scorpions were out during the day. Normally, the little beasts are nocturnal," Aurelius mused while stroking his chin in deliberation.

It took Linus nearly a week to fully recover from his injury, and Julius was tempted to leave him behind, but Linus insisted that he was in perfect health and would watch carefully where he stepped. Therefore, on a bright, clear morning, Aurelius and Julius were accompanied by his two secretaries armed with writing implements, four slaves armed with shovels, and two guards armed with swords to make their way back to the pomegranate orchard.

Gaius stared at the mounds in concern once they had alighted from the cart. He squinted and asked Julius, "Did you excavate one of the mounds when you were here last week?"

"No. Why?" Julius asked in confusion.

Gaius pointed into the distance. "The fourth mound has been dug up and is now flat. Whatever was there is gone now."

Julius looked at the manager in anger. "Did you exhume one of the mounds?"

"No, Master! The day after you left, two men pulled up in a cart like yours. They told our servants that you had sent them to dig up one of the mounds and take you the contents. They further said that you would be back to excavate the other three soon."

Julius fumed for a second in exasperation. Every time they were close to answers, an obstacle was thrown in his path.

Aurelius grasped his arm. "It is alright, we can still unearth the remaining three mounds and will hopefully uncover some answers."

Julius nodded and gestured for the slaves with shovels to begin digging.

It took remarkably little time for the three men to excavate the first mound, which contained two barrels lying lengthwise in the hole. As the other men approached, the diggers pulled the first barrel upright and used a tool to pry it open. Julius looked inside and groaned in disappointment when he found this barrel to be empty.

The slaves repeated the process with the second barrel, and Julius saw that this one contained a large bag, which he reached into the barrel to retrieve. It was much lighter than Julius expected as he withdrew and opened it. Everyone gasped at the beauty of the vibrantly colorful Chinese silks that he removed. They were stunning and costly fabrics that were widely sought after in the Roman Empire. In unison, Julius and Gaius both said, "Smuggling."

The other barrels they dug up held beautiful roof tiles from Africa, gorgeous gems from India, and various other valuable goods, all from outside the empire.

Julius watched as they loaded up the barrels of treasure into the cart. They left the two empty ones there and commenced on their drive to the centurion's home to give him the news. Julius knew he needed to pay the fair tariffs on these goods that Festus had obviously smuggled in to avoid paying the Roman government their fourth of the goods' worth.

The centurion invited Julius and Aurelius into his tablinum and listened with interest to their findings of the day.

"Hmm, I'm very curious about what was in those two barrels that were removed before you could check them. What was so valuable that they would take those and leave the rest behind? ...Well, at least part of the puzzle is solved anyway. I shall write a report that you should take to the magistrate to pay the tariff. Then you can sell or keep the goods."

CHAPTER 17

The spring turned into summer, and Octavia grew uncomfortably round about her middle. Yet, every day was a blessing as she felt her baby moving often and growing stronger. Baracha checked on her at least once a week and told Octavia to expect to have some cramping as her body prepared for birth. Octavia spent time with Aelia and her baby in preparation for her own, and Claudia helped her to purchase the items she needed for the baby.

One day, in mid-summer, she woke up early in the morning with a familiar cramping feeling. As it immediately eased, she noticed the smallest bit of orange light from the sunrise streaming through the edge of the curtain, and she looked at the crib that was next to her side of the bed. It was made of wood and had a mechanism that somehow made it rock back and forth to soothe the baby. Julius had surprised her with the extravagant gift last week.

As she thought about her husband, she turned and looked at him as he slept. She smiled as he began to blink himself awake.

Then another cramp hit her, and her face turned to a grimace. Julius was right in front of her instantly.

"Are you okay? Is it the baby?" he asked urgently.

"It's fine. I'm just having the practice cramps like I have been having for weeks now," she was quick to quell his fears.

He smiled and returned jovially, "You know that one of these times, they won't be practice ones, right?"

"Mmmhmm." She smiled back at him with an impish grin.

Throughout the day, her cramps continued to intensify until she sent one of the slaves to fetch Baracha. When the midwife arrived, Octavia was sitting upon her birthing stool in her room with her mother and Julius, who were holding her hands as she struggled through another round of contractions.

The labor lasted well into the night and early the next morning, but in the end, Octavia held the most beautiful baby girl she had ever seen. Julius sat next to where she lay upon the bed, resting and holding Tatiana. He rubbed Octavia's arm and looked at their baby.

"You did such a great job, Love. She's absolutely perfect," he encouraged his wife.

Octavia looked at him with a radiant smile and then turned her eyes upward. "Thank you, God."

"Amen."

When Tatiana was several months old and had proven herself to be a healthy child, Julius and Aurelius began making arrangements for their families to travel back to Rome. One day, Octavia entered the tablinum while Julius was working on plans for their voyage. He looked up at her with a smile, and when she looked over at

Linus and Onan, Julius dismissed them from the room so they could speak privately.

"What is it, Love?" Julius asked his wife as he gestured to a chair for her.

"I had an idea. I know that we have given quite a bit of money to the church to help those who have a need, but I was just thinking about this large villa we have here. We scarcely make use of any of the rooms, and maybe we could rent them at very low prices to families who have a need or missionaries who come into town. The money could go toward paying for the extra food and preventing the renters from becoming idle."

Julius smiled and rubbed his chin in thought as she spoke. Then he said, "That sounds like an excellent proposal. I could leave Dido in charge of it and have Onan send me reports on the progress. Ideally, with the investment properties around the city and the miniscule rent, the villa would still be self-sustaining.

"I will bring the idea before the church elders on the Lord's Day and get their advice on the practical matters and make sure that they are vetting the tenants to ensure they have actual need."

Julius walked over to his wife and massaged her shoulders. "You are such a kind and gracious wife. I love you."

"I love you too," she responded as she felt the tension easing from her shoulders under his hands.

During the next couple weeks, five Jewish families and a missionary who had sold his home and was preparing to leave for Joppa came to stay with them at the villa. Octavia spent her time getting the families arranged in their rooms and working out details with the staff for feeding them. The families were so grateful and kind to Julius and Octavia for the living quarters, which were nicer than any they had ever seen.

At the time of their departure, Julius, Octavia, Aurelius, and Claudia left with their combined guards, Felix and his family, and the rest of the slaves they had brought with them from Rome, minus Atticus, of course. They left on another merchant ship in the fall, after the summer storms were over.

The voyage across the Mediterranean was again uneventful, and when they reached Tarentum, the women stayed with a few guards at the same inn that Julius and Octavia had occupied on their way to Jerusalem. Then, the men took a fast cart back to Julius's olive orchard to check on the mounds there. However, when they arrived, they found that all the mounds were vacant, and once again, the manager told them that men claiming to work for Julius had come and taken the contents months previously.

Julius turned to Felix, who was with them. "Which of your previous masters buried wine in their olive orchard?"

"His name was Albas Hortensius," replied the guard.

Aurelius looked over quickly, "I knew Albas. He was a friend, and he owned several olive orchards. It was quite sad what happened to him."

"What happened?" Julius inquired.

Aurelius answered, "His son, Tiberius, was always a bad seed. He was lazy and always pursued the married ladies, which got him into quite a bit of trouble with a few jilted husbands. I think it was about fifteen years ago when he murdered one of those husbands and disappeared. The publicity and inquest surrounding his crime and whereabouts caused Albas no end of consternation. Soon, his health began failing, and he died of a heart malady just six months after the murder. His inheritance went to a nephew, I believe."

He paused and thought for a moment. "I think that Tiberius was friends with Festus for a time, in spite of being younger than Festus by at least five years."

Felix nodded, "I worked for the family up until Albas's death. Tiberius managed the olive orchards. He was the one who told me that the mounds were to cover aging wine. When the nephew inherited Albus's estate, I was sold."

"Hmmmm." Julius hummed in concentration as they returned to the cart.

On their way to Rome, Julius and Octavia once again rode in their carpentum, which they secured from the boarding stables. Claudia and Aurelius rode with them and Tatiana while their staff rode in two raedas, each drawn by four horses. Their carpentum was situated between the two raedas, so that they would be guarded from the front and back. As the caravan traveled through the peninsula, the four passengers in the extravagant carriage passed baby Tatiana between themselves. The young girl did little but sleep and eat as the swaying of the carriage kept her in a perpetual state of stupefied relaxation.

One day, Julius was holding Tatiana and was deep in a good-natured argument with Aurelius over the benefit of olive oil in treating soreness of the muscles when a shout went up among the drivers, and the carpentum lurched forward in haste. Julius looked out the window and could see that they were passing by cliffs on his side of the road.

It took him a moment before he was able to detect the reason for the alarm and increase in speed, but he soon spotted a group of around a dozen bandits riding their horses in pursuit of their caravan. The men were on fresh mounts and unencumbered by luggage, so they would certainly overtake the carts soon. He pulled Octavia closer to himself in an effort to shelter his family. Then he watched as the men circled around their caravan and forced it to a stop.

The guards from the raedas jumped from their carts with swords drawn. Two of Aurelius's guards were armed with bows and arrows and immediately began firing off a slew of arrows in rapid succession. They hit several of the bandits before the raiders could leap into action, clearly not expecting such a formidable defense. Some of them aimed their horses toward the archers and lowered their swords to cut the archers down.

The other caravan guards lunged with their swords pointed at the horses of the charging foes. The horses fell with loud cries of agony, and the guards used their swords to run through the bandits who were partially trapped under their injured or dying animals. The fight continued for only a few minutes more as most of the remaining bandits recognized that they were outmatched and turned their horses to flee.

The archers shot two of the retreating men out of their saddles, and in total, only four bandits managed to escape. As the guards took the weapons from the corpses so that their cohorts could not retrieve them later, Julius jumped down from his carriage to check on his staff.

"Do you think that was random or coordinated?" Julius asked Gaius who was cleaning his blade while gazing at the surrounding carnage.

He turned his calculating eyes to Julius and answered, "Frankly, I think that the fact that bandits have only tried to attack us once in all of our travels is incredible. As a guard, I have been attacked by bandits twelve times. They run rampant out here. Chances are they saw the caravan and thought we were carrying valuables instead of a whole team of guards."

"Good point. Thank you, Gaius."

Miraculously, there were no injuries, and the caravan continued upon its way in a slightly more somber mood than before the attack. Octavia sat stiffly and clutched their wiggling daughter as Julius explained Gaius's theory to his fellow riders. He pulled her close and comforted her with the knowledge that they were far better guarded than most travelers and, therefore, unlikely to face any party of bandits strong enough to harm them.

Fortunately, there were no more incidents on the way to Rome. When they arrived back at their domus, Octavia was pleased to be reacquainted with the little kitten who had now grown into an adult cat and strutted around the grounds just as his predecessor had done. Her parents returned to their nearby domus and promised to come visit them and their grandbaby often.

Julius immediately purchased a new rocking crib for his precious baby girl, and while the family settled back into life at the domus, he made plans to travel to the property in Raetia with Aurelius. He was concerned about how long the trip would take because he would be gone for at least a month, possibly two, depending on the weather. He knew that Octavia was worried about the possibility of him encountering more bandits, but he needed to leave sooner rather than later to avoid traveling in the winter.

One evening, he took a stroll in the olive orchard, searching around the perimeter for any more mounds. Gaius had offered to come with him, but it was his evening off, and with the spy captured, Julius supposed that the domus and immediate surroundings were secure. It was difficult for him to never be alone, and he relished the few minutes of solitude that this excursion offered him.

He made it halfway around the trees and thought that it would have been unwise for Festus to bury goods on his own property. Better, though, to check than to assume and be wrong. He felt the breeze on his face and took a second to enjoy the final rays of the sun as it was about to complete its journey for the day. He thanked God for another beautiful day and continued on his way.

As he passed around a tree, he felt rather than heard movement behind him and began to whirl to face the person, but before he could make it all the way around, he felt a hot, slicing pain in his side. He cried out and finished turning to face his attacker. The man had a turban covering his head and face and flourished a long blade that now dripped with blood. He lunged before Julius could pull out his own dagger, and Julius dodged behind a tree to his right and ducked down to grab a heavy branch from the ground.

As the man rounded the tree, Julius jabbed the broken end of the branch upwards into his attacker's face and hit him in the nose with a satisfying crunch. The blow knocked the assailant backward, as he let out a yell of surprise and pain. Julius used that distraction as an opportunity to stand and kick the blade from his hand. As he used the branch to hit the man in the head, Julius saw Felix and another guard run into the small clearing. The attacker was clearly disoriented by the defense and was incapable of putting up much of a struggle before he was subdued by the two guards.

Julius felt no pain and moved to help when he suddenly found that he could no longer stand, and he heard Felix call his name before he slumped to the ground unconscious.

Octavia heard a commotion from the garden and was stunned to see Felix and Gaius carrying her husband in through the back gate of the home. Her brain tried to make sense of the scene as another pair of guards entered the gate, restraining a man between them. This man was wearing a turban around his head that dripped with blood. She stood and focused her attention upon Julius, who she now realized was unconscious, and as the guards walked, blood trailed in a line on the floor behind them.

She ran to the guards and looked desperately at Gaius, but before she could say anything, he answered her unasked question.

"He still lives, but we need to lie him down and try to stop the bleeding."

"Yes, of course. Take him to that chamber there," she said as she pointed to the closest room.

It was a guest room that no one had used in many years. As the men carried Julius into the room, she saw several of her staff, including Esther, who was holding Tatiana, and Isaiah and Linus, who had come into the atrium to investigate the commotion. Meanwhile, the second pair of guards still held the bleeding stranger between them and looked to her for instruction.

Octavia pushed aside her fear and began to bark out urgent orders. She looked at Esther and sternly said, "Take Tatiana to play in the garden."

"Isaiah, go get a medicus! Quickly!" she commanded.

She addressed the guards, "Is this the man who attacked Julius?"

"Yes, Mistress," they both answered quickly.

"Tie him up and hold him for the soldiers," she responded.

They nodded their assent, and she turned to address Linus, "Send word to the centurion Cato about the attack. Ask him to bring soldiers to guard the domus again."

Then she looked at another slave and said, "Send word to my parents to come quickly."

As she issued her directives, her staff quickly dispersed to follow her orders. Then she ran to the guest room, where she held her husband's hand and watched the blood saturate the cloth that Felix was holding against his wounded side.

The medicus arrived quickly and, with a placid expression, inspected the wound and perused over him in search of more injuries. Then he looked to Octavia and gave his report.

"Fortunately, he only seems to have sustained the wound in his side. I will clean it and sew it closed to stop the bleeding."

Octavia nodded, unable to speak, and the medicus commenced mending Julius's injury. Octavia kept her eyes on her husband's face, doing her best to ignore the medicus's work. She spent the time praying that God would heal Julius and keep him with her. The medicus finally finished his ministrations and again spoke to Octavia.

"You will need to keep the wound clean by washing it with clean water and soap, covering it with oil, and changing the dressings twice a day. I am concerned that the blade might have been treated with poison, but it is too early to tell for certain. If he was poisoned or if he gets an infection, he will have redness and swelling around the incision and will develop a high fever.

"I will return daily to check on him until he improves. It is concerning that he hasn't woken up, but he may just need to recuperate from the lack of blood. If he takes a turn for the worse, send for me, and I will come immediately."

"Thank you, Medicus."

He nodded at her and packed up his bag. Then he took one last look at his patient and turned to leave. After the medicus left, Gaius strode in and told Octavia that Cato had arrived and requested to speak with her. He offered to remain with Julius until she returned.

Octavia left the room and went into the atrium where she witnessed three soldiers and the attacker tied up between them. His turban had been pulled off his head, and she could now see his chiseled features clearly. He would almost look handsome if not for the furious expression and obviously broken nose.

Cato stood to the side of his soldiers with Felix and asked her, "Do you recognize this man?"

"No, I haven't seen him before," said Octavia.

"Okay, we will take him and work on finding out who hired him. I will also send five soldiers to watch the domus and prevent further mishaps... You know, there were no problems here when you two left, and I was hoping your predicament would have been resolved before you returned."

Octavia frowned, "So were we."

For that night and the next day, Octavia stayed with Julius as much as she could. She lay next to him at night, praying for him to wake up, and she brought Tatiana to babble to her daddy. Her parents came to stay with her as she continued her vigil. On the second evening after the attack, his wound began to fester and swell in spite of her care. When she beckoned the medicus, he told her that it was as he had feared; the blade had been dipped in some kind of poison. He had told her that based on his experience, Julius might live, but it was just as probable that he would imminently die.

Octavia took in this information with a fortitude that she didn't know she possessed. She was determined to spend every moment with her husband and trust God.

His fever rose to a dangerously high temperature, and the medicus gave her ground white willow bark to brew in hot water in order to reduce the fever. He also instructed her to put cool compresses on him and change them every thirty minutes. Octavia had the slaves rinsing the rags in cool water and bringing them to the room. Then Esther would help Octavia to exchange the old ones for the new. Claudia and Aurelius took shifts with one being with their daughter in the room with Julius and one taking care of Tatiana.

Octavia tried desperately to get Julius to drink small amounts of water and the tea that the medicus gave her and was concerned that he would perish from thirst before the poison could end his life. As word of Julius's condition spread, fellow believers came by to pray and bring them flowers and other small gifts of encouragement.

Claudia glanced from where Tatiana slept in the crib on her side of the bed over to her husband, who was preparing for sleep.

"I am afraid that he won't survive this. What will become of Octavia if he doesn't?" she worriedly asked Aurelius.

He responded, "We cannot give in to those worries. The man is not dead, and we don't know if he will die now. God is in control, not us. If he does die, Octavia will have us, her staff, and all the other believers to help her, but I am hopeful that God will heal him yet."

He pulled his wife into a hug as she sobbed upon his shoulder. "I am sorry that I wasn't there for you through previous trials, but I will be here for you now and through whatever may come," he said reassuringly.

"I love you," declared Claudia.

"I love you too, dear Wife."

CHAPTER 18

For three more days, Octavia continued nursing her husband, switching out the compresses and allowing small amounts of water to trickle into his mouth. She prayed but did not despair, and she committed to trusting God even if he took Julius from her. She knew that if he died, he would be in heaven with their Lord. Still, it was a daily, sometimes even minute-to-minute, struggle to focus on God's love. Meanwhile, the entire household waited with bated breath as their master battled for his life against the poison.

One afternoon, Octavia sat at the bedside and felt her eyes burning with tiredness and her back aching from sitting for such an extended period. Her mother had left the room to check on Tatiana, and Linus opened the curtain door.

"May I come in and sit with him, Mistress?"

"Yes, of course, Linus," she answered and gestured to the vacant chair next to her.

As Linus sat, Octavia watched as he looked forlornly at his master in silence.

"He is the best man I've ever known," Octavia said as tears filled her eyes.

Linus looked at her with profound sympathy and replied, "He is the best master I have ever had."

She responded in a shuddering voice, "I don't know what I will do if God takes him home. Life will be so different, so much duller."

Linus picked up her hand and held it for a moment in wordless compassion. Then, he silently slipped from the room as her mother returned.

On the sixth day after Julius was attacked, Octavia noticed that his fever broke, and his wound looked less swollen. She could see his eyes shifting behind his eyelids and eagerly hoped that he would wake soon. When the medicus came that evening, he was quite encouraged, although not entirely convinced the danger was over.

He addressed Octavia and Aurelius, "I have seen some victims apparently improve before ultimately succumbing to the poison; however, in my years of experience, more often, I have seen that when patients make this much of an improvement, they are usually on the path to a full recovery. You no longer need to use the compresses or willow bark. Just clean the wound and watch for any changes. I will check back tomorrow morning. You are doing an excellent job of ministering to him."

Exhaustion from her long hours of vigil wore on Octavia as she sat in the chair by the bed where Julius lay. Her head drooped forward onto the bed, and she dozed in short bursts as she held her husband's hand with one of hers and cradled her head with her other arm. A lamp burned on the table, and when she roused periodically in the night, she was reassured of his continued breathing.

She was awakened in the middle of the night, and as she raised her head to check on Julius once again, she felt something squeeze around her hand. In her disoriented state, it took her a moment to realize that Julius was responsible for the sensation. She quickly sat upright and looked intently into his face.

"Julius, can you hear me?"

As she watched him, he didn't open his eyes, but he squeezed her hand again. She smiled and jumped forward into his arms, carefully avoiding his injury. He made a slight grunting noise, and she quickly shuffled off of him.

"I love you," she gasped out as she choked back tears.

He squeezed her hand before his breathing evened back out, and she knew he slept again.

The next morning dawned with the brightness of a cheery day for Octavia, and she woke to see Julius with his eyes open, looking at her sedately but with a pained expression. She saw Esther sitting on his other side with a wide smile of delight, having woken before dawn to sit with her mistress.

Octavia sat up and rubbed her hair to try and smooth down her frazzled locks. "It is so great to see your eyes open! How are you feeling?" she asked.

Julius opened his mouth and tried to speak, but all that came out was a hoarse, half moan.

"Can you drink water?" Octavia asked as she raised a glass to his lips.

He shifted slightly with a wince and opened his mouth to allow the cool water in to soothe his parched throat.

Octavia's parents, Gaius, and other members of the household took turns coming into the room to check on their friend, and all the believers said prayers of gratitude for God's healing. When the medicus arrived mid-morning, he was thrilled with his patient's progress and declared him to be on the road to a full recovery.

For the first time, the medicus addressed Julius, "It is good to see you awake. You were poisoned by your assailant's blade and have spent most of the last week clinging to life. Now, you simply must rest and recuperate. You should spend at least a week more in bed and must not attempt vigorous activity of any kind until at least a month has passed. You may now take mandrake and opium mixed into water for the pain, but you must use it sparingly. Your wife and staff can surely handle mixing the medications for you. She has attended to you incredibly faithfully. I cannot recall a better demonstration of care than I have witnessed from your household."

Julius nodded his head in agreement with the physician's recommendations and looked pleased at the praise for his family and staff. Octavia was nearly faint with exhaustion and relief at the encouraging outlook for Julius's health. When the medicus left, Esther mixed his medications while Octavia climbed into bed next to her husband and slept with the assurance that her mother would look in on him throughout the day. Octavia finally allowed herself to fully rest.

Over the next few days, Julius was able to stay awake for longer periods of time, but when he was conscious, the pain roared through his side and curled through his body like smoke from a blazing fire. He took sparing amounts of the medication when the pain became unbearable, but it just took the edge off the worst of the agony and made him drowsy.

One day while he was still confined to his bed, Julius craved some time in which no one was staring at him as if he might die at any moment. He sent Octavia to her room for some rest, assuring her that he would ring for a slave if he required anything. Then he sat and read a story from a scroll for an hour before he felt the needling pain begin to intensify in his side, and he rang the bell.

Linus walked into the room so quickly that Julius was certain he must have been stationed outside waiting for a summons.

"Hail, Linus, I need more medication. Are you able to mix some for me? It is one spoon of each of the powders blended into the full glass of water on the table there."

"Of course, Master, unless you object, I will add some wine to flavor it for you," Linus replied as he moved to the table.

"That would be good, thank you."

Linus combined the powders into the glass and stirred them thoroughly before delivering the solution to his ailing master. Julius began to raise the glass to his lips when Linus swiftly struck the glass out of his hand and yelled, "NO!"

The glass flew out of Julius's hand and shattered against the stone wall, splattering water, wine, and medicine all over the floor and bed. Julius stared at his secretary, stunned into silence by his abrupt actions. As if to further perplex his master, Linus promptly bent over and began to weep.

Just then, Gaius ran into the room, having been alerted by the crash of the glass and the secretary's shout. The guard halted in his tracks as he took in the scene before him.

Linus continued to weep as he stuttered out, "I am ssso ssorry, Master. I just cccan't do it."

Julius and Gaius stared at the man and then looked at each other, baffled by his outcry. Julius looked back at him and sternly commanded, "Sit down, Man. Tell us what you can't do and why you broke my glass."

Linus took a seat and shrunk under the scrutiny of his master and the guard. "He told me to kill you with poison. I put seven spoonfuls of the opium into the glass and added the wine so you wouldn't taste the difference, but I couldn't do it! You see, you have been the only master to treat me kindly. I could send the information to him, but I couldn't kill you!"

"You were the spy?! What about Atticus?" Gaius fairly shouted at the sniveling man.

"Atticus was a spy, but I was one as well."

Julius's expression had hardened from shock into a thunderous glare. "Who hired you?! And when?!" he demanded.

"I will tell you everything from the beginning, Master. Some twenty years ago, I was purchased by a man named Rufus Salvius, who was incredibly cruel. He beat me and all of the other slaves whenever he felt the desire to do so, regardless of our performance. After suffering through his employ for five years, I was ordered to bring him a glass of wine."

He paused for a moment and took a deep breath before continuing, "I poisoned his wine. I will not try to excuse my actions. I know I shouldn't have done it, but I will say that I was tired of his mistreatment and of witnessing him abuse my fellow slaves.

"I was sure that I would be caught and killed, but I was never found out. I was sold to my next master and the next, each being difficult men but not as cruel as my first. The master I worked for before you was named Otho. I became his secretary, traveled with him, and recorded all of his business acquisitions.

"One day, a rather short, overweight man came to my master and asked to see him alone in his tablinum. When Otho and the man emerged, my master told me that this stranger had purchased me, and I was to go with him. I was somewhat surprised, never having been purchased in such a manner, but of course, I went with the unidentified stranger.

"He had me board a litter with him. Then he immediately began to speak to me, 'You are Linus Martinus, slave for the late Rufus Salvius.' I was stunned by this statement, as you might imagine. I am sure my face showed my shock, for he laughed at me and said, 'You should not be surprised. I know many things. For instance, I know that you killed him, and if you do not want me to turn you over to the soldiers for punishment, you will do all that I command.

" 'I will sell you today to a slave market here in Rome. A man will arrive there tomorrow to buy a whole new household full of slaves. His name is Julius, and I need you to appeal to him. You are a qualified secretary, and you need to present yourself as one. Even if it is not as a secretary, you must be purchased for his home! Do you understand me?'

"I replied, 'Yes, of course.' Then he continued with his demands. 'You will then send me weekly reports about everything that is happening in the house. You will send the reports to this address.' And he handed me a slip of parchment that contained an address for a property here in Rome. I agreed, of course, because I had no choice.

"Then he took me to the market, where he sold me and purchased the other secretaries there so that I would be the only one available. As you know, his plan worked, and you purchased me for your staff. I reported to him about your schedule, and I am sure that he sent someone to vandalize your room and to put the picture of the couple on the crosses in the domus. However, I played no active role in those incidents.

"I reported on your search through Festus's records, and when we left for your countryside villa, I received my first note back from the man. He told me to prevent you by any means necessary from sorting through the records in the villa. He said that it was most imperative for you to not see any scrolls that mentioned the property in Raetia.

"You told me that we would be going through the scrolls starting the day after we arrived, which limited the amount of time I had to act. So, I went into the tablinum and found two scrolls that discussed the Raetia property, and I set the fire by knocking over a candle onto the scrolls on the desk. I needed it to look like a mistake to avoid an inquest, so I could not set fire to all of the piles of scrolls.

"I hoped that the fire would burn the scrolls and move to the piles. Then, I planned to raise the alarm and, therefore, be above suspicion and prevent the conflagration from spreading to your room. However, you were awake, and I heard you leaving your room as I ran around the corner of the corridor. You found and extinguished the fire so expeditiously that only those two scrolls burned. Then, you set a guard over the tablinum, and I was unable to further prevent your perusal.

"When we went on our trip through Italia, I was instructed to do whatever I could to prevent you from inspecting any mounds of earth on your properties. He told me that if I were asked, I should say that they were barrels of wine left to age in the fields and that they should be left for several more years. At the property in Tarentum, I urged you to make haste in preparing for the sea voyage to avoid you checking the mounds there.

"In Jerusalem, I received a letter from the man giving me an address in Jerusalem to which I should resume sending my missives. He also said that he was paying Atticus to watch and send him reports, as well, and he told me to wait until Atticus was assigned to guard the tablinum. Then, I could go in to find a particular scroll about the Raetia property.

"However, when we arrived at the villa, I found that you had hired new guards to watch the tablinum, and there was no opportunity to access the scrolls. I continued to report on your movements, but I had nothing to do with the attack on you in the city or the assassination attempt that led to Apollos's murder. I was disgusted by these incidents of increased violence and slowed my letter writing to my blackmailer.

"However, he sent me another letter and was adamant that I was to find the scroll. He threatened me once again, so I found a little street urchin who was starving and trying to care for his siblings. He was desperate, and I was desperate. He only ever saw me with a turban over my face, so he wouldn't recognize me. I hired him to search for the scroll silently so as not to attract the attention of the guards, and I had Atticus 'misunderstand' Felix's assigned post and so leave that window free for the boy to access. Every night, I was scheduled to meet with the urchin at the Brook Kidron to check his progress and hopefully pay him the rest of the money for finding the scroll.

"But as I was working in the house, I heard that a young man was caught attempting to steal one of the master's scrolls. I knew that instead of solving my problem, I had done the opposite and drawn your attention to this particular scroll. That evening as I was contemplating a plan, imagine my shock and terror when you arrived home escorting the same boy that I had hired! My heart nearly withered inside my chest for fear that he would somehow recognize my eyes or my voice or some such thing. You even assigned me to work with him!

"I thought that my heart might cease beating and I would die right there in the villa. I even thought for a time that Onan had told you that he suspected me when you had me work outside of the tablinum on busywork. But fates were on my side that time, and Onan did not show any sign of recognition. Then Atticus got caught, and I was terrified he might reveal my part in the plot. Once again, I was spared, however, and continued on.

"I then had to find a way to keep you from looking into any mounds we might find as we explored your properties around Jerusalem. The man did not know where the properties were, or which properties contained mounds. I knew that you were suspicious of the last mounds we had seen and that I would need a distraction in case we found more, so I purchased three scorpions from a man at the market. I carried them in a box until we found the mounds. I then let them out of the box and incurred a sting right before you planned to excavate them.

"It was quite excruciating, but it did make for an effective distraction. After my fever passed, I kindly asked the midwife to take a letter to town for one of the slaves when she left. I often asked her to do this and found it an effective means of evading the scrutiny that outbound letters might incur. Other times, I would tell all of the staff that I was collecting letters to be sent out, so that if anyone inspected outgoing mail, no one would be sure who wrote my letter, which I used my left hand to pen so as to disguise my normal writing style. Then I would have one of the slaves take letters to the post. After the blackmailer received the missive about the mounds, he was able to hire men posing as your slaves to take away some of the barrels. I have no idea what was in them or why he chose to take those and not the others, but I had succeeded in my directives.

"I know nothing about the bandit attack on the way back to Rome and tend to believe that it was a coincidence. I also was not informed about the assassin in the olive orchard. The man only wrote to me again when he realized that you did not die after the attack. He said that after you were dead, he would cease to contact me ever again and my secret would be safe but that if I did not help you reach Hades, he would bring proof before the magistrate that I had murdered my old master. Then I would be flogged and crucified for all of my crimes.

"My fortitude failed me, and I felt torn between the person I wanted to be and the person who I had become. I told your wife while your life hung in the balance that you were the best master that I had ever had, and I meant it. But I was terrified... am terrified of facing the punishment for my crimes. I tried to push the reality of the situation from my mind and waited for my opportunity.

"When you called me in to help with your medicine, I knew that I had the ability to end this entire part of my life and move on, away from the deranged blackmailer who follows my every move. But when I handed you the glass, it was as if I had just woken from a terrible nightmare, and I realized with startling clarity what I was about to do. I could not let you drink that cup, and so I knocked it from your hand, ensuring your continued survival and sealing my fate."

Linus abruptly ceased his monologue and glanced up from where he had been studying his wringing hands. Julius and Gaius both stared, motionlessly digesting all the information that the secretary had revealed.

Julius, who had sat upright in bed, found that his pain was mostly forgotten as the rush of desire for action moved through his veins. "Are there any more spies in my home?"

"I do not believe so, Master. If there are, I have heard nothing of them," Linus was quick to respond.

"Maybe we can use this to our advantage," Julius said as he looked toward Gaius.

Then he turned back to Linus and said, "We will keep you under guard until we decide what to do with you. Your change of conscience does you credit, but I am sure you understand why I can no longer trust you."

Linus nodded defeatedly, "Of course, Master."

Then Julius called Felix and another guard into the room to escort Linus out and keep him under watch. When they were gone, Gaius took a chair by the bed, and the two men began plotting their next moves.

Julius began, "I think we should get the address here in Rome where Linus has been sending his messages. Then we should set up surveillance at that location. We will have Linus send another message, and we will catch the perpetrator. What do you think?"

Gaius responded, "I think, Master, that the responsible party will not show up in person but will send a slave to collect the letter. However, we can follow the slave to his master without revealing that we know about Linus's treachery."

"Very true. The question is, should we involve Cato or try to orchestrate this alone?" Julius inquired.

Gaius considered for a moment and responded, "If we involve Cato now, soldiers will surely be spotted and will spook our target. I think it is best to use our guards in disguise and acquire more information at present. As for Linus, I suggest that we lock him in the slave quarters in a room without a window. Tell the staff that we were forced to quarantine him but that he is not currently ill and none of the staff are in any danger. It will be logical that we would have a guard stationed outside the door to prevent anyone from breaking the quarantine. The guard can pass food and water into the room, and we can have him write letters that we dictate to him."

"That is an excellent plan. They will assume that the quarantine is for an illness when it is actually designed to prevent the spread of information. Please have him locked up immediately and then return with Octavia so we can plan out our letter and next moves," Julius agreed as he nodded appreciatively.

While he waited for his wife and Gaius to return, his mind was spinning, and he thought through all the time he had spent with Linus in the last nearly two years. He wondered what his secretary had been thinking. Unlike when Atticus had been revealed, Julius felt truly shaken. Atticus had been a mostly silent fixture around Julius, protecting but not directly working with him. Linus, however, had worked personally with his master almost every day since he had married Octavia.

At this point in his musings, his wife and Gaius walked into the room. They each took a seat by the bed. Julius spent the next several minutes catching his wife up on the information that Linus had exposed. Her face showed her shock and dismay at hearing the report about a man whom she had considered to be a trusted member of the household. Julius concluded his story with the plan that Gaius had made for the sequestration of their secretary.

Then he asked her, "What do you think?"

"I can't believe this! How could he have done all those things? I trusted him."

Julius reached out and held her hand. "I know, Love. I'm so sorry. I trusted him, too. Now we have to formulate a plan using Linus's connection to our adversary in order to expose him."

Octavia nodded as silent tears ran down her face.

Then, Gaius jumped into the conversation, "If you do not mind my suggestion, I would recommend that we have Linus write a note saying that he needs help in poisoning you. He can indicate that two people are always in the room with you and ask if the man has replaced Atticus with another spy in the household.

"We will have a slave take it to the post as Linus would have. Then, we will post sentries at the letter's destination in order to observe and follow anyone who picks it up. You can even temporarily trade guards with Aurelius and use some of his trusted men who could not possibly be spies for our enemy. Hopefully, the individual who picks up the letter will lead us to your enemy, and we will receive a report back about whether or not there is another spy in your house."

"That sounds like a great plan," Julius stated while Octavia nodded in agreement. Then he continued talking to Gaius, "Please send for Aurelius, and I will ask him for the use of his guards. Since he has been staying with us, I doubt he will mind us using them."

When Aurelius entered the room, he listened to the plan with rapt interest and concern. He easily agreed to the use of his guards, and Gaius swiftly went to compel Linus to write out the entrapping note.

CHAPTER 19

The address to which Linus's letter was sent was revealed to be a shop that sold clothing, bags, and jewelry for wealthy patrons. It was located upon the ground floor of an insulae, which was situated in a large square plaza. Gaius volunteered to watch the shop with Aurelius's soldiers every day until the letter's recipient arrived. He had made the point to Julius that none of the other sentries would be able to identify someone that Gaius may recognize, and his master lent him some of his own clothes to wear as a disguise.

The next two days dragged on as Gaius sat stationed at a table on the patio of a café near the clothing shop. He had brought writing utensils and pretended to be working on business while the other sentries were stationed around the plaza, surreptitiously keeping watch on the shop. As they pretended to inspect goods or sell their own wares, Gaius let his eyes carefully scan his surroundings while he appeared to be focused on the scrolls in front of him. He could feel the stiffness in his neck and back from sitting and trying to look inconspicuous for such an extended period of time.

In spite of his discomfort, he gladly spent many hours in the corner of the shaded patio where he would be less likely to be spotted. He drank his beverage from the café, where he had a perfect view of the entrance to the shop. His master was still confined in bed, recovering from the poison and waiting for news from the surveillance, and Gaius was determined that he would solve this mystery for his master and friend.

In the afternoon of the second day, Gaius had not seen anyone he recognized and watched patiently as patrons entered and left the shop. If anyone picked up the letter, one of the guards, who was temporarily working in the shop, courtesy of an excellent reference from Aurelius, would follow the currier. That would, in turn, signal to Gaius that their man was on the move, and then, he and the other sentries would begin to follow the letter carrier to his master.

Carts and carriages came and went through the plaza with regularity, and Gaius had an essedum waiting between the shop and the café that he had hired to stand by in case the currier was traveling by cart. He thought through everyone he had met during his tenure in Julius's household and could not think of anyone who would have the means and motive required to explain all of the strange happenings surrounding his master and mistress.

As he was considering this, he detected movement from his left near a tree by the edge of the patio. His right hand moved swiftly to the dagger concealed at his waist, but he ceased to retrieve it as he recognized his wife coming his way with a palla covering her head.

"What are you doing here?" he asked abruptly as he swung his eyes back to the shop to make sure he did not miss the signal during the momentary distraction.

"Julius and Octavia are a bit restless and asked if I could come check on you. They said that it would seem natural if a slave came to bring you a message, and as long as I kept the palla over my head, I would not be recognized and could ferry messages back and forth," she answered in a low voice.

Gaius nodded but did not respond further as he continued to watch the shop. Just then, a large man emerged from a nearby street between the essedum and the café. He walked with his back to the café and made his way to the store. As he paused at the door of the store, he turned and looked around the plaza, not showing any sign of noticing the men watching him. As he slipped into the store, Gaius heard his wife gasp and hurriedly whisper, "That's Julian!"

Gaius did not take his eyes from the door as he asked his wife, "Who is Julian?"

"He was Festus's secretary and household manager for the domus. On the day that Octavia married Julius, he fired Julian and the rest of the staff, except for me, for their past acts of cruelty against Octavia," she answered in surprise at seeing the former staff member.

Before Gaius had the chance to respond to his wife, the portly man reemerged from the store followed immediately by Aurelius's guard. As the two men walked toward the side street Julian had come from, Gaius stood and moved forward at a determined but casual speed so as not to attract the man's attention. Julian looked all around him cautiously, and he saw Gaius who had just left the shelter of the patio.

The slave's eyes darted furiously until they landed upon the essedum which Gaius had hired and was stationed only about six paces from him. He then grinned snidely, and more quickly than Gaius would have thought possible, he loped to the cart. Gaius increased his speed as he anticipated the man's attempt at escape but did not have time to prevent the large man from jumping into his essedum. As Julian leapt in, Gaius heard him promise the driver a hefty sum for taking him out of the city as fast as possible.

Gaius was only a few feet now from the front of the cart and had to jump out of the way to avoid being run down by the horses throwing up dust in their haste to escape the sting of their master's whip. He glanced up at Julian's face, who smiled down at him with a wicked grin as he whirled by, leaving Gaius in the dust. Gaius growled in frustration even as he understood the temptation for the driver to take the large sum of money.

He searched around desperately, but there were no other carts for rent in the plaza. He ran down a side street and then another but still saw no available carts, and when he, at last, decided that it would be a futile pursuit even if he found a vehicle, he returned to the café discouraged and furious that their opponent had outmaneuvered him.

The other guards had assembled at the café with Esther to await his return, and when he arrived, he shook his head to show the failure of his chase. Then he motioned to them to wait while he went into the shop. The proprietor was helping an older woman select a new bag, and Gaius waited impatiently for his attention. Finally, the patroness and the man walked over to his table, and she made her purchase and left the shop.

Then the man turned his gaze to Gaius and asked him, "How can I help you, Sir?"

Gaius responded, "There was a large man who just came and picked up a letter. I need to know how often he comes here to pick up letters and why."

The man looked at Gaius with a calculating, greedy gleam in his eyes until the guard pulled a small bag from his tunic and retrieved a few of the denarii that Julius had given him for his task. The proprietor stared at the coins as Gaius used his large hand to shuffle them around before setting them down upon the wood table with a loud clink. He left his hand covering the coins as he asked, "So, do you have information for me?"

"Yes, Sir. I do," the man answered while licking his lips slightly.

Gaius released the money, and the man struck out his hand like a cobra in his haste to retrieve the coins before he began to speak.

"About two years ago, that fat man came to me and asked to use the address of my shop to get messages. He said that his master did not want certain letters coming to his home, and the man paid me a handsome sum for the use of my address. He would receive a letter about once a week, and every week, on a certain day, he would arrive and pick it up. Then, there was about a year-long period in which no letters arrived, and he did not come to collect any. A few months ago, I was startled when another letter was delivered, but the fat man dutifully came to collect it and has resumed his pattern of picking up the letters weekly since then."

Gaius nodded at him encouragingly and inquired, "Did the man ever introduce himself or tell you who his master was?"

The man shook his head as he replied, "No, part of the fee he paid me was for his and his master's anonymity."

Gaius fixed a conspiratorial smile on his face as he leaned closer to the man, "And you never got curious about what was in the letters? I know I would have found it difficult not to peek."

The shopkeeper shrugged and looked around before answering, "There wasn't any profit in it for me. Even if it contained damaging information, I did not know any of the key players and didn't want to risk getting caught over what was likely of no benefit to me."

Gaius nodded and gave his thanks before leaving the shop and returning to the assembly waiting for him at the café. On the walk home, he asked Esther to tell him about Julian.

She responded, "He was arrogant and rude and ran the staff as if he was the master. He even spoke to Festus as if they were equals rather than a slave and master. Festus often sent him out of town to check on his businesses and investments, and I always dreaded his return. He was only surpassed by Festus himself when it came to the abominable treatment of Octavia.

"He would ignore her outright if she ever attempted to address him and took pleasure in giving her commands from Festus. He also set the tone for the other slaves and told them to treat her as if she was subservient to them. It amused both Festus and Julian to see the slaves treat her poorly. They certainly made her the lowest ranking member of her home."

Gaius grunted in exasperation and responded, "And now we know he works for whoever has been tormenting the family for the past two years."

The guest room was overflowing as Gaius, Esther, Octavia, and her parents crowded around Julius's bed and listened to the guard's report of his and his wife's discovery and their target's escape.

Octavia's eyes widened in astonishment. "Julian!?" she exclaimed. "I saw him with Marcus in the market soon after he was sold. Could he be working for Marcus? He could have committed the vandalism at Marcus's behest and would have even been angry enough after being sold to take the opportunity to kill Grumps."

Julius stared at the wall in concentration as he considered this, while Aurelius looked sorrowful at the thought that his old friend could be responsible.

"It's certainly possible," said Julius. "Marcus may have been Festus's business partner in the smuggling ring."

Aurelius jumped in, "But how can we prove that Julian works for him or that he invested with Festus? Has his name been found on any of the records that you've searched?"

"No, it was not on the investor scroll either," Julius responded in frustration.

"I can ask to meet with Marcus under the guise of reconciliation and ask him if he knows whatever happened to Julian. I can tell him I have questions for the man about an investment I had with Festus," said Aurelius.

"It would be wrong to lie, Dear," responded his wife.

"Right," he agreed. "I can come up with a true reason I want to talk with him, or I can be vague. We have time to come up with what I should say."

Julius asked, "Or should we involve Cato with the information that we have and let him interview Marcus?"

Gaius answered, "I know soldiers like Cato. He is not driven to find the truth unless it is obvious or there is something in it for him. It would not be beneficial for him to further antagonize Marcus without more evidence. I think Aurelius asking him would be the best option, and we can have some of the guards who were at the plaza today staking out Marcus's domus. They would be able to recognize Julian if he arrives, and they could discretely inquire of one of the slaves whether Julian works for Marcus."

Octavia responded, "I like that plan. It seems our best option to ascertain the probability of Marcus's involvement."

Everyone agreed that this was the ideal approach and began brainstorming on how Aurelius should frame his query to best disarm Marcus.

CHAPTER 20

Aurelius walked up to the front door of Marcus's domus. He had sent word that he wanted to catch up with the man and hoped that their long friendship would not be brought to an end over a woman. He had expressed his gratitude for the years of friendship that Marcus had graciously provided him and noted that he was catching up with old friends after being abroad in Jerusalem for a year.

Marcus had jumped at the opportunity to show off his more magnanimous nature, and so extended an invitation for Aurelius to join him at his domus for the midday meal. Aurelius was met at the door by a slave who led him to the dining room. Upon entering, he saw Marcus give him a sickeningly innocuous smile from his couch.

"Hail, my Friend! It has been too long!" Marcus gushed as he stood and pulled the other man into a hug.

Aurelius tried to mask his discomfort. "Hail, Marcus! It has been incredibly long, hasn't it."

"Please recline with me!" Marcus invited in a friendly tone. "How was Jerusalem?"

"It was good. My daughter came, and we stayed with them for several months through a difficult period of time," Aurelius said as he tried to reveal enough information to invoke sympathy while not betraying any actionable information about his family.

"I am sorry to hear that. I hope that she is well," Marcus probed with an inquisitive gleam in his eye.

"They are doing quite well now. How have you been doing?" Aurelius returned.

"I am quite well, actually. I got married about six months ago," he gave the other man a conspiratorial grin. "I hope you don't mind the comparison, but she is several years younger than Octavia, and I believe that her more demure personality is a better fit for me after all."

Aurelius swallowed his outrage at the impertinence of the other man and fixed his smile firmly upon his face. "I am glad that she suits you."

He was saved from further comment by the distraction of three slaves bringing in a banquet of food for the two men, and as they began their courses, Aurelius chatted with the man as he wondered how Marcus had ever been his close friend. Every topic of interest to Marcus was now detestable and unconscionable to Aurelius, and he mentally thanked his Savior for freeing him from his former life of sin and misery.

About an hour after the food was served, Marcus seemed quite at ease with his guest, and Aurelius began to pose the question behind his reconnection with the man.

"Oh, by the way, I was wondering if you knew whatever became of Festus's secretary, Julian. I had heard that you may have purchased him. He seemed to handle Festus's business affairs so effectively. I was quite startled when I heard that Julius had sold all of the staff on his first day in Festus's home!"

Marcus laughed a bit as he answered, "Julian is a man who will always land on his feet. I met him at the market shortly after

Julius sold him, and I asked him how he was. He said that he was immediately snatched up by a wealthy new master who treats him well and recognizes his talent. He is the most impertinent slave I have ever met, and I joked with Festus that if he didn't watch out, he would find Julian running his estate one day. I am certain he is doing well wherever he may be."

Aurelius laughed, "I hadn't seen him enough to make that kind of judgment, but I had wondered if you might have purchased him."

Marcus finished taking a drink from his goblet before answering with a smile. "I am the only one in my home permitted to be that demanding and particular. I certainly didn't need a snide secretary."

"Agreed." Aurelius capitulated with an obliging chuckle.

After a few days, Julius and Octavia received more confirmation that Julian did not, in fact, work for Marcus when Aurelius's guards reported back. Two of them were able to gain the confidence of Marcus's slave girls, who revealed that they had never met Julian and that their master had never spoken of him in their presence. While Julius and Aurelius continued to have a sentinel posted close to the domus, they decided that Marcus was not Julian's master.

After receiving counsel from the elders at his church, Julius decided that he had no choice but to hand Linus over to Cato with an explanation of his crimes. It was an incredibly difficult decision because Julius had considered him a friend. However, he could not be imprisoned forever in the domus or trusted to be around Julius or his family. Additionally, because he was an admitted murderer, he could not be freed or sold to another unsuspecting family.

Julius explained the gospel message to Linus and told him that he could be with God in death if he repented of his sins, but Linus just looked at him with a crushed expression and asked to be handed over quickly so he would no longer be forced to listen to such blasphemy before his death. When Julius gave him to the centurion, he petitioned Cato for a swift punishment instead of a public spectacle because Linus had spared Julius's life at the cost of his own crimes coming to light. Cato agreed and held his private trial the next day, after which he received a mercifully swift execution.

Both Julius and Octavia mourned over Linus and the man they had believed him to be. It was difficult for Julius to live with the fact that he was responsible for bringing the man to justice, but when he thought about Apollos's murder and all the torment that his enemy was able to inflict upon his family because of Linus, he was assured that it was necessary for the man to face the penalty for his crimes.

Over the next few weeks, the household members were encouraged by the considerable progress with Julius's recovery, as he was finally able to get out of bed and walk around his domus. He did have to stop often to rest but only took his pain medication right before bed so that he could sleep. During the rest of the day, he was able to push through the pain and work to regain his mobility. The medicus cut down his visits to once a week and was pleased with his patient's continued progress.

Unfortunately, winter was coming on quickly, and the prospect of traveling to Raetia was delayed until the following spring. This delay caused Julius considerable consternation because he believed that property held the key to the great mystery that had plagued them for so long.

In light of Julius's recovery, his in-laws returned to their domus, and after he was healed enough, Julius and Octavia began to attend church services with Gaius and Esther again. They would almost always see Aurelius and Claudia there as well. The couple also began having their friends from church back over to their home for meals and fellowship. They were encouraged to hear from Onan about the many families whose homes were confiscated or who could no longer safely live in their old neighborhoods because of the persecution but were able to take refuge in their Jerusalem villa.

Six-month-old Tatiana was growing into a sweet, spunky little girl who never ceased to charm those around her with her wide green eyes and giant grin. Julius thought she looked just like her mother. Tatiana loved to sit up and wave her little arms at Felix's son, and Esther became a close companion for her when her mother needed a break from trying to keep her out of trouble. Julius was astounded by how often he had to take things out of her mouth before she could choke on them. Every leaf or bug on the ground became a potential hazard because she could now crawl around on her chubby little legs faster than he would have expected.

As no further incidents occurred after they had spotted Julian, he allowed Octavia to go out to the marketplace with him and several guards. She enjoyed her time out of the domus, but after his attack, Julius was always on alert when he left the safety of his walls, and he never went anywhere without protection.

One day, when they were at the market, a slave began to approach him and Octavia, and Julius did not detect any danger until he noticed his wife lean into him. He looked down at her and saw fear in her eyes as she stood mutely beside him. He pulled his wife behind him, and Felix stepped in front of the couple as the man got close.

"I mean you no harm," the slave began as he raised his hands in the air to demonstrate his lack of a weapon and leaned over so that he could see Octavia and Julius around their guard. "I am not sure if you recognize me. I worked for Festus and was sold when you two were married."

Julius tensed at this but began to relax as the man continued.

"I wanted to say that I am so sorry for the way that I treated you, Mistress. I have no excuse for my actions, and looking back, I can see how terribly I and the others treated you."

Octavia looked surprised at this outpouring of remorse. "I forgive you, Favian, and I appreciate your apology."

Favian nodded and began to retreat back to where he had originated when Julius called out, "Stop! I have a question for you."

The slave turned nervously, and Julius continued, "Do you know of the whereabouts of Julian, Festus's household manager?"

"No sir," the slave responded. "He waited until you left the market, and then he bought his freedom. But I have not seen or heard of him since."

"So... he is a freedman?" Julius asked in obvious surprise.

"Yes, sir."

"Thank you, Favian, and thank you for having the courage to apologize to my wife."

The slave bowed and quickly scurried away before he could be detained further.

Later, Julius spoke with Gaius and Octavia, but none of them understood the meaning of this new information.

"So, if he is not working for someone, he must be working with someone. He, as a former slave, could not have the funds to hire so many ruffians and murderers." Gaius asserted.

Octavia replied, "I still think that he was responsible for the initial vandalism. That didn't cost anything, and he was just the right level of angry and entitled to be the likely suspect."

Julius nodded, "I agree with you both. I think once the spring comes and I can travel to Raetia, we will be able to find the answers we need."

Octavia spent the winter months raising her daughter and helping Julius prepare for his trip to Raetia. She was comforted by the number of extra guards they had purchased and had Gaius training for their protection details. Half of the guards would stay with her, Tatiana, and Claudia at the domus while the other half would join Aurelius's guards and travel to Raetia with the men.

She and Julius continued to send funds to the apostle Paul and to the suffering churches around the empire through missionaries who visited their church. Their church even received a thank you letter from Paul, who told them of how he was stoned at Lystra but was roused after being left for dead and how he and Barnabas were now preaching in Derbe. Julius suggested that they allow needy families from the church to move into the apartments at their insulae for lowered rent until they could get back on their feet, and the church was blessed by the resources God had given them.

One day, Julius asked Octavia if she could sketch out a portrait of Julian so that the guards would be able to recognize him if they saw him. She agreed and worked on the portrait for several days, asking Esther to critique her work because working from such a distant memory was challenging for her. At last, Esther and Octavia were satisfied with the likeness, and Octavia took it to Gaius and Felix, who stood outside training the new recruits.

Gaius nodded in approval of the likeness while Felix stared at it in thought.

"That man is Julian? He looks vaguely familiar to me, as if I saw him a long time ago," Felix muttered in concentration.

Gaius looked at him quickly and asked, "Could you have spotted him surveilling us at some point?"

Felix nodded, "That could be it. I will keep thinking about it. Maybe the exact incident will come to me."

Gaius then showed the sketch around to all of the staff so that everyone would be able to recognize one of their enemies.

The next week, disregarding the cold, Octavia and Julius decided to take a leisurely ride around town to get out of the domus. They rode in their carpentum, which, in spite of its showiness, Gaius had assured them was the safest way for them to travel, provided they were accompanied by two guards. Octavia asked Julius if they could travel along the edge of the city so she could see more of the countryside. He easily acquiesced to her scenic route and told the driver where to go.

After passing by many domuses and insulaes, they reached the edge of the crowded city. Soon, Octavia was enjoying the sights of farmland and mostly bare trees upon a lonely road bereft of the constant traffic from carts. However, her delight turned to alarm as they passed a large refuse dump.

"Stop the carriage!" she shouted, loud enough to be heard over the cacophony caused by the horses and wheels upon the stone road.

The carriage stuttered to a jerky stop as Julius held Octavia against her seat so she wouldn't be thrown forward into the guard sitting across from her.

"What is it?" he asked in grave concern.

"Shhh, listen. Do you hear a baby crying?"

She really needn't have asked the question because the moment the carriage had stopped, the loud wail of a child echoed through the countryside. Octavia instinctively threw open her door in her haste to reach the poor baby, who she was sure required immediate assistance.

Julius reached for her and held her in the carpentum. He rushed to assure her, "We will go, but let the guards get out first, Love."

She reluctantly nodded as the two guards jumped from their positions and scanned the area for any sign of peril. When they determined that there was no imminent danger, Octavia and Julius scrambled out and joined them. They followed the wails of the child and picked their way over rotting food remains, tattered fabrics of many different colors, and broken furniture.

Soon, the four spotted a squirming bundle of fabric in the middle of the refuse. Octavia pushed forward and, in her haste, nearly tripped over a protruding couch leg. Julius grabbed her arm to steady her, and she winced at the pain.

"It is okay, Love, we will reach him soon. Be careful," Julius warned.

At a more measured pace, they continued forward until they reached the squalling infant. Octavia reached down and scooped him up as rapidly as she could. She began soothing the poor child, who was surely desperate for food and shelter from the bitter wind.

"Let's get him back to the carpentum, and we will check him there," Julius suggested as he helped to turn her around.

He then led his wife through all of the garbage, and Octavia was gratified to hear that the baby's frantic screams had subsided into a throaty sob. When they reached their carpentum once again, she knew that they were filthy and smelled awful, and she wondered how anyone could abandon their baby in such a place.

As she climbed into their ride, carefully cradling the baby with one hand and holding Julius's steadying hand with the other, her husband instructed the driver to take them back home by the quickest route. As the vehicle rolled forward, Octavia unwrapped the soiled blanket from a perfect little boy. She looked him over and saw no sign of injury or defect. The guards averted their eyes as she began to nurse the baby, who quickly latched on in the haste of hunger and thirst. Tears streamed from her eyes as she questioned how his parents could have discarded him as easily as another person discarded a broken couch.

Julius held her hand and comforted her, "I know you are wondering how this could have happened, but we should thank God that he had us drive on this route that we never traverse at the perfect time."

Octavia nodded as the tears continued, and Julius began to pray, "God, thank you that we were able to find and save this innocent little boy. Please help him to grow healthy and strong. Please give us wisdom as we decide upon his future. Amen."

Octavia said in a voice barely above a whisper, "I want to keep him."

Julius hugged her reassuringly and said, "I think we should pray and sleep on it before we make a final decision, but I tend to agree with you."

When they arrived back at the domus, the babe was fed to satisfaction and sleeping in the warmth of Octavia's arms. Gaius and Esther came into the atrium as their friends arrived back from their jaunt around town. They both wore shocked and questioning faces as they took in the little baby and their friends' disheveled appearances.

Julius explained their adventure as Esther approached to admire the little boy, and Gaius stood soberly at a short distance. Then Esther and Octavia took the baby to the baths in the domus to get him and Octavia cleaned up from the trash heap before Julius and the guards took their turn.

Octavia had never been as grateful for the heated bath as she was at that moment. She knew that it was difficult for the slaves to maintain the fires under the bath, so they did not have it heated during warm days, but in the winter, the fires were always being tended.

Once the baby was cleaned and dressed in some of Tatiana's old baby clothes, no one would have ever guessed that he had been in a garbage heap only hours before. Octavia prayed again, thanking God for allowing them to find him safe. She then took him to the cradle in her room and laid him in it, and he immediately fell back asleep, exhausted from the day's hardships.

Octavia then sent Esther and Gaius to inquire of the believers if anyone knew of a wetnurse they could hire for the boy, since her milk would not be enough to sustain both him and Tatiana.

Fortunately, one of the women at the church, Sabina, had just weaned the child she was hired to nurse and was grateful for the continued employment. She arrived just as the baby woke with a hungry cry and was given a room near Octavia's chambers. The baby slept in the room with Sabina in a hastily purchased crib so she could nurse him through the night while Tatiana retained her position in her parents' room.

That evening, Julius and Octavia prayed again for wisdom and, in the morning, decided that they would adopt the baby and name him Antonius.

CHAPTER 21

Antonius proved to be a challenging baby as he adjusted to his new life. Octavia, Esther, and Sabina lavished him with the love and attention he deserved in spite of his nearly constant crying and fussing. His new mother patiently cared for him, knowing that everyone he had ever known was gone, and it would take him time to acclimate. Octavia estimated that he was probably about one month old, and because he wasn't malnourished, she assumed that he had been cared for by his mother up until his abandonment.

After she found Antonius, Octavia was determined to find some way to help the poor rejected children of Rome. She and Julius spoke with the other families in the church and coordinated a search effort for these babies. Every day, slaves from their home went to the two closest dumps while fellow believers searched the other refuse pits around the city.

In the two weeks since they had helped organize the search, their household had rescued two babies and found them homes in the church. One baby had been found too late. Octavia grieved over the lost little one, and Julius made sure she was buried in the catacombs with their last name as an adopted family member, not as a rejected outcast. The church worked together, adopting as many of these unwanted children as they could find, whether in life or in their death.

One fine, warmer day, Gaius and Esther were enjoying a much-needed day off of work together as they walked through the olive trees near the domus. Esther noticed the sunlight filtering through the trees and the early spring breeze rustling through their leaves, but she struggled to enjoy the sight as thoughts rapidly churned through her mind. She observed that her ever-perceptive husband kept looking at her inquisitively.

Finally, Gaius said, "I know you are thinking about something, Beautiful. What is it?"

Esther smiled at the moniker and said with some shyness, "How do you feel about adopting one of the abandoned babies?"

Gaius halted his stride and looked down at her with a slightly pained expression.

"I know that you were abandoned, and I know this might bring up bad memories for you, but we have been married a long time now with no..." she cut off and then uttered, "I think I might be barren."

She could not stop the flood of tears that rushed down her cheeks, and her husband pulled her into a comforting embrace. He rubbed her back while she sobbed.

"We don't know that you are barren. It can take some couples a long time to get pregnant." Gaius soothed.

"But it has been well over a year!" his wife lamented.

He took a deep breath before responding, "We will pray about it, and you are right that it is difficult for me to see these babies and to be near them, knowing that they were abandoned like I was. I thought that I had moved past any negative feelings I had about that abandonment long ago, but seeing these children renews my anger at my parents and my longing to know who they were and why they left me to die. I don't often feel sadness and pain. I have bottled it inside for so long, and I don't know if I can invite an abandoned child into my life and love them like I was never loved."

Esther stared up at her husband, knowing how much the admission had cost his pride. She rubbed her hands down his cheeks and stood up on her toes to kiss him.

"We don't have to make a decision today, but I would appreciate it if we could pray about it. It is also difficult for me to be around babies all the time while I long for one of my own to love and cherish," she said sadly.

"I am sorry, and I understand that too," Gaius said, and then he prayed for wisdom and for God to give him the ability to love an abandoned child or for them to get pregnant.

The days were getting warmer, and as Julius sat in the atrium watching Tatiana crawl around, he reflected upon his eager anticipation for his trip to Raetia in one week. He was not thrilled about leaving Octavia behind, but he felt it was safest for her and the children to remain in Rome with plenty of guards and with her mother, Esther, and the believers from church to keep her company.

As Julius was considering his plans, Gaius walked in and asked him a question regarding how many of the guards would ride on horses and how many would ride in carts for the expedition.

After answering, Julius turned back to the atrium, where, to his surprise, he could no longer see his daughter. He swiftly stood.

"Gaius, did you see where Tatiana went?" he inquired urgently.

Gaius answered, "No, but I will call for all the servants to begin searching. She could not have gotten far."

As Gaius raised the alarm, Julius ran over to the curtain door closest to her last location. The room was Festus's old bedchambers, and Julius had rarely ever been inside. He checked it once for anything important and could not remember entering after that. As he looked around the room, he did not see her, so he dropped to his hands and knees to look under the bed, which was the perfect height for the little troublemaker to hide under.

He did not see her under the bed, but he was surprised to see a box that he hadn't seen before. He pulled it out, and after seeing that the girl wasn't behind it, he left it on the floor and rapidly moved back to the atrium just as Octavia entered from their room carrying the mischievous little girl who was unharmed and clearly loving the attention from her impromptu hide-and-seek game. Octavia smiled at him, and he was relieved by her obvious understanding of the situation.

With the crisis averted and everyone returning to their tasks, Julius returned to Festus's room and opened the box, which was about the size of Octavia's new cat, Prince. The contents of the box were two scrolls, a large cut and polished ruby, and a bag holding a substantial number of gold aureus coins.

He opened the first scroll and saw at the top the coordinates for the Raetia property. Underneath was a drawing of a map with sketched landmarks and with seven Xs written on them. A name was written next to each X. Julius noted with concern that the names appeared to be the same as some of the names with Xs by them from the scroll that was nearly stolen from him in Jerusalem. He put the map scroll in his tunic to compare the names later.

Then he opened the second scroll and read the following hastily scrawled message:

*"I have made a mistake. I killed my lover's husband
and am now being hunted by the soldiers. If you will
give me refuge, I will pay you 200 aurei, a large cut
ruby, and will welcome you into my business which is
sure to make you wealthier than your wildest dreams.
Send your answer to Justinian at the inn we frequent.
-Your Friend, Tiberius"*

Julius stared for a moment in stunned silence as he reread the scroll before putting it in his tunic with the first, closing the box of treasure, and thrusting it back into its hiding spot under the bed. Then he scrambled to his feet and rushed to the atrium, where he ordered a slave to have Gaius and Felix meet him in his tablinum.

When the two guards arrived, Julius motioned to the chairs where they sat, and he placed the scroll from Tiberius to Festus upon the desk in front of them. After the men had read the message, they looked at one another with a hopeful yet cautious understanding.

"So, Tiberius Hortensius is behind the smuggling and, therefore, the attacks?" Gaius asserted the question they were all wondering.

"It certainly seems that way, doesn't it?" answered Julius. Then he looked at Felix and asked, "Does this seem like something he would have done... or something you saw any evidence of when you worked for his father?"

Felix rubbed his chin as he thought. "I do remember that he was a very secretive man. He would often disappear from his domus, and his father would vainly ask the slaves where he went, but no one knew. Once, I witnessed a man come to the domus asking for Tiberius, and when I sent word to him, Tiberius came to the door in a rage and began beating the man in the street for daring to come to his home. It would also make sense why his olive orchards had those same mounds in which you found the smuggled goods. So, yes, thinking back... he certainly could have been smuggling goods even when I worked for his father."

Julius nodded in agreement, "If he was in business with Festus and did not know where all the smuggled items were hidden on Festus's properties at the time of his death, it certainly makes sense why he would desire to thwart my efforts at checking Festus's records or visiting his properties."

"We have to assume that even now, he is watching from a distance if he has not been able to hire another spy in the household," said Gaius.

Julius nodded in consternation and unrolled the second scroll upon the desk in front of the men.

"You should also inspect the second scroll that I found. It appears to be a map of the Raetia property... and compare it to the stolen scroll," he said as he unrolled the other scroll next to the map.

They all took a moment to compare the names on the map to those of the other scroll. All seven of the names on the map corresponded with names beside Xs on the other list.

"Do you think he was killing investors and burying them there!? What about the other five names on the list that have Xs by them?" Felix uttered in shocked amazement.

"It certainly makes sense that they are buried there if they all truly disappeared. I think the other five met with their deaths in what appeared to be tragic accidents but were actually orchestrated events," Julius answered grimly.

"I think we have to assume that Festus was the only one with the map of where the bodies were buried. I imagine Tiberius would do anything within his power to keep this scroll from the authorities. A dead rival husband is one thing, but killing this many prominent publicans would set off an empire-wide manhunt, which would surely lead to his capture and public execution," Gaius declared in a grave voice.

"Festus probably kept this as insurance to protect him from Tiberius getting greedy and wanting to cut him out of the deal or ratting him out if Tiberius got caught for the smuggling," Julius added.

"I think we need to show this to Cato and give him all the information we have. It would also be better for us if we have soldiers with us in Raetia," Gaius suggested.

"I think you are right," Julius agreed. "Send for him now. Tell him that we desire his family's company for dinner tonight and that I have a situation I would like to discuss with him after dinner. Also, send invitations to Aurelius and Claudia. We will see what Cato proposes."

In the meantime, Julius filled Octavia in on his discovery and its implications.

When Cato, his wife, and children arrived at the domus, the centurion kept his demeanor impassive, but his eyes shone with delight at the invitation to such a grand home. The family jubilantly dined with Julius, Octavia, and her parents, who found them to be delightfully charming. After dinner, Octavia and Claudia led his wife and children to the garden and read them a two-act comedy that had everyone giggling.

Meanwhile, Julius, Aurelius, Felix, and Gaius held court in the dining room, where Julius laid out his entire predicament before Cato, including every incident he had experienced in Jerusalem. He described what he had learned about the smuggling and showed the stolen scroll and the two new scrolls he had uncovered. He revealed that he had confirmed that all of the names with Xs on the first scroll matched the names next to the Xs on the map.

Cato took in all of this information in silent contemplation. Only when Julius was finished with his tale did the centurion finally speak.

"So, it appears that Tiberius and Festus were murdering investors who spoke out or were complaining about not being repaid and buried them at this property."

Julius nodded in affirmation, "That is our theory."

Cato responded, "The murder of his lover's husband occurred ten years ago when my predecessor was stationed here. I have not seen any sign of Tiberius in my time here." Then he looked at Felix and asked, "What does Tiberius look like?"

"The last time I saw him ten years ago, he was rather short and of average weight for a man of his size. He had dark hair, a strong nose, and a small, almost sunken chin," the guard answered.

"I assume that does not match the description of anyone you have encountered in the last two years?" Cato asked as he looked at Julius.

"No, it certainly does not," Julius confirmed. "And we have been planning to go next week to the Raetia property because it seems to be at the center of this mystery."

Cato nodded and looked at the scrolls. "This list consists of many prominent publicans. Only some of them are from this area, but I do recognize two of the names with Xs as men who disappeared years ago. Their families came to me, but my investigations did not bring any resolutions to the disappearances. I will appeal to the emperor for a certificate for us to use the cursus publicus, so we can ride from one postal station to the next, picking up fresh horses at each one. I know that if these men were actually killed and a murderer of high-ranking Romans is on the loose, as we fear, the emperor will be adamant that we urgently resolve the issue."

"Will we be able to go with you? I personally would like to visit this land with you if possible." Julius asked.

"Yes, you, your father-in-law, and three of your guards can come. I will be bringing a dozen soldiers, so we will be very well guarded," Cato agreed.

"How fast will we arrive using the cursus publicus?" Aurelius asked.

"We should be there within a week, provided that we do not encounter any hardships along the route," Cato answered.

Julius noticed Felix's eyes widen in amazement as he thought about the speed they could travel using the state-run transportation service normally reserved for high-ranking officials. Cato then went over more details of their impending travels and said that he would take this matter before the emperor tomorrow.

The next day, Cato sent word that the emperor had approved their request and wanted them to leave immediately. Therefore, they would leave at dawn the following day. Aurelius and Julius each went about accumulating the supplies they would need and could fit into a light bag. Julius assigned Gaius and Felix to accompany him, while his father-in-law brought his most trusted guard, Quintus, one of the archers who had nobly defended their caravan from the bandits.

The next morning, Julius bid Octavia a loving farewell and left with the rest of the expeditionary party. The first two days of travel went as smoothly as planned. They rode their horses from post station to post station, turning in their tired mounts for fresh ones throughout the day. In the evenings, they made camp and cooked their food over a fire. Cato used this time to get to know more about Julius's group and spent many hours philosophizing and asking questions about the Jewish God in whom these Romans believed, to the centurion's bewilderment.

On the third day, when they stopped for their midday meal, one of the soldiers walked a short distance from the group and was standing by a little stream when he screamed out in pain and fell to the ground.

As Cato and other soldiers rushed to his aid, the centurion stopped abruptly near the fallen soldier. He cried out, "Halt! Snake!" and pointed to a long gray snake with dark lines parading down its back perpendicular to its spine.

One of the soldiers cried out in alarm, "It's an asp viper!"

Cato motioned to one of the soldiers who circled around, moving to his side behind the injured man's head. Then Cato and the other soldier picked the fallen man up under his shoulders and dragged him to safety. One of the other men, who had been introduced to Julius as the medicus, began sucking the poison out of his wound.

Julius stood with Aurelius, observing the ministrations and silently praying for the man's recovery, when Cato walked up to him and said, "Have you ever been bitten by one of the asps? They say it is the most painful bite in Italia."

Julius shook his head, "No, but I once had a donkey that was bitten and succumbed to the poison."

"Fortunately, we are only an hour from the next station. We will leave him there to convalesce, but he should be fully recovered by the time we come back on our return trip," Cato predicted.

After dropping the soldier off at the station, they continued upon their way, noticing that the warmer weather of spring that they had been enjoying began regressing to the cooler temperatures of late winter as they pressed north. The next few days grew colder as they moved closer to the mountains of Raetia. They traveled rapidly on the Via Claudia Augusta, the road over the Reschen Pass through the Alps. On the evening of the sixth day, they reached the last station before their destination and stayed the night so that they would arrive at the property the next morning.

Julius found it difficult to fall asleep that night as he wondered about what the next day would bring. Would the mystery finally be solved so Cato could issue a search for Tiberius, or would this journey only result in more questions? Would his visit to the property bring an end to the attacks on him and his family, or would they further enrage his hidden foe? He prayed that God would bring a resolution to his problem and allowed his trust in God's sovereignty to comfort his soul and bring him the rest he needed.

The next day, the group of men rode up onto the ridge overlooking the property, which was a large valley amid the mountains. There was a dazzling blue lake in the middle, but they did not take time to admire the beauty of their surroundings. Instead, they were shocked to see a small dwelling on the edge of the property.

Cato rode to Julius and asked, "Did you know someone lives here?"

Julius answered in obvious confusion, "I did not even know there was a structure of any kind on the property."

Cato nodded and motioned to his men as they followed him toward the home. It was small, probably only large enough for two bedrooms, and it had obviously fallen into disrepair. When they reached it, one of the soldiers dismounted and knocked on the door. Everyone's hands were on their weapons as the door swung open.

A grizzled old man opened the door cautiously. His eyes widened with fright when he saw the company of soldiers on horseback on his front porch. Cato did not wait for the man to speak and immediately launched into his questions.

"Do you live here? What is your name?"

"My name is Bjarni, and yes, Sir, I live here," the man croaked out with a strange accent.

"Who owns the property?" Cato persisted.

"His name is Gallus. I maintain his property, and he allowed me to live here with my two sons," the man explained while his eyes darted around the large company.

Cato glanced at Julius in surprise until Julius reassured him, "Festus used the name Gallus Domitius to buy some of his properties."

Cato nodded and looked back at the old man. "When was the last time you saw Gallus, and what do you do to manage the property?"

The man rubbed his chin and squinted his eyes as he thought before responding, "I have not seen him in over two years, but his business partner has come a couple times in the last year or so. I guard the property against intruders, and my sons buried the wine barrels where Gallus instructed. Although, like I said, it has been a couple years since he has come with the barrels."

Cato's eyes narrowed at the mention of the business partner, and he asked, "Do you know the business partner's name, and what did he want when he came?"

"The partner never gave his name. Frankly I wouldn't have known he was Gallus's partner except that he came with Gallus on one visit. The man wanted to know where the wine barrels were buried, but I told him that only Gallus knew that information. Gallus made a map and kept it a secret. My sons buried them so deep that they are not visible or marked in any way."

"Why did he not inquire of your sons where these barrels were buried?" Cato asked.

The old man's eyes took on a misty sheen as he answered, "Soon after Gallus came with the last barrel, both my boys took ill and died."

"I am sorry for the loss of your sons, but we are here because Gallus passed away over two years ago, and this man inherited his property," Cato declared as he pointed to Julius. Then he continued, "We have the map and will be digging up the barrels now."

The man nodded in agreement, "Yes, Sir."

CHAPTER 22

Julius took out the scroll with the map and looked around at the landmarks, matching them up with the corresponding marks on the drawing. Aurelius jumped in once or twice to lend his aid before they were able to find the first area referenced by an X. Four soldiers with shovels began to dig at the location, but after twenty minutes of digging, Julius began to fear that there was nothing buried there and that the map was false. However, his fears were shortly alleviated when one of the soldiers exclaimed that they had hit something.

It took another fifteen minutes before the barrel was freed from the dirt enough for the soldiers to tie ropes around it. Then, the ropes were attached to the saddles of two horses who walked forward and hoisted the barrel from the earth. One of the other soldiers produced a tool for opening the barrel, and the lid was promptly removed. A dank odor of long-ago decay poured from the barrel, and the soldiers retreated a step back. Bjarni stood at a distance observing the scene, and Julius noticed that he looked confused by the soldiers' reluctance to look inside the barrel.

Cato stepped forward and confirmed everyone's suspicions by declaring that there was a body in the barrel, at which point Bjarni cried out in terrified opposition, "No, that can't be. It was wine! He told us it was wine!"

Julius walked over to the older man before Cato joined them. The man was shaking and crying in shock from the discovery. "I dddidn't know! I swear to you, I had no idea. I would never have lived on a property with the dead so casually buried." Then he fell to his knees, crying, "No wonder the gods took my sons!"

Julius and the others watched the man weep, unsure of how to proceed. Then Julius turned to Cato and whispered to him, "I tend to believe that he is innocent in all of this."

Cato responded, "Your feelings are irrelevant on the matter. We will have to bring him back with us and present the entire case to the emperor. We will also need him to identify the partner once we have caught him."

Julius nodded and bent down to comfort the grieving father.

After five hours, the soldiers had worked in teams and exhumed all seven of the barrels. Unsurprisingly and tragically, each contained the remains of a body. Cato had one of his soldiers write the name upon each barrel that corresponded to the name of that barrel's location on the map so they would know whose remains each barrel contained when they returned with them to Rome.

When they had finished with the task and filled in the holes, dusk was starting to fall. Some of the men were uncomfortable sleeping near the dumping grounds, but the pragmatic Cato ordered his men to set up camp near the lake. Julius and his party bivouacked on the edge of the soldiers' encampment, and all except for Felix, who sat and listened, and Quintus, who stood guard outside, prayed for the families of the men whose fates they had uncovered that day.

The entire party was eager to leave the next day. Julius, Aurelius, and Gaius found the land to be a bleak reminder of the sinful nature of men, and the soldiers were certain the land was cursed by the gods and the tormented souls of the murdered men. To the distaste of the soldiers, they purchased a wagon from a nearby village onto which they loaded the barrels to return them to Rome for the inquest and proper burial.

The procession now arranged themselves with Cato and two soldiers at the lead, followed immediately by Julius and his party; then came the rest of the regiment. The wagon trailed at a distance and was driven by a soldier who was assigned to the task and was rotated with a different soldier at every stop. They traveled back through the mountain pass and had just arrived at the border of Italia when a loud crash behind Julius sent the horses skittering forward in fear.

As he looked back, he saw that the wagon was tilting to the ground in a manner consistent with a broken axle. He and the rest of the group turned their horses and returned to the section of road that now hosted the immobile wagon. To further impede their progress, one of the barrels had been jarred loose when the corner of the wagon had hit the stone road. The barrel's splintered remains now lie in the road in three pieces, and its unfortunate occupant now reposed in the midst of the wreckage.

As Cato took stock of the damage and made his plans, everyone else dismounted and prepared the midday meal. As they ate, Julius overheard several of the soldiers muttering about curses and ghosts of the dead seeking revenge. He hoped that Cato could control his men, especially when they seemed to be half-crazed by fear.

After they were all refreshed, Cato announced that he was sending four soldiers to the next village or post station to arrange for a new axle and barrel. Then, he had two of the remaining soldiers cover the body with an animal skin they had purchased to shelter the wagon.

The rest of the party erected their camp in a small clearing in the woods along the road. The remaining seven soldiers were increasingly jittery as they set up the tents, and Cato eyed them with a calm and commanding expression. Once the camp was set, he addressed his soldiers.

"Men, I have heard your whispers that you are worried about ghosts and other such nonsense. These men are in Hades, where all of the dead go. They cannot harm us. The only ones who can are the men responsible for their deaths, and we must be on our guard and ready to avenge these miserable souls at a moment's notice. Do you understand?!"

The soldiers rallied at their leader's speech and gave a strong war cry in assent. Then, with the men more at ease, Cato organized two pairs of soldiers to act as hunting parties. The prospect of fresh meat for dinner raised everyone's spirits, and the group remaining at the campsite prepared a fire as they laughed and joked for the first time since they made their gruesome discoveries. Bjarni was the only person who did not join in the merriment. He sat to the side of the camp and curled in on himself in his private world of grief.

It was about an hour after the hunters had left when Gaius and Cato both came to alert simultaneously, apparently having sensed something in the woods. Then, without further warning, Julius heard a whizzing sound coming from where they had tied off their horses and saw one of the soldiers toward his left fall to the ground with an arrow protruding from his throat. As soldiers and guards alike scrambled to grab their weapons, the two surviving soldiers met a similar fate as their comrade.

Aurelius's guard, Quintus, was on his feet, firing arrows back into the trees where the assault was originating, and his efforts slowed the volley of projectiles while the rest of the group took shelter behind trees. Julius noticed that Bjarni was still sitting on his log, looking stupefied a couple of yards in front of Julius's shelter, so he lurched forward and grabbed the man, pulling him back to cover. He also saw Quintus catch an arrow in the top of his chest right under his collarbone. The man fell but was able to shuffle backward, prop himself up against a log, and continue returning arrows.

After what seemed to Julius to be an eternity but was only the course of a few moments, arrows ceased flying and the scene in the clearing was one of complete devastation. The soldiers all lay where they had perished in the initial volley, and Quintus was propped up, still clutching his bow with one hand, although his eyes remained fixed open and glazed over in a warrior's death. Cato was lying on the ground, unconscious or dead with an arrow in his shoulder and one projecting up from his thigh, where he was bleeding vigorously.

Gaius, Felix, Aurelius, Julius, and Bjarni were the only visible survivors and were separated behind trees around the clearing. All except the old man held their swords at the ready for whatever came next. Before his guards had time to get to him, Julius heard a sound from behind him, and he turned to see several men advancing toward him with swords. He was forced to retreat back into the clearing and pulled the old man with him. As he backed into the clearing, he saw his guards and father-in-law had already been herded there by more men with swords.

Julius could see that they were in a defenseless position and shouted at the mercenaries, "What do you want?!"

One of the men stepped forward from the rest and commanded, "We have you surrounded. If you put down your swords and surrender peaceably, we will take you with us unharmed."

The looming threat of a disagreeable outcome should they not surrender led all of the ambushed men to drop their swords and allow the men to bind their wrists. Then, the mercenaries led their captives to two carpentums which were sitting empty on the road near the broken-down wagon. There, they forced Felix and Gaius into one carpentum with two of the mercenaries. Julius, Aurelius, and Bjarni were prodded into the other vehicle with one mercenary to complete their company.

Julius supposed that the rest of their attackers mounted their horses and rode alongside the carpentums, but he was unable to see because wooden planks had been nailed over the windows. He was surprised to notice that an opening had been cut into the roof of the carriage to allow light inside for visibility, probably to allow the sentry to be able to watch them.

Any attempt that Julius or Aurelius made to question their guard was returned with stony silence, so they eventually gave up their quest for answers from this man. Julius prayed that God would protect them and that if they joined the others in death that God would keep Octavia and their family safe. He had a sinking feeling that he was about to meet Tiberius, the madman behind the majority of his troubles during his marriage. He had wished to have the meeting on his terms with many more guards, but he knew that, for some reason, God had planned it to be this way.

"God's ways are better than your ways," he whispered to himself quietly.

An hour or two after their abduction, the carpentum came to a halt, and the men from both carriages were unloaded into the bright sunshine. As they turned to observe their surroundings, they were shocked to see a sprawling villa on the side of an azure-blue lake. Their abductors led the bound men up the steps into the entryway of the gargantuan domicile.

Julius took a moment to study the expansive entryway as one of the mercenaries went deeper into the home and left the others to guard the prisoners. Unfortunately, nothing about the décor helped him to identify its owner or their location.

They were only made to wait a few moments before Julian shuffled into the room, sporting a giant smile of success. When his shifting eyes landed on Felix, they widened slightly in surprise, but when the guard said nothing, he moved to stand in front of Julius.

"Hail, friends," he exclaimed in his nasal voice that ended with a chuckle.

He seemed a little put out when no one responded to his little joke and scowled while motioning to the abductors so that they brought the group forward into a large dining room. There, he invited everyone to sit and put their bound hands upon the table where they could be seen. Then, he dismissed the mercenaries, seemingly not wanting his conversation to be overheard. Finally, he took his place standing at the head of the table about six feet away from the nearest prisoner, and he began to speak.

"My master needs to know what you have revealed to the authorities. He has been less than pleased by you probing into matters which are none of your concern," Julian declared as he glared at Julius.

On Julius's left, Bjarni looked up at the fat man and snorted before saying, "You lie. You have no master. I saw you with Gallus at the graveyard. You were his partner."

Julian's face twisted into an angry snarl as he glared at the old man in a fury and screamed, "SHUT UP!"

In response, the old man began to laugh hysterically, and as Julius swung his gaze to look at Bjarni, he caught a glance at Felix's face, which held a surprised look of recognition. When Julius looked back across the table, Felix looked at his master and nodded his confirmation.

Julian pointed to Bjarni, presumably to deliver what Julius feared would be a death sentence.

"So, you must be Tiberius," Julius swiftly injected into the conversation with a calm smile.

Julian looked miserably upset that he was rapidly losing control of the conversation. Then, a look of acceptance came over his face, and he took a deep breath and smiled.

"I am, in fact, Tiberius, and the fact that you had no idea who I was is a comfort. If you had no idea, the authorities certainly could not," Tiberius responded with another of his nasally laughs.

CHAPTER 23

As Julius stared at the tyrant who had dogged him for years, he still could not believe it was the same man he had fired over two years prior.

"The authorities know that you murdered twelve men at least and buried seven of them at Festus's property," Julius said defiantly.

Tiberius again looked enraged, and his voice deepened to a low baritone as he shed the affectations of his alter-ego, Julian.

"I did not kill any of those men!" He practically shouted, "That was all Festus. The greedy simpleton! All I was responsible for was killing my lover's husband, but in my defense, he caught us in his room and came at me with a dagger. I had no choice but to use my own dagger and save my life. I never murdered anyone else."

"What about Apollos? What about the soldiers you had killed today!" Julius accused furiously.

"Who is Apollos?" Tiberius screwed up his face in confusion.

"My guard who was shot defending me from your archer!" Julius sternly answered.

"Oh, right, the guard. I may have paid to have a few plebeians sent to Hades before their time, but they were nobodies. I never murdered another publican, because it is far too messy. There is too much of a cry for justice, unlike with plebeians. If you kill one of those, another just rises up to fill his place."

Julius felt Aurelius reach over beside him to cover Julius's hand with his own as he noticed his son-in-law begin to rise from his chair in righteous fury. Julius looked at his father-in-law, who gave him a meaningful stare, reminding him to be careful, so he resumed his seat and schooled his features to be calm once more.

"Why would Festus kill all of those men and then leave a scroll from you with the map, implicating you in the murders?" he asked passively.

Tiberius pulled out the seat before him and sat in a huff, "I only wanted him to join me in my smuggling business. He knew that he held power over me as long as he held that letter, but I had little other choice. None of my other friends would have been greedy enough to risk the penalty for sheltering a murderer. One thing I knew I could count on was Festus's greed. He had even asked me previously how I had so much wealth when my father owned olive orchards.

"I knew that if I paid him off and brought him in with me on the smuggling, he would hide me, so I sent the letter to him. He sent his agreement back to the inn where I had been taking refuge for the last month and doing nothing but eating to drown my sorrows. I realized that I had gained some weight, and I worked to gain as much weight as I could in the next few months as Festus allowed me to live in one of the villas he had recently purchased on credit. He told the slaves that I was another slave and had me work as a household manager. I finally gained enough weight that I was not recognizable as the man I once was.

"Then I moved back to Rome and continued with the smuggling operation I had been running. I would get investors and have them pay to bring the items into the empire secretly to avoid paying the high tariff rates. Then, I would sell the items into a network of fences that I had established, and I would pay off my investors with interest. I told all my old contacts that my master had purchased the business from Tiberius and that I would be making all transactions in the future. None of them recognized or even questioned me!

"We would hide the smuggled goods in barrels in existing properties and some that Festus bought under an assumed name. Then, when the right buyer was lined up, we would sell him the goods. We were making so much money, and I thought that all was well. Occasionally, a plebeian would get suspicious of the mounds, and we would have him buried in his own mound. But for the most part, it was clean and easy.

"Then imagine my shock and horror when I discovered that my greedy partner had decided that he would solicit investments from more investors on his own and in much larger amounts than we could repay with the smuggling! The fool! He would take a small investment and then use the next investor's money to pay the first one back while retaining some of the second investor's money. He continued to do this until several investors were not getting paid back. When they came to him wanting their money, he put them off or threatened that they could be arrested for their involvement in an illegal smuggling business. My secret business!

"The man had no propensity for caution. So, when one investor got too loud and Festus feared he might tell someone, Festus had him meet with an accident. Then, he purchased that asinine property in Raetia. He told me it was for smuggling more goods, but it was so far away from customers that I told him it was of no benefit to us.

"I did not realize what he was doing until he took me once on a trip there with an investor. I believe his name was Plinius."

At this statement, Julius sensed Aurelius tense next to him. Tiberius didn't notice and continued with his narrative nonplussed. "Festus dined Plinius and kept him entertained all along the route. When the man would question where we were going, Festus would just ply him with more wine or tell him that his investment was about to pay off more handsomely than he could imagine. I could tell that the man got uncomfortable at times but felt as if he didn't have a choice if he didn't want to be stranded in the middle of nowhere. I know I felt the same," he whined as he looked sorrowfully at his captive audience.

"And so, we continued on our doomed trip to the northernmost part of Italia. There, Festus rented a cart and purchased a wine barrel. Then he led us to a field to show the investor 'our business' he told him. I was thoroughly confused at this point, not knowing of any business ventures we had near there. However, sometimes Festus would purchase a property without telling me, like the ones in Jerusalem I didn't know about," he growled in frustration before continuing.

"When we were in the middle of the field, Festus came up behind the man, took out his dagger, and stabbed him several times. I stood by in shock as he killed him. Festus laughed at my surprise and dismay. He said that he knew I had killed a man and asked, did I not enjoy it. I told him, of course, I didn't enjoy it. He gave me a funny look as if he could not understand this and then commanded me to help him with the body. Having no other options, I helped put the man into the wine barrel, which we loaded onto the cart and drove through the Alps to his property, where some men buried the body. Festus did not let me see where he buried the man and told me that several more were buried there.

"He assured me that my name was attached to documents about the property and any revelation of the bodies would lead the authorities right back to me! I couldn't believe it! I knew that

I had been in business with a greedy man, but I had no idea the depths of his depravity. Now, he was trying to implicate me in a string of murders that I had no knowledge of or portion in!"

Julius was surprised that the man kept telling them of his crimes, but it seemed as if he felt the need to justify himself to someone. Tiberius continued his story, looking at the group as if for reassurance that he was the one in the right and for sympathy with his predicament.

"For the next few months, I stopped all the smuggling and tried to decide how I could extricate myself from Festus's clutches. I traveled to his properties and his countryside villa under the guise of working on the smuggling business when, in actuality, I was looking for any evidence against me. The slaves at the villa would not let me in the tablinum, saying that Festus had given them strict instructions that not even I should be allowed in without the master. All I found in my search of his bedroom at the villa was a list of the investors and how much they had paid Festus. I didn't realize he had two copies of that list. And I found a riddle about the dead man in the fourth pomegranate barrel."

Tiberius began to rub his temples as he continued dryly, "Apparently, Festus thought that he was quite a clever poet... the fool. Anyway, I was deliberating my next move when Festus suddenly dropped dead of a heart malady. I am sure you can understand why I was relieved, but now I had the widow to contend with. I admit that I may have made a tactical error in making her an enemy for so many years, but it was just so fun to abuse her."

At this, most of the men at the table clenched their hands into fists or stiffened in controlled fury at the man's cruelty, but the narrator did not skip a beat in his story.

"Had I ingratiated myself to the wench, I may have been able to find her a husband that I could control. However, I had also not anticipated the bizarre terms of Festus's will. What a half-wit! He really thought he could have her kicked out onto the street — that no one would step into his shoes. I thought that Marcus was going to ask for her hand and encouraged him in that direction. He is also a simpleton, and I knew I could easily manipulate him and destroy any evidence against me without his awareness."

Tiberius sighed and rubbed the corner of his eye. Then he continued, "But as I said, the man is a fool, and he kept stringing Octavia along, intending to swoop in at the last moment and be the conquering hero. Apparently, I did not give the woman enough credit. I always believed her to be a simple, stupid creature, but she proved me wrong when she snuck out and purchased herself a slave to marry!"

At this statement, everyone at the table turned their eyes upon Julius in shock.

"Oh, so you didn't make that common knowledge?" Tiberius asked with a feigned innocence that quickly morphed back into anger as he continued, "But then it took me a month! A month... before I was able to find your marriage declaration and the paperwork showing she'd freed you! Oh, I definitely underestimated the little harlot!

"When she came home with you, I was convinced that I could persuade you around to my side. But imagine my shock to realize that she was actually able to find a husband who cared about her, and you immediately sold me for the crime of what... mistreating a woman?!

"I, of course, couldn't let you know that I was actually a wealthy publican disguised as a slave, so I waited until you left before I purchased my freedom. Then, I had no access to the domus or Festus's other properties, so I did everything I could to thwart your progress in learning about your predecessor's illicit investments and the murders. I knew a juicy bit of information about a secretary and immediately went and purchased him to set him up as a spy in your home.

Tiberius gave a mischievous grin and looked triumphantly at Julius. "You had no idea that you had bought a spy, and he was so, so useful to me. He told me everything about you, your little wife, the baby she couldn't carry... everything."

As he dragged out the last word, it took all of Julius's will not to show his anguish outwardly, and Tiberius looked a little disappointed with the lack of response from his barbs.

"I was responsible for the vandalism, of course. Then I incited Marcus against you and your wife and indicated that he should go to you," he looked pointedly at Aurelius before continuing, "Of course, the fool blundered his attempt to interfere in the marriage, and I am not surprised you wouldn't want him for a son-in-law." Tiberius shook his head as if exasperated.

"I then set about paying back all the investors so that they would not come to you seeking their money from Festus's estate. It was quite expensive, but I had known of a property or two that Festus had put into a false name and given me the paperwork to file. Being a clever man, though, I kept the scrolls and hid them away just in case. I was able to sell the properties and use the proceeds to keep the investors satisfied.

"Then you went to your countryside villa where Linus was only able to burn two of the scrolls that might mention my involvement in the smuggling or murders, and I was not certain if there were more there to implicate me. However, the gods smiled upon me that day, and there were no more.

"Then you traveled all over Italia, where I was forced to follow you instead of relaxing at one of my villas in peace! Linus was able to distract you from the barrels in Tarentum, but you then traveled to Jerusalem. I get seasick! Do you get seasick?!

"Because of you," He accused as he jabbed his finger toward Julius, "I took a miserable journey to a godless land where I finally decided to end your life, because Octavia would be much easier to control on her own. I knew from Marcus that you made her your heir. She must have bought your loyalty along with your life because you actually named a woman as your heir!"

He looked disgusted at the prospect and threw his arms up in disbelief. Then he continued his monologue. "But you just wouldn't die! First the ruffians I hired couldn't kill you because your guard thwarted them." He glared at Gaius, and Julius noticed that the edge of his friend's lip twitched as if he was holding back a smile.

"Then the expert archer I hired managed to only kill some donkeys and your guard!" He took a deep breath as if to reign in his anger as he continued, "I decided at that point that the gods must want you alive for some reason, so, through threats, I urged Linus to find a scroll with any mention of the Raetia property. That plan backfired spectacularly when it led you straight to the scroll. Then you captured Atticus, who fortunately did not know my identity or whereabouts. I paid off the soldiers holding him, so they treated him well in exchange for him not disclosing that Linus was also a mole.

"Do you see the level of hardship I have had to go to just to escape punishment for the crimes of the madman Festus?!" He looked at them urgently as if seeking exculpation for his sins. When all he received was blank stares, he continued, presumably still attempting to gain commiseration from his captives.

"After the assassination attempts, you never went anywhere without guards and took an excessive number of precautions. Then you found the investment properties that Festus had in Jerusalem, of which I was annoyingly unaware. When I learned from Linus that you were going to visit a pomegranate orchard, I knew that there was a body there."

He looked at Julius as if exhausted by just the retelling of his adventures and said, "I'm sure Linus told you about his plan. I'll give the man credit; scorpions were a clever and painful distraction. I allowed you to find the other barrels, hoping that you would realize Festus had been smuggling goods and then having the answer to your mystery, you would have been less likely to further pursue answers about the Raetia land.

"Also, if you kept the smuggled goods, I would have some way to blackmail you into backing off, but you immediately went to the authorities and paid the tariffs! And, of course, you didn't stop searching for me. Then you can guess the rest: more following you around, other assassination attempts, Linus betraying me instead of killing you. Then you had him killed, so I didn't have to." He shrugged his shoulders as if he couldn't care less.

"I was surprised that you used Linus to try to trap me, but as you experienced, I am too clever for that." He grinned triumphantly at Gaius, who stared calmly back as if indifferent.

"Without a spy in your domus, I was no longer able to counter your moves and did not anticipate you using the cursus publicus to travel to Raetia. I, of course, pursued you when I learned what direction you were headed. I know that you were on your way back from the property when I had my men detain you. So, now I need to know, what did you tell the emperor that convinced him to grant you permission to use the cursus publicus?" He inquired commandingly to Julius.

Julius considered his answer carefully before replying. "I was not in the meeting with the emperor and can therefore not testify to you about the petition."

Tiberius looked at him in disappointed annoyance and spoke in a monotone voice. "Do not talk to me as if I am a fool. I do not want to have to harm your father-in-law in front of you. Just answer my questions. I have explained my actions to you, and I need honesty from you in return. You have nowhere to go... no way to escape me now."

Julius looked across the table at Gaius who gave him a slight nod.

"I found your letter to Festus and the map of the burial sites stored together. It made it seem as if the business you invited Festus into was murdering investors. The centurion took this information to the emperor who wanted it resolved immediately and sent us by cursus publicus."

Tiberius shook his head and thrust his fingers into his hair in vexation as he stared down at the table. Julius noticed that a calculating look came into Felix's eyes, and Julius shook his head urgently to prevent the man from acting hastily. Even though they would be able to easily overpower the man, the mercenaries in the hall would surely detain and possibly kill them all. Felix acknowledged his master's message with a slight frown and a nod.

Their enemy raised his head and asked, "What did you find in Raetia?"

"We found the seven bodies in barrels." Julius answered before continuing, "I do not know how you plan to cover that up, though. We were bringing the barrels back with us along the Via Claudia Augusta and had made it into Italia when the wagon broke, and a barrel fell out. Even now, all the barrels and one body are just sitting on the road. Surely, more soldiers have come upon the scene."

Tiberius looked at Julius with his mouth agape in fear and indecision for a moment before he answered weakly, "But no one will know who those men are for sure, not without the map, which I am sure you still have, correct?!"

Julius shook his head as he answered his enemy's assertion. "The X marked locations on the map had the names of the deceased written next to them. The centurion from our party marked each barrel with the corresponding name from the map. Also, the map is still in my saddle bag."

Tiberius looked deathly pale at this revelation and called out for one of the mercenaries to enter the room. He then stood and walked over to confer quietly with the other man.

Julius used the reprieve to pray again silently, "God, please protect us and bring justice to Tiberius for the crimes he has committed."

Then as the mercenary left the room, Tiberius returned to stand at the head of the table and declared, "My men will soon take care of those barrels, and no one will be able to find me or prove that I was in any way involved. However, I may need to inquire of you further, so I will have you held for now."

He smiled in churlish delight as he continued, "When I purchased this property to keep a watch on that blasted Raetia land, I had a prison room built underground here. You will be my first guests there."

CHAPTER 24

Tiberius clapped his hands to summon several of his guards who led the prisoners through an expansive courtyard. Julius noticed this courtyard was furnished with a large impluvium surrounded by trees. Next, they were escorted down a staircase into the hot basement of the villa. The prison room was near the furnaces that warmed the baths upstairs, and the heat was oppressive, as was most certainly their captor's intention. As the guards led them into the room, each prisoner had both their arms and legs shackled with long chains that were fixed into the stone wall at their backs. Bjarni and Aurelius were on the ends, with the rest of the members chained up between the older men.

The prisoners sat propped against the stone wall and silently digested all they had learned from their enemy. The heat soon exacerbated the men's thirst, and Julius wondered how long Tiberius planned to keep them down here and if he planned to give them water. Suddenly, guilt for the predicament his friends were facing flooded through him, and he began to apologize.

"My friends, I am sorry that it is because of your association with me that you find yourselves in this situation."

Gaius turned to his friend and said, "You bear no responsibility for our current position. You have done more for me than I had ever imagined, and I am honored to be here with you fighting for justice for Apollos and Cato and all the others whom this man is responsible for killing."

Felix nodded in agreement and added, "I appreciate all you have done for me and my family and am glad to be with you here."

Julius took a deep breath before responding, "Thank you, friends." Then he turned to Aurelius and asked him, "Are you angry that I did not tell you about the circumstances behind my marriage to your daughter?"

Aurelius barked out a half laugh and answered, "Of course I'm not the least bit upset at you. I'm angry with myself. If even half of what that despot upstairs said about Festus is true, how can I live with myself knowing that I condemned my own daughter to live with him and under his power? She begged me not to force her to marry that man, and I ignored her. I believed it was the whims of a silly girl's imagination and fancy that she wanted a younger man who might love her. What a fool I was. I have never really apologized to her. Will I ever get the chance to now, or will my daughter forever think of her father as a man willing to sell her off to a monster?"

Julius was quick to respond, "She does not think of you in that way. She thinks of you as a new creation in Christ. She knows that you sinned against her, and while an apology would be good and right, you have demonstrated in the past year that you are sorry for your mistakes and want the best for her. And she has already forgiven you. Besides, if you didn't give her to Festus, I would still be an unmarried slave."

Gaius jumped in, "So would I."

Felix also answered, "I would never have met my wife or had my family either."

"So, the actions you took that you did not realize at the time were evil, God used for the good of everyone in this room. He also used me to tell you about him and his saving love," Julius concluded.

Aurelius seemed deeply moved by this outpouring of grace. "Thank you all... and thank you God."

After a time of silence among the men, Felix spoke up, "I have often heard you three speak of your God. Why do you believe that he is the only God?"

The men spent the next several hours explaining the gospel and all they had learned from witnesses about Jesus. Then they prayed with Felix who repented of his sins and believed in the Savior of souls, Jesus.

Bjarni was the only one who was not engaged in the conversation. Instead, he remained silent and morose as he sat with his eyes closed and his head down.

The bright light and the heat from the furnace kept the men awake for much of the night. No one came to their prison to bring food or water, and it was impossible for the prisoners to tell how much time had passed. They grew weak from the conditions and lack of sustenance. The next day, Julius found that he was sleeping more and more, and he felt as if the life was draining from his body. He prayed once more to his God to protect Octavia and his children and fell asleep again.

Suddenly, he was awoken by an urgent grabbing at his arm. Then, he was vaguely conscious of water being poured into his mouth. He slowly roused himself with the thought that he was about to be swallowed by a ferocious dragon. However, as his faculties returned to him, he realized that a soldier was removing the shackles from his hands and feet. The soldier then supported most of Julius's weight as he walked upstairs from the empty prison.

Once out of the basement, Julius observed his fellow prisoners, who were also freed and being plied with food and water, except for Bjarni.

"Where is Bjarni, the old man?" he asked the soldier supporting him.

"I am sorry, Sir. He did not survive the heat," the man answered sympathetically.

Julius drooped his head in sorrow for the old man and took a seat next to his fellow captives. They were all slick with sweat, and they quickly gulped down the wine, bread, and cheese provided to them by a slave girl. As they ate, the men were startled when they saw Cato striding toward them.

"Hail, Cato! We thought you were dead!" said the stunned and much-revived Julius.

Cato grinned and walked with a slight limp over to the freed prisoners. "So did the mercenaries, I expect. It was sloppy work, and they were clearly in a hurry. The two hunting parties returned and patched me up, and the other soldiers I had sent out returned to the site of the wagon accident. Then, I sent word to the nearest large regiment in the area. They joined us in the woods, and we waited for a day to see if the murderer would come back to hide the evidence of his past crimes.

"I realized that the murderer had likely just sent mercenaries to kill and capture without realizing that we were carrying crucial evidence that could lead to his capture. When the mercenaries, therefore, returned, we were able to capture them and compel them to lead us here. The slaves told us where you were, but it seems that Tiberius left soon after his mercenaries and no one has seen him since."

"Of course not," groaned Julius in exhaustion and defeat.

"Do not despair," replied Cato. "All of Rome will soon be looking for him, and he will be found."

"He has proven to be a rather challenging adversary, as I'm sure you will discover," predicted Aurelius.

"That may be, but he will find that he is no match for the might of the Roman Empire," Cato declared steadfastly.

As all the men and soldiers ate, Julius filled Cato in on all that Tiberius had told them about his and Festus's roles in their criminal enterprises.

Cato was quiet for a moment before responding, "My next step will be to update the emperor and then interview the living members of the investor's list you showed me. They can verify Tiberius's story about Festus being the mastermind behind the investment scheme. Regardless, however, he is still wanted for murder and will receive a public execution when we find him."

All of the men and soldiers stayed in the villa for the next two days, hoping that Tiberius might reappear. However, when there was no sign of him, the expedition began their return trip to Rome escorted by the regiment of soldiers. Half of the group, with Cato, Aurelius, Julius, and his guards, used the cursus publicus while the other half escorted the wagon of remains at a much slower pace.

When the faster group reached the station where they had left Cato's injured soldier, they found him mostly healed from the snake venom and ready to make the return trip with them as the centurion had predicted. As they came to the city of Firenze, Cato allowed his company to take a one-day break because Julius's party was still recovering from their prison experience.

Julius was grateful for the reprieve and decided to briefly walk around the city with his two guards while Aurelius rested at the inn. When they reached the city, he gave each of his guards some extra money as a reward for their loyalty, and he invited them to shop along with him.

As they strolled the city streets, Julius reminisced about when he was a child, and his father had left to take the harvest to a market far away; he would always return with some small gifts for his wife and children. Young Julius had eagerly awaited his father and the gifts.

His mind returned to the present as he thought of the smile of delight he would see on Octavia's face when he walked through the door of the domus, and he looked through the jewelry selections displayed by a vendor before moving over to another booth on the street that sold children's toys and games. As he perused this booth's selection, he saw a blur out of the corner of his right eye and looked up to see Tiberius rushing toward him, holding a large dagger.

Before he had time to react, his view of Tiberius was blocked entirely by the broad back of Felix as his guard jumped in front of him. Julius saw Gaius try to rush forward to aid Felix, but his progress was impeded by another attacker brandishing his dagger at Gaius. Julius turned back toward Felix and pulled his own dagger from his tunic just in time to see Felix slump to the ground. Tiberius circled around the prone body of the guard and advanced toward Julius, whose back was up against the booth where he had been browsing.

Julius noticed a quick movement to his right and glanced over while trying to keep his attacker in view. He was barely able to distinguish Gaius, who held his attacker's knife arm as he bent down and picked up a large rock. Julius turned his full attention back upon his assailant and immediately witnessed the same rock hurl into Tiberius's left arm. The shock and pain of the projectile made the man lower the dagger but not drop it to the ground, and his gleaming eyes never left his opponent.

Julius used the momentary distraction to rush forward, and he simultaneously used one arm to immobilize the man's knife-wielding arm so that he couldn't raise the dagger while the other hand plunged the blade into the man's chest. Julius was surprised by the fight that Tiberius still possessed, and the other man tried to take advantage of Julius's weakened state by grabbing him and attempting to thrust up his own dagger.

"The gods must want me to kill you myself," the attacker breathed out.

Then Julius thrust the knife further into the man's bulk and twisted until he felt Tiberius drop his arms in defeat and saw the life draining from his venomous eyes. The large man finally fell to the ground, lifeless. As Julius looked again toward Gaius, he saw that both his guard and the second assailant had managed to disarm each other. But in the next moment, before he could rush to help his friend, he saw Gaius swing back and ram his giant fist into the man's temple. The sound of the crushing blow reverberated through the street, and the hit knocked the man to the ground, where he remained unmoving.

Gaius rushed over to his master, and they both knelt down to check on Felix. As soldiers began to stream down the street in their direction, Julius observed that Felix was still breathing but had sustained a substantial wound to his abdomen from the other man's blade. Then the soldiers arrived, and they had a medicus look at Felix while they questioned Julius, Gaius, and the vendors who witnessed the fight.

Soon, Cato was sent for, and when he arrived, he vouched for Julius and Gaius. Then he walked over and looked at Tiberius.

"So, this is him? This is Tiberius?" he asked.

Julius nodded as he continued to watch Felix, "That is the man."

"Well, it looks like his execution wasn't as public as I planned, but I imagine the emperor will be satisfied nonetheless," Cato stated sardonically.

"He was a very calculating man. I think he probably knew we had to come through this city on our way to Rome, so he had someone watch for a large group of soldiers to arrive. Then he and his man followed us until they could find a time when we were alone to attack," Gaius speculated.

Cato nodded in assent before returning to where Felix lay with the medicus over him. "What is the prognosis for this man?" he asked.

"I have his bleeding reduced and need to get him to surgery immediately, but I think I can help him," the medicus responded in haste as the soldiers lifted Felix onto a cot. They all moved hurriedly down the street toward the local valetudinarian or military hospital encampment.

Julius looked at Gaius and said, "Thanks for the rock."

"Thanks for not dying," Gaius responded dryly.

Julius gave a half smirk as his friend retrieved his dagger and restored it to its place at his side.

As Cato escorted them back to their inn, Julius prayed for Felix to recover quickly. He decided that he and Gaius would stay at the inn with Aurelius until Felix was well enough to travel. His father-in-law was grateful for the extended reprieve from the horseback riding.

The day after his surgery, the men were able to visit Felix in the valetudinarian and found him awake, in good spirits, and praising God that the surgery was successful and that they had all survived the attack. The medicus said that he would be able to leave in four or five days if he had no infection but that he could not ride a horse for at least a month. Julius assured Felix that he would rent a carpentum to take them home to Rome.

That afternoon, Cato left with his soldiers and the body of the fallen Tiberius. He told them that he needed to report back to the emperor but that he would also go by Julius's domus and update Octavia on the men's current situation. He finished up by saying, "When you return to Rome, you have an open invitation to my home for dinner."

Julius grasped his outstretched arm and responded, "Likewise, my friend."

CHAPTER 25

Octavia cradled Antonius against her chest as she watched Tatiana crawl around the garden with Felix's son, Cassius, who was trying to pull himself up on the stone benches. Sabina was resting after another long night of comforting the babe. Esther quietly entered the garden and sat beside her mistress.

"I know it has been less than a month, but I had hoped that Gaius and Julius would have returned by now," Esther said plaintively.

Octavia clutched her friend's hand and reassured her, "I know, I did too, but we have been praying earnestly, and hopefully, we will hear news soon."

"Have you heard any word from the church about a home for baby Cicero?" Esther asked.

The baby she inquired about was the only child that Octavia's slaves had found in the garbage heaps since Julius had left on his expedition. The child was growing normally but was born missing three fingers on each hand. Most Roman families would not consider keeping a child with only thumbs and pinky fingers instead of fully formed hands, and he had likely been immediately rejected upon his birth, considering how tiny and weak he was when discovered.

Octavia sighed and answered, "No, I'm afraid that he will be a difficult baby to adopt. He will certainly require more care than other children and is sure to face a life of difficulty and bigotry."

Aelia walked through the garden just then to collect Cassius for his nap and thanked the other women for watching him. When she left, they continued their conversation.

"We will make sure that he finds a home, though, Mistress."

"I know, and if no one else will take him, I am sure that Julius would be amenable to us raising him as well. He would never thrust a child out onto the streets," Octavia replied.

The friends looked up as Claudia strolled into the garden, holding Cicero and humming to the child.

"He is such a happy child," Octavia's mother gushed as she sat on a bench opposite the other two women.

Esther got up quickly, "Tatiana, Dear, what do you have in your mouth now? Spit it out."

After wrestling a leaf from the little one's gums, Esther returned to her seat with a smile and a shake of her head and commented, "Always getting into trouble at this age."

Octavia nodded in agreement and watched as her mother gazed down at the baby in her arms with pure joy and love.

"Have you ever considered adoption, Mother?"

Claudia looked up quickly, and Octavia thought she saw tears in her eyes. "I am not sure if your father would ever acquiesce to such a taboo request."

"Well, it does not hurt to ask him if you are interested. He is quite the changed man, and I see the way you look at Cicero," her daughter urged gently.

Claudia nodded and said, "When he returns, I will inquire as to his opinion on the matter."

Esther and Octavia ducked their heads and smiled conspiratorially while her mother played with the baby on her lap.

"I saw that," Claudia replied dryly.

The next day, a messenger summoned Octavia to the atrium where she found Cato waiting for her. Her heart leapt into her throat, and she feared the news that Cato was there to deliver. However, before she could allow fear to consume her fully, Cato began speaking.

"Do not fear. Your husband and father are well. They are in Firenze and are waiting for your guard, Felix, to recover from an injury. The last that I checked, he was doing well and should make a full recovery. All the others are healthy, and the man who caused your family so much trouble is dead."

Octavia lit with joy at the news and thanked Cato profusely before he left. Then she ran to tell Claudia, Esther, and Aelia the news. The women gathered in the dining room, and when Octavia relayed the information that Cato had delivered, the other women looked relieved, except for Aelia, who clutched at her arm nervously.

"Do you think that your God will listen if you pray to him for me?" she asked hopefully.

"Of course, he hears, and you should pray to him as well," Octavia assured her as she took her slave's hand comfortingly.

They all prayed together that their husbands would return quickly and safely and thanked God that their enemy was brought to justice.

In the middle of the next week, Octavia sat sketching in the garden while Claudia held Cicero, and Aelia and Esther watched the other children. Without warning, a messenger rushed into the garden and announced that the master had returned home.

The women sprang to their feet, collected the children, and ran to greet their husbands, eager to reunify after such a long separation. The reunion was sweet and full of tears as the men hugged their wives and children.

Julius kissed Octavia and took Tatiana and Antonius from her arms. As Octavia cried with joy, he reassured her that he was unharmed.

Gaius stood holding his wife against him firmly with a face filled with the peace of God's providence in allowing them to return home.

Aelia looked over her husband, checking for his injury before he assured her that he was mostly recovered and pulled her to his uninjured side for a hug. Then he kissed the boy in her arms and told her, "I came to some important realizations about God while I was gone."

"So did I," Aelia said in surprise. "I prayed with the other women for your safe return, and he has answered my prayers!

Aurelius looked confused at the baby in his wife's arms and asked, "Who is this little one? I am sure he was not here when I left."

His wife looked at him with hope and trepidation. "His name is Cicero. Octavia's staff found him abandoned because of his deformity, but I have developed a fondness for the boy."

Aurelius smiled at his wife and said with certainty, "You want to adopt him, don't you?"

She looked a little surprised at his abruptness but answered, "Yes, he needs me, and I think we can give him a good home."

He continued to smile as he agreed, "I think you are right, my Dear."

That evening they invited Cato and his family to their home, and all the men regaled their families with the stories of their epic adventure along the Roman roads. After all of the story was told, the group spoke of brighter topics and laughed together.

That evening, after Cato and his family had left for home, Aurelius asked to speak to his daughter privately. Octavia led him into the library, unsure and slightly anxious about what he might say. They both sat in chairs facing each other, and he looked at her with such sorrow that she became even more fearful of his message.

"Daughter, I must seek your forgiveness. I thought that I was doing the right thing when I married you to Festus with no regard for your feelings on the matter. I want you to be assured that I had no idea of any of his illegal dealings or his murderous nature. Had I known, I would not have given you to him, but even if he hadn't been a treacherous despot, I still should not have trapped you into a life with a man you didn't want. Can you ever forgive me?"

"Of course I do, Father. You are not the same person now that you have been redeemed by our Savior, and I know that you would never do something like that as a believer. God used your sin for good and for his glory. If I had not been married to Festus, I would not have met Esther, who led me to Christ, and I would not have married Julius or had Tatiana," she consoled him.

His eyes filled with tears and his shoulders slumped as he allowed her forgiveness and the assurance of God's good plan to wash over him.

Then he looked back up at her and spoke again, "I know that you bought Julius's freedom in order to secure your own, and I need to tell you that I admire you. You made a good choice in him, and I am pleased to have him in the family,"

"Thank you," Octavia moved to her father's side and wrapped him in a hug.

The day after their return, Gaius and Esther were once again strolling through the olive orchard when Gaius sat on the ground under a tree and pulled Esther down in front of him. He settled her sitting between his legs with her back leaning up against his chest and hugged her to himself as if he never wanted to let go.

After several minutes of silent embrace, the guard began to speak, "I had a lot of time to think and pray while traveling and sitting locked in the prison. We talked to Aurelius about how God used his sin in giving Octavia to Festus for the good of all of us, and I thought about how if I hadn't been abandoned, I never would have met you. I believe that God will use my past and give me the strength to love a child who was also abandoned. I have begun to learn that God likes to use our brokenness for his own glory, and I am certain that God is glorified when we take in the orphans."

Esther could barely speak past the lump in her throat, but she half turned in his arms so she could see into her husband's eyes.

"I love you so much, and I think you are right. God has used all the sins committed against us to help us gain our freedom in Christ and freedom from slavery. I couldn't ask for a better husband than you."

He gave her a smile as he felt the acceptance and love he had never dared to dream of and that he hoped to give to a child as well. He leaned down to kiss his wife as a tear slid down his cheek.

Over the next few weeks, Julius and Octavia returned to their routines and looked for ways to honor God with the wealth that Festus had accumulated through his illicit means. They sold the hidden ruby and used the proceeds to benefit the church and missionaries. They also raised the wages for their slaves so that those who desired freedom would be able to purchase theirs sooner.

Together, they considered all of the properties they owned and considered how to best use them to benefit their fellow believers and help the poor. They sold the Raetia property and gave the money to the poor, and they were pleased to be rid of such a painful reminder of Festus's madness and sin.

Octavia's parents came to visit often with Cicero, who was clearly flourishing under their love and attention. Octavia had to fight back a little envy when she saw her father affectionately doting on his new son with a love that he had never shown her as a child. However, she prayed that God would forgive her and release her of her envy, and in time, it became easier for her to see their displays of affection toward her adopted brother.

Two weeks after the men returned from their Raetia adventure, one of their slaves returned to the domus with a tiny baby girl who had been left in one of the refuse heaps. Esther took the baby from the slave and looked at Gaius hopefully as she walked toward him. He nodded at her with a smile of acceptance and hesitant joy.

They cleaned her up and named her Mary in honor of the mother of their Lord. Fortunately for them, Aelia was weaning Cassius and agreed to nurse Mary for the couple. Octavia knew that Esther was pleased when Gaius quickly overcame his fear and bonded with his new baby, carrying her with him whenever he could.

The following day, Julius called Gaius into his tablinum where he sat with two glasses of wine placed on the desk in front of him. After the guard was seated, Julius said, "First of all, congratulations on your new daughter. She is beautiful."

Gaius smiled and nodded at the compliment, "Thank you. She is delightful."

Then Julius took on a serious affect and continued to speak, "Gaius, as you know, I do not own you, and I feel that you have risked your life to save mine enough times that I want to release you and Esther from your agreement to work for me until you've paid for your freedom. I would like it if you and Esther agreed to live here with my wife and me, but as family, not as employees. I consider you a brother, and I want to give you ownership in this estate."

Gaius's normal impassive expression was replaced with one of shock as Julius continued with his speech, "I know that you are a very smart man who is quite skilled at commanding men and strategizing. Octavia and I were talking about helping you to start a training center for guards—if that is something that interests you, of course."

"That sounds incredible! I never thought that I would own anything," Gaius stated with a grateful smile.

"Well, as you know, I was a farmer and then a slave who was given all of this wealth, so I would like to use it to help others," Julius said.

"I will have to talk to Esther, but a training center sounds like a great endeavor," the guard said as he nodded thoughtfully.

"Excellent. Do you think you could use all the extra guards that I have accumulated but no longer have a need for?" Julius inquired.

Gaius thought for a moment before nodding. "Felix and I have trained them well, and they would make great sparing coaches and practice partners."

"Perfect. That resolves what I am going to do about all the guards. Someone might think I'm hoarding gold here or some such thing."

Julius and Gaius both chuckled before Julius continued, "I am planning to free Felix and his family as well. He nearly died to save my life, and I think he might be an excellent instructor at your training center if you and he are agreeable to it," Julius suggested.

Gaius nodded in agreement and picked up the glass of wine closest to him in a toast.

"To freedom and the future," he declared.

"To freedom and the future," Julius echoed happily as he raised his own glass.

Felix was allowed to convalesce in peace with his wife and son for a few weeks. On the day that Felix prepared to return to duty, Julius summoned the man into his tablinum and gave him and his family their freedom in exchange for their excellent service and for Felix's bravery in saving his life, nearly at the expense of his own.

"I would be pleased if you would continue to live here with us. As you know, Octavia and I do not have much family, and this domus and all the villas we own are meant to be family homes. Now we are making our own family," Julius asserted to a stunned Felix.

"Yes, of course, thank you, Master!"

"Not master, Felix, friend," Julius corrected with a grin.

That day, Gaius, Esther, Felix, and Aelia, along with their children, moved out of the slave quarters into their own rooms in the main living area. Later, the former slaves dined with Julius and Octavia as equals in rank and as a chosen family. Together, they celebrated their freedom in Christ and their adoption into his family.

THE END

EXHORTATION FROM THE AUTHOR

I hope that you enjoyed this book! I relished writing it for you, and I was thoroughly inspired when delving into the world of the early church. I strongly encourage you to read the Book of Acts. I am sure you will be uplifted to read about the early Christians as they dedicated themselves to their church and fellow believers. We should all strive toward their example of aiding families in their churches, helping widows and orphans, funding the church, and supporting missionaries.

In John 13:35, Jesus says that we will be known by our love for each other. I encourage you, dear reader, to use the gifts that God has given you through your talents and your finances to benefit your church. We are all members of the body, and God has given us specific abilities to benefit our church body (1 Corinthians 12:12-31). As an example, my husband and I have been inviting church families to our home for dinners on a weekly basis since the beginning of this year. This time of fellowship has been a great blessing to our family, and we have been thrilled with the opportunity to connect with other church members.

I would also like to advocate for you to support your leaders. Paul tells us in 1 Thessalonians 10:12-13 that we should esteem our church leaders "very highly in love because of their work." Consider doing something kind for your pastor or elder's family, like inviting them over for dinner or treating your pastor to a lunch. Too often, we only approach our pastor if we have a problem, but I know from personal experience as a former pastor's wife that ministry work can be very isolating. We should pray for and consider the well-being of the shepherds that God has given us.

In the United States, we thankfully live in a time in which orphans are not being abandoned in garbage heaps. Still, one can volunteer time or resources to help children in foster care or donate through organizations such as Compassion International (a favorite of mine). We can also support missionaries through mission's organizations like HeartCry Missionary Society or Reformed Baptist Missions (links below).

Do not be discouraged if you cannot support all of these worthy causes! Instead, use these suggestions to brainstorm ideas about what you are able to do and ask God to provide you with opportunities to bless others. Even if you are not in a financial position to give monetarily, God has endowed you with time and talents to use for his glory and the benefit of your church family, and never cease praying!

I will conclude my exhortation with this Scripture passage:

"Let us hold fast the confession of our hope without wavering, for he who promised is faithful. And let us consider how to stir up one another to love and good works, not neglecting to meet together, as is the habit of some, but encouraging one another, and all the more as you see the Day drawing near." Hebrews 10:23-25, ESV

In Christ,

Jeanette Stahlheber
https://www.compassion.com/
https://heartcrymissionary.com/
https://reformedbaptistnetwork.com/missions/

ACKNOWLEDGMENTS

I want to express so much gratitude for my husband who excitedly read my book as I wrote it and is always so encouraging when I try something new. Also big thanks to my mom, Becci Martin, and my friend Victoria Jensen who read my manuscript and gave me invaluable constructive criticism. Thank you so much to my graphics designer Yoko Matsuoka who turned my olive branch sketches into digital illustrations, my book cover designer Nada Orlic who rocked it out with this stunning artwork, and my incredibly encouraging editor Maureen A. Campanile.

ABOUT THE AUTHOR

Jeanette Stahlheber lives in Texas with her charming husband, three hilarious children, and two sweet dogs. She spends her days home-schooling and managing her home. She also collects and sells antiques online.

She loves everything artistic and crafty, including painting wall murals and making elaborate cakes (which she occasionally sells). She enjoys rock climbing, cultivating her indoor plants, and trying out new hobbies like watercolor painting, oh and writing a novel for fun. Her faith and relationship with God are central to all her endeavors.

Learn more at her website: jeanettesrelaxingreads.com

SCRIPTURE INDEX